DEATH OF
A LUCKY LADY

VIRGINIA RATH

DEATH OF
A LUCKY LADY

VIRGINIA RATH

COACHWHIP PUBLICATIONS
Greenville, Ohio

Death of a Lucky Lady, by Virginia Rath
© 2019 Coachwhip Publications

Published 1940
No claims made on public domain material.
Cover image: Gold coins © Donald Swartz

CoachwhipBooks.com

ISBN 1-61646-480-1
ISBN-13 978-1-61646-480-6

DEATH OF A LUCKY LADY

PART ONE

"Come, tell me all that thou hast seen,
And look thou tell me true!
Since I from Smaylho'me tower have been,
What did my lady do?"

WILLIAM GORDON m. LUCILLA THATCHER (1847)

ALICE (1858–1938) m. DAVID KEITH (1856–1905)

HUBERT (1884–1918)   STEPHEN (1886–1925)   AMALIA b. 1889
m. MOLLY FLANIGAN   m. LONA CARLSON   m. ANTONIO
                                                  COLONELLO 1908
        NORA   Divorced 1913
                                                   m. JAMES
                                                   LANDRETH

I

Amalia Landreth tucked the telephone receiver into its cradle and sat back against her piled-up pillows. She rested the telephone on her plump knees, smiling at the Amalia in the blotched old mirror across the room.

"You're a fool for luck, my girl," she said, and saw the edges of her smile crumble a little because unconsciously she had mimicked her husband's pseudo-Oxford accent.

He'd told her so often she was lucky even while he complained: "You count your chickens before they're hatched, m'dear—so loudly anyone who cares to listen can hear you." And that was true too: throughout her life she had been almost equally optimistic and indiscreet.

But this time . . . She thrust one hand under her pillows and smiled again as she felt the sharp edges of the box there. Surely even a pessimist would admit this chicken must break out of its shell by tonight. And no one could say she hadn't been as discreet as it was possible for her to be, though she supposed there were people who would say she had still talked more than was necessary—

The square marble clock on the black marble mantelpiece chimed a peevish nine o'clock. Patton had orders not to wake her until ten, but this morning the sun in her eyes had roused her before the telephone rang.

Amalia appraised the day and approved it. She had forgotten in thirty years away from San Francisco that its Novembers were like this. She wouldn't wait until tonight to celebrate; she would go out this morning and buy gay, insane, expensive clothes.

Perhaps Nora could go with her. She should let the child know she'd shaken off the depression that had had her by the throat last Thursday. You shouldn't inflict your troubles on a niece you hoped would like you for yourself and not from a sense of duty—

Nora's voice, when she finally answered the telephone, had a definite "Oh-lord-what-now?" sound. Blue Monday, poor child, Amalia thought sympathetically. She said:

"I won't keep you, darling, but isn't it a divine day?"

"Is it? The sun doesn't penetrate into this sunny housekeeping room, you know."

"I forgot to pull the shades last night, so it woke me early this morning. I wanted to stretch luxuriously—"

"Why not?" Nora said politely.

Amalia chuckled. "You've never slept on your grandmother's horsehair mattress. I'm not too impressionable, but if anyone ever left her imprint on a house or a room, Mamma did on this one. Even the clock sounds like her scolding me for lying late in bed."

She thought she heard Nora shift from one foot to another and said penitently: "You must stop me when I begin chattering, pet. Have you much to do this morning?"

Nora sighed. While her aunt was talking she had buttoned her blouse and finished drinking a cup of very weak coffee. She would have been very curt with anyone but Aunt Amalia, who had been an undigested lump in her conscience during a busy week end.

It hadn't taken her a month to decide that Aunt Amalia was a buoyant person. And after being practically submerged in gloom on Thursday she had bobbed up to skitter cheerfully on her way again. She needn't have worried about Aunt Amalia, Nora thought, or suggested having dinner with her tonight when she couldn't find time to see her over the week end. An engagement she suspected and hoped Amalia had forgotten—

"Much to do?" she repeated. "This is Big Game week—the Stanford-California game, you know?—and I must get material for an article on what the richbitches will wear to the game. And there will be an enlarged woman's section Thursday: Thanksgiving. I must help fill that, which means several hours' cruising about the stores besides producing the daily low-down on what the well-dressed woman is and will be wearing."

"Poor child," Amalia said. But rather absently, Nora thought. "Thanksgiving is early this year, isn't it? So quaint of Mr. Roosevelt. But it can't come too early for me. I'm ready to celebrate today. I think we must have an old-fashioned Thanksgiving dinner here. And I must have new raiment, darling. What is the name of the shop whose owner does the designing?"

"Gisele's? You can't do better but—well—"

Nora hesitated, not wanting to ask: "Can you afford to go there?" Because she had wondered on Thursday if perhaps Amalia was facing the fact that at fifty she had nothing that could be called an income. Stray remarks of hers had made Nora think James Landreth hadn't left much when he died a year ago. And Amalia's mother, Nora's grandmother, had certainly left only a few hundred dollars and a heavily mortgaged house that would be hard to sell.

"Well, dear?" Amalia said.

"Oh, I like Michael Dundas but I tell him the only difference between him and Jesse James is that Jesse had a gun."

"Oh—that." Amalia laughed. "They're always highway robbers if they're good, pet. I don't mind—today. I'm aching to be extravagant."

"Have you sold the house?" Nora asked bluntly.

"The house? Oh no. Everything is in shape so I can vacate it any time now, but if it is sold I'm afraid there will be very little left for me. It's not that. It's just the most amazing— But you're coming to dinner tonight?"

"I'd planned to. But if you'd rather I didn't—"

"No, I want you to," Amalia said quickly. "I'll be back for dinner and then we'll talk—"

Nora swallowed a tart: "It would be odd if we didn't talk"—looking over her shoulder toward her tarnished alarm clock. It did occur to her Amalia's manner was suddenly that of a person wanting to be coaxed to tell something she shouldn't tell. But the clock said nine-fifteen, and Nora wanted to be downtown by a quarter of ten.

"Would you like me to take you to Gisele's?" she said resignedly. "If you'll meet me downtown at the glove counter in the White House we'll go out from there. But I'll have to leave when I've talked to Michael. He's always good copy, though he'd be better if you could quote him verbatim. He's allergic to all fashion reporters but me. Some silly fool raved in print once about the white streak in his hair and his 'amazingly blue eyes.' But he thinks it's amusing I have no clothes sense and keep my job only because I have a photographic eye and can walk all day without my feet hurting—much. Will eleven-thirty do?"

"That will be splendid, pet. And I know you're used to eating earlier than I do, so I was going to set dinner ahead tonight, but I might just possibly be late getting home, so—"

"Eight o'clock will be perfectly all right, Aunt Amalia," Nora said desperately. "And I simply must go—"

She slammed the telephone onto its stand, pulled her stockings up and her suit skirt down. Why, she wondered, hunting for her hairbrush, do my skirts always hike when I have a twenty-two-inch waist and no hips? There's nothing wrong with my legs, either, but my stocking seams never stay straight any more than my blouse collars will lie flat.

Clothes simply don't like me, she decided, brushing her hair vigorously. She pulled it back over her ears, twisted it into a knot and skewered it with two hairpins. She slashed lipstick across her mouth and bit it off while she shrugged into her coat and clapped a blue beret on the coppery hair that was already beginning to feather into little curls about her face. She snatched her purse from a chair, gave a last harried look at her unmade bed and closed the door on it.

It was close to noon when she stepped into Michael Dundas' office. "I've been warned," she said quickly. "The high priestess of this temple told me you arrived early and in half an hour reduced the entire staff either to tears or profanity. She told me I came in at my own risk."

"Did Fanchon also tell you I rose at an uncivilized hour to put my wife on the Daylight Limited to Los Angeles?" Mr. Dundas inquired. "And don't worry about the staff. They find a good shaking-up very stimulating. It gives them material for conversation among themselves."

"I'll bet it does! And whatever drove Valerie away from you and her new house? I didn't think anything would."

"Neither did I, Miss Keith. But I hadn't foreseen my mother-in-law would decide to try matrimony a third time—and with a phony Austrian count."

"Oh. Do you know he's a fake?"

"I paid a detective agency to tell me so. Valerie has gone to place the proofs before Mamma, though I'd say the hell with it and let Mamma have her fun."

"Relatives are a problem," Nora said. "I brought my aunt here just now. Not Lona: Mrs. Stephen Keith. This is a real aunt, my father's sister, Amalia Landreth. You may have heard of her—"

"Should I have?"

"She was the Contessa Colonello once, and people seem to remember that kind of thing."

"They do, don't they? And of course," Michael said blandly, "the Keiths are one of San Francisco's proud pioneer families. You've mentioned that casually now and then: say several dozen times."

Nora flushed. "I'm very sorry I bored you!"

"My dear child, I'm married to another of the species. What the Mayflower is to New England the trek across the Isthmus, the voyage around the Horn and the covered wagon is to a San Franciscan. I can't say I blame you for liking to point out to southern Californians that though they may not always be riche they are usually quite *nouveau*.

Your aunt Amalia seems to have been places and done things. Are you afraid her credit isn't good?"

"I don't know. She says she feels like being extravagant today. She's only been here a month: the first time she's been back here since she went off in 1908 to make the grand tour and married in Italy. She divorced Colonello for infidelity—"

"Does an American wife ever divorce an Italian husband for any other reason?"

"She may have put one over on him at that. Because she married James Landreth as soon as she could. He was one of these Americans who think Europe is the only civilized place to live. That's where they lived until the Munich crisis. Then they came back to New York."

"Wasn't your grandmother living then?" Michael asked. "Didn't an Alice Keith die at a very ripe old age last year?"

"Yes. And they meant to come here at once, but they were in an automobile smashup, and Mr. Landreth was killed. Aunt Amalia was in the hospital for months with a broken hip, and Grandmother died during that time so there wasn't any reason for her to hurry out here. But she inherited the family mansion on Union Street, and someone had to go through things there and decide what's to be done with them."

"And what did you inherit from Grandmamma?"

"I never even saw Grandmamma," Nora said grimly. "If you don't want to hear this, say so. . . Well, my great-grandfather Gordon came here from Georgia, just married, in '48—"

"Which makes you one up on the forty-niners," Michael suggested, grinning.

"Oh, be still! I'm not bragging. Anyway, Great-grandfather Gordon prospered but had only one child, my grandmother. She married David Keith. His family were old settlers too but not well to do. It was Grandmother's parents who built the Union Street house for her wedding present. So, though it's called the Keith house, it was paid for with Gordon money, and it was always Grandmother who had the money.

"She was just an old hellion. She didn't care a hoot for a daughter but ate her sons alive. She kept my father and Uncle Stephen away from girls she'd have had to admit were eligible—"

"Until they were easy pickings for any fairly affable and moderately comely female?"

"Y-yes. Though Mother was more than moderately comely. She—" Nora colored deeply. "She was an Irish maid."

"Splendid! I'm surprised your father retained so much good judgment—and guts."

"Hiring Mother was Grandmother's first little error. She disowned Father and never saw him again. She held onto Uncle Stephen until he was in his thirties. Then she made another mistake: she engaged Lona as a companion!

"And Lona married Uncle Stephen?"

"Um-hum. But a companion is a cut above a maid," Nora said. "And maybe Grandma thought a son with a wife was better than no son at all. So they went on living with her until Uncle Stephen died. Which he did in two years—"

"The emotional strain of marriage seems to have been too much for the Keith constitution," Michael remarked.

"My father was killed in the war! He had some stamina in spite of Grandmother. Well, when Uncle Stephen died Grandmother threw Lona out on her ear. She'd made a will that disinherited me, so she had to fall back on Aunt Amalia. She got the works which isn't so much after all. Grandmother's lawyers say she never really understood the depression and had been living off her principle for years. After all, Great-grandfather Gordon's money wouldn't last forever when no one ever added anything to it.

"Of course what Grandmother really wanted was a substitute son or two. So she cultivated one of the distant cousins for a while—or he cultivated her," Nora said scornfully. "Roger Keith: he's a writer."

"And not at all a bad one," Michael said. "Though not, I imagine, very successful financially."

"He says not. Well, I'm sure there would have been far more for Aunt Amalia if it hadn't been for Roger. I know Grandmother helped him through college—as long as he went. After he had his first book published either he walked out on Grandmother or she threw him out. Probably the book shocked her to death."

"And Aunt Amalia is a problem?" Michael said.

"Oh, I'm very fond of her. For one thing, she can talk both French and Italian, but she never does strew her conversation with it. And I suppose I needn't worry about her. I was last Thursday, she was so depressed. She'd been trying that day and Wednesday to decide what to save in the house and what to throw away. Because it's to be sold, and it's crammed full of useless things. Well, it isn't cheerful work, coming across things that belonged to your brothers and parents and your own baby clothes—"

"'You will do this, won't you, Mother? Put my little shoes away—'" Michael crooned. "'Give them all my other to-oys, but put my little shoes ahwa-ay.'"

Nora scowled at him and then laughed. "Aunt Amalia isn't slushily sentimental. I thought Thursday she might be depressed for financial as well as sentimental reasons. But today she's cheerful as a lark, wants a new wardrobe and is planning a family Thanksgiving dinner."

"Would that include Cornelius?"

"Oh yes. Aunt Amalia seems to be suffering from a rebirth of family feeling. She's gotten in touch with everyone that could be said to be a Keith or related to a Keith. Most of the ones she knew have died, and one is reported missing, so there aren't many of us, and she's glad to welcome even a niece's semiofficial fiancé into the fold. She knew Neil's uncle, and she likes Neil. And he," Nora said sadly, "finds Aunt Amalia exhausting. How is he?"

Michael raised his left eyebrow. "Don't you know?"

"I spent the week end in Berkeley with an old school friend."

"Well, you've only to step next door to see Cornelius. I haven't talked with him myself since Friday."

"Oh, I simply haven't time now. I had dozens of questions to ask you, but relating the Keith family saga has driven them from my mind," Nora said. "Let's see. . . . Are you showing straw hats yet?"

"We aren't rushing the season that much. Besides, our best straws have always been imported, and the war is playing hell with all imported materials—"

There was a tremendous thumping on the outside of the door at Michael's back. "Are you in?" a powerful bass inquired. "If you are, open up and get ready to give me a drink."

II

From its original cubbyhole in Maiden Lane, Gisele's had expanded into larger quarters some distance out on Sutter Street. Michael's office had a back door opening onto an alley used by delivery trucks. There entered from this alley a tall, heavily built young man: Cornelius Sturtevant, owner of Gisele's left-hand neighbor, "Sturtevant—Antiques."

He had fine, straw-colored hair on a squarish head, china-blue eyes and cheeks that looked as if they had just been treated with red nail salve and buffed to a high shine. He looked at Nora meditatively and finally gave signs he recognized her as the girl he intended marrying.

"I didn't know you were here. I called you last night but I guess you weren't home yet."

"I didn't get home until after eleven," Nora said. "Are you in the doghouse again, Neil?"

Mr. Sturtevant groaned softly, ambled over to a chair and sat down after first automatically testing its solidity. Mr. Sturtevant had not been born to antiques. Sturtevant's was his by inheritance from his uncle and godfather.

He had an office that roughly corresponded to Michael's. But where Michael's office was a lair into which the staff of Gisele's entered timorously, Cornelius' was dominated by his late uncle's faithful handmaiden, Martha Ferris. When Martha's plainly stated opinion of his sins and omissions as a dealer in antiques ruffled even Cornelius' placidity, he bolted out his own back door and in at Michael's.

"You know," he said now, "I thought my luck had changed when I inherited this business. I'd had six years to find out one machine can do the work it used to take six expert accountants to do. Besides it was darn nice of Uncle Cornelius to leave me everything. But if I'd known he was leaving me Martha along with the business—"

"The successful businessman is he who hires a woman to run his business for him." Michael took a bottle of whisky from a desk drawer and poured drinks for himself and Cornelius. "Do you think I could struggle on without Fanchon Weiss? But of course she damn well knows I'd fire her if she ever forgot I do own this business. If Martha annoys you too much, why don't you dispense with her?"

"Oh, Uncle wouldn't have liked that. Besides, I didn't realize at first how much there is to learn about the antique business—if you think it's worth learning. Martha says I haven't any flair for it, and I don't guess I have."

"What is your latest misdemeanor?" Nora asked.

"Oh, I went to an auction Saturday, and Martha Bays I bought all the wrong things and paid too much for them. She says it's foolish for me to go to auctions when I don't know old Wedgwood from late Woolworth. Well, I do know the difference between profit and loss. Uncle made a good living out of the business a good many years. He needed to because he spent it. He had a swell apartment that looked every dollar it cost. But I'm not making it to spend. Those things on silver you call hallmarks may be a mystery to me, but I can keep books."

"I suppose to some extent the good will of the business was dependent on your uncle," Michael said thoughtfully. "But it doesn't seem to me his death should make such a great difference. You still have Martha who knows all the old customers, and people don't quickly shake off the habit of patronizing one certain shop once they've acquired it."

Cornelius shrugged ponderously. "Seems like we never have what the important customers want any more. And you can't make money off people who come in just to look around or pick up knickknacks. I guess I'm pretty methodical, so I'd like to see things neatly arranged so you'd know just what you had and where it was without digging around in dark corners an hour or two."

Michael grinned. "But that comes under the heading of atmosphere, and all antique shop-ies must have atmosphere."

"If you mean dust we've got plenty of that. Uncle didn't even leave a decent inventory. Martha says she knows what we have, but that isn't me knowing." Cornelius turned to Nora. "Did you have a nice week end?"

"No. It's a mistake to visit old school friends when you haven't seen them for years and have nothing but old times to talk over. That subject doesn't last forever."

"You should 've stayed over here like I wanted you to. We could have gone for a nice long hike Sunday."

"Still just a country boy at heart."

"I was raised in the country," Cornelius said seriously. "I like to get out and breathe air that's air and see blue sky over me and feel the dirt under my feet."

"'The leaves, the little birds, and I, the fleecy clouds and the sweet, sweet sky,'" Michael suggested.

"I think you're making fun of me—"

"And it won't do any good, because he's incurable," Nora said quickly. "But I walk enough during the week to satisfy me, Neil. So I hope you had a good workout by yourself."

"Hunh? Oh—yes, I did. I went to bed early Saturday to get an early start Sunday over to Marin County and—"

Fanchon Weiss tapped perfunctorily on the office door and came in, with a disapproving glance for the whisky glasses.

"Mrs. Landreth asked me to see if you were still here, Miss Keith. And she wants to meet the maestro—"

"I'm leaving," Cornelius said promptly, heaving himself out of his chair. "Oh, I like your aunt, Nora. Only she kind of tires me out."

"Wait: I'll go with you. Will you tell my aunt I'm gone?" Nora said to Fanchon. "She'll want me to have lunch with her, and Aunt Amalia doesn't just eat lunch. She 'lunches' and not hastily. I simply haven't time—"

"Then come on. It won't be any lie for Miss Weiss to say you've gone if you hurry," Cornelius said, jerking the door open and whisking Nora through it.

"He seems in an awful rush," Fanchon remarked. "Well, will I tell Mrs. Landreth you just stepped out too?"

"No. I want to meet her."

"You want an excuse not to work." As Fanchon had been Michael's first and at one time his only employee, she looked on herself as his guiding angel, and there was nowhere she feared to tread. Fortunately, she also knew when she was walking on shaky ground and very seldom did. "If you're going to do the Harris girl's trousseau—"

"Her papa may be filthy rich, but she still reminds me of something made with four toothpicks and a potato to amuse the kiddies," Michael said morosely. "You run along and collect Mrs. Landreth. . . ."

Amalia, settling her small plump body into the chair closest to Michael's desk, assured him that she was "mad about your things. They're really quite amazing. I'm sorry Nora's gone. There was a blue ensemble I wanted her to try— You don't think she'd look well in it?" she asked as Michael grinned briefly.

"Theoretically, yes. But I have never been able to decide what it is that Nora does to clothes. Perhaps she was meant to be a woodland nymph and wear none."

Amalia laughed and showed dimples that were still dimples and not merely depressions. "Well, Nora's father was the kind of man whose shirt was always parting company with his trousers, and his ties were always under one ear. I suppose you're right about Nora. I'll have to think of some other little surprise for her."

She sighed. "I love to surprise people, yet I hate to know anything I can't tell. It's never long before a secret ceases to be a pleasure to me and becomes a nuisance. And a good story and good luck are no fun if you can't share them. Oh, you have a telephone book. Would you mind—"

Michael handed it to her across the desk, and she opened it at the yellow classified advertising section. He couldn't and didn't try to see what page she was interested in, but she found it without going very far into the alphabet.

"You'd think there 'd be more, but I suppose almost any of . . . Just where is the Phelan Building? Oh of course, any taxi driver will know. I've lived so many years in Europe I didn't even know the laws of the United States—"

Amalia opened a purse the size of a small knapsack. She took out a compact, two handkerchiefs, lipstick, a key ring, cigarette case, two folders of matches and finally a forlorn stub of pencil.

"I know what you're thinking," she said, seeing Michael grin again. "Mr. Landreth always said I carry everything, including a week's emergency rations, in my purses. They remind me in that way of my grandmother's workbags. I was very fond of my grandmother. She wasn't at all like my mother— Has Nora ever spoken of her?"

Michael nodded. "Well, I never could like Mother," Amalia said. "But my grandmother— Nora's great-grandmother Gordon—was very different. Mother was a very stupid woman. I don't suppose she ever read or learned anything new in the last forty years of her life. Grandmother was thrifty because she'd come from a poor family. I suppose it took time for her to get used to there being so much money, and perhaps she thought Grandfather Gordon's luck might run out some day."

"Fortunes were certainly made and lost with equal rapidity from '49 on," Michael agreed uncomprehendingly.

"Grandfather's luck never ran out—I think I must have inherited it—so Mother never needed to be thrifty. But she always held onto things because they were hers. Mother," Amalia recalled, "always thought she drove a hard bargain—"

"Was Colonello one of her bargains?" Michael said.

"Oh yes. But I wanted him myself. He had beautiful black mustaches, he paid divine compliments and kissed one's hand so gracefully. But I've never been a bargainer—"

Michael, looking at her generous, full-lipped mouth, believed her. She must have been a pretty thing once, he thought: a girl off a lace-paper valentine. And probably she had always wanted to be taller than she was—and still did. Hence the four-inch heels on her glossy opera pumps and the tall hat that looked rather like a mistreated lamp shade with half a red-and-green bird clinging to it. . . .

"I've always hated bargaining," Amalie. went on. "And I play a very poor game of poker. But sometimes you feel you must strike as hard a bargain as you can. I doubt if I know how, but I've just been thinking we used to say: 'Two strings to your bow.' Well—"

She delved into her purse again, drew out an envelope on which Michael glimpsed a postmark and foreign stamp and looked at it irresolutely. He tore a sheet from his memorandum pad; pushed it and a pencil toward her.

"Did you want to copy an address?"

"Oh, thank you. Men always have notebooks. Notes scribbled on old envelopes aren't very impressive, are they? That is, when you intend referring to them impressively. And it doesn't impress people either if you can hardly decipher them."

She put the envelope back in her purse whose contents, judging by its contours, Michael thought she had only skimmed. And wondered, watching her scrawl a few words on the paper he had given her, what it was she so badly wanted to tell someone. He doubted if she would be able to hold out against questioning, and when he looked at her again she was watching him with a smile that freely admitted her own weaknesses.

"You don't know how many times today I've come close to breaking a good resolution," she said. "That I haven't is due less to my own will power than to others being either polite or not curious—"

"That is my pet pencil," Michael broke in, holding out his hand as Amalia prepared to inter the pencil in her purse.

"Oh, I'm sorry. My husband always said a man should attach a chain to any pencil he loaned a woman. But I don't think chains are attached to pencils in public places to keep just women from walking away with them. . . . By the way, Nora was speaking of your wife in the taxi coming out here. I knew her father, though he was younger than I. I'd like to meet her sometime."

"I know she would be delighted," Michael said, so politely that Amalia smiled again.

"And you would be grateful if I'd take myself away. I came in here to talk clothes, but there will be lots of time for that. Would you mind telephoning for a taxi?

"I'm not always so rattled, Mr. Dundas," she added when he had put the telephone down. "I'm a little—excited today. Trying to pass time— Though I won't claim I'm not talkative, because I am." She got up. "Remember, I do want to meet your wife. Good-by: I'll wait outside for the cab. . . ."

Before Michael could put on his hat to go out to lunch, Fanchon reappeared. "No, you don't," she said firmly. "This is one of those days when you're apt to go out and never come back. And there's one or two things you have to decide."

"Very well. But get on with it. I wish I had asked her to have lunch with me—"

"Who? Mrs. Landreth? She just went off in a taxi. I wouldn't want to haul that purse of hers around," Fanchon said reflectively. "It felt like she was carrying lead weights in it when I handed it to her. Well, look. About the Harris girl . . ."

III

When Nora was between six and seven her mother had taken her for a Sunday afternoon walk that led them past the old Keith house. Molly Keith, pointing it out from across the street, had said: "That's where you'd be livin' if you had your rights, darlin'."

To which Nora, the child, had answered quickly: "I wouldn't want to live there. I—I don't like
it."

And she still did not like the house, though she
was three times seven before she decided it resembled a grayish, pot-bellied incense burner heavily
patterned with dark green leaves. It was neither
truly octagonal nor completely circular but something between the two. Its gray paint was apparently as imperishable as it was ugly—what could
be seen of it above and around the edges of a thick
mantle of ivy.

The ivy flourished, along with four evergreen
trees that shut light and sun away from every window on the lower floor except those in the kitch-
en. The front yard was bald and slick. Nothing
but a fine scum of moss would grow on the damp
earth under the trees.

The furniture inside the house was apt to be
slick too, and, Nora often felt, damp as the earth
outside. She usually shook herself furtively after
sitting for any length of time on the sofa or chairs
in the ceremonial parlor.

"I don't see how Aunt Amalia's borne living
here even a month," she thought, going up the
front steps. "Even her personality doesn't make a
dent on the place. But I suppose personality isn't
an adequate substitute for a furnace—"

She rang the bell and stood waiting until Patton opened the door: Patton trim and sturdy in a dark dress, cotton stockings and low-heeled shoes. As always, her sorrel-brown hair looked as if it knew its place and meant to keep it. Nora wondered how Patton did it, coming from the kitchen and the preparation of a not-too-simple dinner.

She was immediately conscious her own hair wanted combing, that her blouse was crumpled and one of its buttons hanging by a thread. That was the effect Patton had on her: she would never be really at ease with a well-trained servant. She despised herself for being grateful that Patton's "Good evening, miss," was less austere than usual.

"I'm not disgracefully early, am I?" she said, stepping into the hall. "My aunt said eight o'clock—"

"Yes, miss. It's half after seven, but Madam hasn't come in yet."

"You don't mean she's still downtown?"

"Oh no, miss. She was here this afternoon, but she went out again. I don't believe there is any cause for alarm. May I take your things? And begging your pardon, but I rather thought Mr. Sturtevant would be with you—"

"Mr. Sturtevant?" Nora said blankly. "He's coming by to take me home about ten-thirty. Do you mean he's expected to dinner?"

"Why—Madam said dinner for three, and that you would be here, miss. So I'm afraid I presumed Mr. Sturtevant would be the third guest, though Madam didn't say so."

"Well, perhaps Aunt Amalia got in touch with him since I've seen him, but I don't think so," Nora said. "Because if he'd been coming here to dinner after all, he'd have gotten in touch with me again to tell me so. Whoever it is should be here soon. I'm earlier than I should be—"

"Oh no, miss," Patton said politely. "If you will step into the living room, there is a fire there."

The fire was a few smoldering chunks of coal in a very small grate. The marble mantelpiece was fully six feet long, but an eighteen-inch log would have strained the seams of the fireplace. Outside it was so warm a light coat was all one needed, but even tonight it would have taken a small conflagration to warm this room satisfactorily. Patton moved a chair close to the fireplace, knelt and stirred the coals into sullen flame.

"If you'll excuse me, miss?" she said then. "I'm certain Madam will soon be here—"

"I wish she'd come," Nora said nervously. "I can't imagine why she isn't here. But don't let me keep you."

When Patton had gone she sat scowling at the row of floridly hand-painted china vases and plates on the mantelpiece. More than likely Roger Keith would be the third at dinner. Lona would have been here by now: she always arrived much earlier than you wanted her to. Whereas Roger would probably turn up, unapologetic, at eight-thirty.

Of course there was Edwin Lacey, the second and last of the "distant cousins." She didn't know of anyone besides Lona, Roger or Edwin—or Neil—that Amalia would be apt to ask to dinner. So far she hadn't tried to get in touch with any old friends. . . .

But perhaps she had—today. She might have been looking forward to meeting someone she hadn't seen for thirty years. . . . Well, but in that case, why hadn't she said so? There were people who instinctively said as little as possible of their personal affairs, but Amalia wasn't one of them.

Nora shook her head. A prospective reunion with an old friend wasn't enough to account for Amalia's cheerful excitement. Meeting Nora at the White House this morning, her first words had been:

"Darling, my feet are barely touching the earth today. I'm fairly soaring, even if I am an elderly woman with a game leg. I was just remembering that Mr. Landreth used to call me Micawber. He said I was too confident something would always turn up. I wasn't feeling too Micawberish last week, but my luck hasn't run out after all.

"And," she added with her peculiarly youthful giggle, "I can almost hear James asking why, if I've held out this long, I can't wait a few hours more. Shall we get a taxi, pet, and see what your Mr. Dundas has to offer? I remember his shop now: it's next door to Cornelius'."

It was silly, Nora thought now, to be so contrary you wouldn't ask questions just because you knew people wanted you to. And she hadn't said to Aunt Amalia: "What's happened?" or, "I'll simply die of curiosity if you don't tell me what it's all about." She'd talked about Michael and Valerie Dundas during the short time it took to go from the White House to Gisele's. Otherwise Amalia might have told her where she was going this afternoon, and if she knew that she might know there was a perfectly good reason for Amalia's absence.

It was already eight o'clock. And that meant, almost certainly, that Edwin wasn't the second dinner guest, because to Edwin eight o'clock meant five minutes of and not so much as one minute after. It would be Roger, and even five minutes alone with Roger was the last thing Nora wanted at any time.

She looked irresolutely toward what she could see of the hall through the living room's open door and finally got to her feet. She had forgotten to put powder in her compact, and its mirror was broken. Amalia wouldn't care if she borrowed powder and a spare comb or brush.

Nora went slowly up the stairway to the second floor, her hand sliding smoothly over the solid mahogany railing that had come from New York around the Horn. One light burned dimly in the upper hall near the top of the stairs. Nora turned toward the big front bedroom, glancing over her shoulder at the door of another bedroom.

This both Lona Keith and Amalia referred to as "the blue room." But Amalia sometimes spoke of it facetiously as "the shrine." If there was anything disparaging about the term, Amalia intended the criticism not for her grandmother Gordon, whose the blue room had been, but for her mother, who had kept the room as the old lady left it.

"That kind of thing is so morbid," Amalia had remarked. "Grandmother would have said so too. But when she died in her sleep one night just before we went off to Europe Mother locked the door and gave orders nothing was ever to be changed or disturbed there—"

And, according to both Lona Keith and Nora's mother, nothing had ever been disturbed even when the room was swept and dusted. "Just one of Mother's little ways of asserting herself," Amalia said. "One way of holding up her hand and telling time to stand still. I'd have liked some of Grandmother's things—to use because she'd used them. That would never have occurred to Mother, so it's left to me to dispose of everything. . . ."

Well, Nora thought, from what Amalia had said this morning—that she could vacate the house at tiny time—she must have decided what was to be kept and what thrown away. She'd said on Thursday there was almost nothing any member of the family couldn't have for the asking, but Nora doubted that anyone would do much asking. The only thing she wanted was a glass letterweight that, briefly inverted, showered snowflakes down on Little Red Ridinghood and her dog.

She opened the door of Amalia's bedroom and groped for the light switch. She felt the round pearl button under her finger and jabbed at it. Afterward she remembered that very clearly. She thought, too, that the light came on and then burst suddenly into a hundred fiery fragments. Their glow blinded her, and one of them seemed to have lodged in the back of her head. But that burned out, too, and then there was only blackness until she heard someone whimpering and knew it was herself.

She was in some airless place that smelled of leather, fur and sachet. Amalia's violet sachet and, of course, Amalia's closet. Nora struggled to sit up, clawing at the skirts of the dresses hanging above her, pulling two of them from their hangers. She managed finally to get to her knees and find the knob of the closet door.

The door was locked. Nora opened her mouth and then closed it. No one would hear her if she screamed; besides, she felt as if the top of her head would fly off if she did. She touched the back of it cautiously and was almost pleased when she discovered a lump there.

That was definite proof someone had hit her over the head and slung her in here. Someone who'd been waiting behind the bedroom door as she opened it; someone who couldn't escape down the front stairs While she was in the living room, sitting so she could see into the hall. And couldn't make use of the back stairway whose door opened into the kitchen as long as Patton was there. . . .

At that point Nora muttered childishly: "My head hurts too much to think." Besides, it was unbearably cold in the closet. She stood shakily erect and tried to find some sort of coat among the garments on the hangers.

Amalia's shoes and hatboxes seemed to be gathered into a heap in the middle of the floor. Amalia didn't leave them that way, Nora thought. She kept the shoes all in a row and the hatboxes on the closet shelf. Someone else had done this—

By touch she identified a padded chintz robe she had seen Amalia wear and threw it over her shoulders. It reached only a little below Nora's knees, for Amalia was barely five feet tall. She sat down again, pulling the robe's full skirt over her crossed legs. Something crackled faintly in a pocket, and she automatically thrust an exploring hand into it. But the thing was only an envelope. . . .

She put her head down on her arms and closed her eyes. She might finally have dozed for a few minutes, for when she started up it was to the sound of a door's slamming. She waited, hands twisted hard together, until she heard a familiar voice say: "Jeepers creepers! What goes on here?" and then she began to scream.

IV

"Don't try to talk till Patton gets back with that brandy," Roger said. "So a big bad burglar hit you over the head? It's a good thing you have thick hair, Leonora."

"What time is it?" Nora asked.

"What time? Nine o'clock."

"Oh." Nora lay back in the old rocking chair where Roger had put her after helping her from the closet. "Well, even for you, coming at nine for an eight o'clock dinner—"

"Look, my sweet," Roger said gently. "Are you suggesting I was asked to dinner tonight? Because I wasn't."

"You weren't! But someone was—"

"So Patton says. But it wasn't me. I just dropped by hoping for brandy and coffee and conversation. And I get—this."

One look at the room explained his "Jeepers creepers! What goes on here?" The bedclothes had been torn apart; cushions plucked out of two chairs and the upholstery ripped away from a third. The door of a three-cornered washstand stood open with a once indispensable article of bedroom furniture resting upside down in front of it like a large china egg with a handle. Every drawer of the ponderous bureau and chiffonier had been pulled out and half their contents tumbled onto the floor.

Since Nora had last been here Amalia had carried in stacks of old family photographs and yellowed letters, several plush photograph albums, a leather-bound diary and a huge family Bible with clasped covers. These, on the floor beside her desk, seemed not to have been disturbed, though the desk itself had been no more gently treated than bureau or chiffonier.

Even the wastepaper basket had been upended, and a miscellaneous collection of articles on a

round, claw-footed table looked as if they had
been handled by careless or angry hands. Two
old-fashioned workbags were turned inside out:
threads, needles, darning cottons, two silver thim-
bles, newspaper clippings, buttons of every color
and shape, bits of unfinished needlework, crochet
and tatting were strewn over the table and floor. A
long box decorated with a painted spray of violets
and a crookedly lettered "Gloves" had obviously
been thrown to the carpet and then stepped on.

"It's—senseless," Nora said. "Unless someone
was looking for something definite he knew must
be here. And how could your big bad burglar know
that—and that Amalia wasn't up here dressing for
dinner as she usually would have been? A thief
who broke in just to see what he could find that
was worth taking would take it and leave. Besides,
Patton keeps the kitchen door locked, and the
downstairs windows haven't been opened for years
and are stuck tight."

"I know." Roger walked over to the bureau and
inspected Amalia's silver toilet articles. "This jew-
el box is full up with stuff that looks good to—"

"Costume jewelry, all of it." Nora barely glanced
toward the bureau. Her eyes still seemed not quite
in focus, or she would have seen at once that at
least one thing had been taken from the bureau.
"Aunt Amalia didn't have any valuable jewelry. She

had the usual string of pearls once, but she sold that to get back to the United States and divorce Colonello."

"She didn't recover any of her dowry from that guy," Roger said absently. "Well—Patton, you're the woman we want to talk to. You might pour me a slug of that stuff while you're at it."

"Yes sir." Patton put an old cut-glass decanter and two glasses on the bedside table. "I must admit I'm beginning to be rather uneasy about Madam," she said, pouring brandy. She brought one of the glasses over to Nora. "When it came to be almost nine o'clock I went into the living room, and you weren't there, miss. I was just starting to come upstairs when Mr. Keith arrived."

"And she thought I was the missing dinner guest," Roger said. "But I swear I'm not."

Why "swear," Nora thought. Does he already think we're going to want very badly to know who, besides me, Aunt Amalia asked here tonight? She watched him furtively as he stood frowning at the disordered desk.

He looked a strong, silent, out-of-doors type, but while he was strong enough—physically—no one had ever called him silent, and he was a contented city dweller. He owed his tan to the exchange of an old typewriter for a used sun lamp and the lines about his eyes to his habit of easy laughter.

Because of that and the fact that a lock of brown hair was usually playing tag with his eyebrows your attention was distracted from his gray eyes. By the time you realized how sharp and inquisitive they were, it was usually too late: you were already well on your way to being in print.

"Maybe it doesn't matter who the missing guest is," he went on. "But it certainly does begin to seem important to find out where Amalia went. If you don't know, Patton— By the way, what is your first name?"

"Gertrude, sir. But I prefer to be called Patton."

"An old English custom. You are English?"

"Yes sir."

"The cotton stockings would tell that if your accent didn't. Though you must have lived in America quite a while?"

Nora smiled unwillingly. It was so like Roger to take this time to try to satisfy his curiosity about Patton—who had so far eluded him. He might have use for an English maid sometime, and she knew he considered Patton a promising specimen.

"I've been in the States ten years, sir," said the promising specimen. "She said this morning that she would lunch downtown, and she returned home at about two-thirty. She laid down to rest for a while—"

Patton glanced toward the topsy-turvy bed and sighed almost imperceptibly. "And she told me she wouldn't be having tea at home today. She came downstairs at about quarter of five: we met in the hall. She said: 'I'm going now. I might be a little late getting back, but if I am I won't bother to dress.' And then she went out—"

"She didn't call a taxi?" Nora said. "She never used street cars—"

"She walked, miss. I must own I was a bit surprised that she did. When I opened the front door and saw no cab was waiting I asked if I shouldn't order one. But she said that she was early and was going to walk; that it wasn't too far, would be good for her and help to pass the time."

"Oh. When did she tell you that I'd be here tonight?"

"This morning, miss. And thinking it over, I'm inclined to believe she may not have intended in the forenoon that there should be a second dinner guest. Because when I brought up her breakfast tray, and she said that you would be here, she certainly would have said dinner for three if she had planned that then. But it wasn't until this afternoon that she asked if I could manage dinner for three."

"And did you see this room after she left?" Roger asked. "She didn't leave it in this state—"

"Oh no, sir!"

"I wanted to ask about the shoes and hatboxes," Nora broke in. "There in the closet— Aunt Amalia didn't leave them in a heap like that, did she?"

Patton looked into the closet. "Oh no, miss! After she walked away I came up here, hung up that quilted robe you have about you now and put her slippers in the closet. Everything was in perfect order then, as it was when I passed by again at seven o'clock and glanced in, wondering if Madam might have returned. I could see well enough by what light there was from the hall to know the room was not like this. It—it looks as if someone might have been looking for something in her shoes."

"That's what I thought." Nora turned to Roger. "I don't think it was any common thief that hit me over the head. I think it has some connection with Aunt Amalia's being missing. I want to report that to the police."

"They won't take you too seriously if you tell 'em Amalia's an hour and a half late to dinner," Roger said. "They handle too many false alarms like that. And you'd have to admit Amalia is no slave to the clock."

"She may be hurt. A car may have hit her—"

"Then we'd have been notified by now. She didn't go out without her purse, did she? There'd be plenty of means of identification in it."

"Madam had her purse," Patton volunteered. "And her clothing is marked with her name. She was dressed just as she was this morning, Miss Keith."

"I'll call the emergency hospital or even Missing Persons, but it won't do any good—this early," Roger said "And if she comes walking in pretty soon it'll be a little embarrassing—"

"And the burglary?" Nora said sweetly. "Would it be embarrassing to report that too?"

"You've just said it isn't an ordinary burglary. If it isn't, and someone was searching this room for some very special item, it's just possible Amalia wouldn't welcome publicity. Could anyone have gotten in by the back door since Amalia left here, Patton?"

"No sir. I very seldom leave the kitchen door unlocked and never in the late afternoon. It gets dark early now, and that overgrown old back yard, if I may say so, seems almost an invitation to prowlers."

"Well, then I don't see how the fellow got in or why he wouldn't wait till later at night. . . . Hey! What are you going to do?"

"There are a few people Aunt Amalia might have talked to today or might even be with now," Nora said, taking the telephone from the bedside table.

"Lona or Edwin? I don't think Edwin is at home—"

"I'm calling Lona. She makes a point of keeping in touch with Aunt Amalia."

"Yes," Roger said thoughtfully. "'My sister-in-law, Mrs. Landreth, who was the Contessa Colonello—'"

"Lona may be funny that way, but *she* has never struck me as being really mercenary," Nora retorted. "She . . . Lona? This is Nora. I'm at Aunt Amalia's and—"

"I'm so glad you are, dear. It's sweet of you to find time for Amalia when you're so busy. I know how it is: I've been rushed myself. I was only able to run in for a few minutes Friday and Saturday. Oh, I did have tea with her on Sunday, but I had to rush away—"

Roger, standing behind Nora, grinned and drew one finger across his throat. Nora grimaced.

"I'm sorry you think I've been neglecting Amalia—"

"But I didn't say that, Nora dear. I only said *I* feel a little guilty because I can't be with her more.

But Mrs. Greer insists she must have her drapes by Thursday, so I've been weaving since early morning, and I'm still at it. That isn't hard work, I know, compared with your job. Have you ever thought it may be too strenuous for you? I know you are naturally thin, and it must be wonderful not to have to count calories. But I'm afraid you don't take very good care of yourself, though you were probably only tired when I saw you last—"

"I didn't call to discuss my health," Nora said rudely. "Have you talked to Aunt Amalia today? Because she asked me—and someone else—to dinner. We don't know who else, but she walked out of here about five, and she isn't back."

"And of course you're worried? I wouldn't be—"

Nora gritted her teeth. She could fairly see Lona looking a little more than usual like a serene Scandinavian goddess chiding a foolishly impatient mortal.

"Because while Amalia wouldn't willingly cause you an instant's worry, people with wonderfully optimistic and cheerful dispositions like hers are apt to do things that worry more practical people," Lona went on. "That is, Amalia wouldn't worry, so it won't occur to her that you might."

"Oh, you needn't be drawing me a diagram. Did you talk to her today? No? Then I won't be keeping you."

"But, Nora, you are so impetuous, dear. Don't do anything rash—"

"Like calling in the police? That makes two of you that don't seem anxious for me to be doing that. But I'll let it go for a while and wait here. Good-by. . . . Why do you think Edwin isn't home, Roger?"

"I ran into him downtown at noon, and he mentioned having to make another will this evening for an old dame who changes hers every time she gets mad at one of her relatives. Why not consult Cornelius?" Roger said. "He is stolid, dependable, unexcitable—and dull."

"He isn't a member of the family yet. And he isn't dull. Except for that, you're right!"

Nora jabbed angrily at the telephone dial, and Patton cleared her throat reprovingly.

"If you'll excuse me, miss? I'm not certain I turned off the oven when I left the kitchen."

"Yes, of course. We don't need you now. . . . Neil doesn't answer," Nora said. "He might be on his way here now. . . . No: it's not ten o'clock yet. Roger, I'm scared!"

"I'll admit I'm beginning to be uneasy myself. But I still say it's too early to do anything. And I don't think you've told me everything that's on your mind. In fact, I have a definite hunch you don't trust me."

"Do you say so? I don't."

"You used to."

"And I'll not be doing it again. I don't think you're interested in anyone except for what you can get out of them: whether it's money or that they're what you call 'good copy.' There's the way you bled my grandmother—"

"She had more ice water than blood in her veins," Roger said coolly. "You weren't very excited about it at the time."

"Why would I be when I was thirteen, and you were nineteen and my idol? But that was eleven years ago. I thought you liked me and Mother too. You did stand by when she died and helped me through that. And then," Nora said bitterly, "you put Mother in a book and t-tried to s-seduce me!"

"I beg your pardon! I made you a simple proposition. If I had really tried to seduce you the chances are I'd have succeeded. Because you were lonely and grateful. So I demand credit where it's due. I was a damned fool, but you were to blame too—"

"I was to blame!"

"Yes. When you were nineteen you tried to give the impression you were utterly modern and emancipated. You had me thinking you meant it. As to putting Molly into a book, that was a compliment, and if you had any literary judgment, you'd realize that. What's more, Nora, you're a snob."

"Me? I'm a snob! Why, you—"

"You are," Roger said pleasantly. "You say your mother was worth all the Keiths put together. So stop remembering she was once 'in service' in this house every time you step into it. Because she was a damned fine woman. But if I told you when you're excited—as you are now—your voice hangs in the air at the end of a sentence, the way Irish voices do, and that you sound just like your mother, you'd be insulted. There are times when you give me a fine, large pain. Now, are you going to tell me what's on your mind concerning Amalia—that you haven't told me?"

"No, I am not! You wouldn't think it was important." Nora took up the telephone again. "I'm going to talk to someone who may think it is and suggest something to do about it."

V

Michael took one look about the living room, shuddered violently and walked over to the anemic fire.

"I take off my hat to the Victorians," he said. "They were a hardy species, physically and esthetically. Though I suppose this room is more Edwardian than Victorian. It should be placed, intact, in the De Young Museum."

"You've got something there," Roger said. "But see here: I told Nora it was an imposition to ask you to—"

"I am not easily imposed on, Mr. Keith. And I am interested." Michael turned to Nora. "Mrs. Landreth is not in the morgue. I got in touch with Sullivan of the homicide squad, and he got that information for me."

"I wonder," Roger said conversationally, "why just the word 'morgue' makes some people turn green. Of course it is one of those words whose very sound is like the thing it stands for. Brace up, Nora: you asked for it."

"It's a relief to have one definite piece of information even if it is on the negative side. We called the emergency hospital after I talked to you, Michael. They've no record of her there. What did Mr. Sullivan say?"

Michael shrugged. "You can't blame him for not being unduly excited. Mrs. Landreth hasn't even stayed out all night yet. But while this doesn't come within his province—yet—he promised to let me know if he hears anything that might be even a lead."

"You're a cheerful guy," Roger complained. "Why should you immediately suspect foul play— if you don't mind that phrase?"

"I do mind. It is unworthy of you, Mr. Keith."

Roger grinned. "I don't talk like I write, if that's what you mean. Whenever I detect anything that can be called a sparkle in my conversation, I note it down for future use. Ordinarily I polish my sentences while polishing the seat of my pants on a chair before a typewriter. But why should you be interested in this business?"

Without actually turning his back on Roger, Michael managed to give the impression he had done so.

"I talked to your aunt after you left the office this morning, Nora. Our conversation was not the usual one between a lady and her couturier. Since I am a friend of yours, and she'd known Valerie's father, she might have waived formality in any case. But she was so happily excited—not worried or afraid—over something that it was all she could do to keep from telling anyone who would be politely interested all about it."

"That's what I felt," Nora said. "So I didn't just imagine it if you felt it too. I'll tell you what she said to me over the telephone early this morning and later when we met at the White House. . . .

"You see?" she ended. "She was happy and excited: she said so. She said her luck hadn't run out after all, though for a while she'd thought it might have—"

"She said to me that a good story and good luck need to be shared," Michael said. "And that several times today she'd come close to breaking a good resolution—"

"Not to talk for a while longer," Nora finished. "She told me it wasn't because she'd sold the house that she could be extravagant. She said: 'it's just the most amazing—' and then didn't finish. Was she going to say 'story' or 'bit of luck'? And then she remembered I was coming to dinner, and I think she decided to put off telling me anything until then. But what had happened since I saw her last Thursday, and why could she tell me what it was tonight but not this morning?"

"As to the first, I couldn't guess. But she did have an appointment somewhere, with someone, at about five o'clock, apparently. And this morning she was considering the technique of bargaining. She doubted if she knew how to strike a hard bargain, yet she felt she must. In that connection it had occurred to her that two strings to your bow are better than one. So she looked up an address in the classified ads, copied it—and also asked me where the Phelan Building is. And, I imagine, went by taxi from the shop to that building."

"The Phelan Building?" Nora glanced instinctively toward Roger. "There are a lot of offices there."

"Our cousin, Edwin Lacey, has one there," Roger said.

Michael frowned. "But isn't he an attorney? And she said: 'You'd think there 'd be more, but I suppose almost any of them—' referring to some section of names in the telephone directory."

"No one could say there aren't enough attorneys," Roger agreed. "But if she's been in Edwin's office she would know where the Phelan Building is."

"She hasn't," Nora said. "Edwin met her at the train when she arrived, and she's never had any reason to go to his office. Could she have been looking for a—a detective agency, Michael? I know that's a crazy idea, but—"

"There are quite a number of detective agencies listed. I remember thinking she hadn't gone very far into the alphabet to find what she wanted. Beyond *a* but no farther than *e,* I'd say. There's no more information I can give you; it's up to you now, Nora."

"Up to me? In what way? Why?"

"You're her next of kin, I believe? I should think it's your place to decide whether you sit here and wait for her to return or proceed on the assumption she isn't coming back."

"If we did know she wasn't coming back we'd notify the police," Roger said. "In a way, you have.

But they aren't here asking questions. We've talked to Patton: she's told us all she can—"

"From what Nora told me over the telephone
you questioned her only about what happened today. You didn't cover the period from Thursday to
this morning."

"You're remembering I said Aunt Amalia was
so depressed Thursday—yet we both saw what she
was like today. . . . When did you see her last,
Roger?" Nora asked.

"Patton can tell you I was here Friday morning
and Saturday noon. When I dropped in on Friday
I hadn't seen her since Tuesday. And she was certainly very cheerful, even for Amalia, those last
two days. Maybe there was an 'I-know-something-
I-won't-tell' air about her."

Nora started to speak, stopped and looked away
from Michael when he glanced speculatively from
Roger to her.

"Well, Aunt Amalia certainly wouldn't expect
us to ignore her bedroom's being turned upside
down—"

"If you'd thought that was a plain case of burglary you'd have notified the police instead of telling Mr. Dundas not to mention it to them. And
if you don't think it was any ordinary thief in her
room—"

"Oh, Roger, I'm tired listening to you being logical and—and consistent," Nora said. "I can't just sit and wait. I've got to be doing something! Michael, will you come up to her bedroom? I told you the state it's in, but you'll be wanting to see for yourself. . . ."

Patton came down the hall as they stepped into it. "Mrs. Stephen Keith just called, miss," she said. "You wouldn't have heard the telephone in Madam's bedroom, so I answered. Mrs. Keith would like to be notified when Madam returns."

Michael looked up and down the hall. "There's no telephone here?"

"No sir. Madam wished a telephone in her bedroom, because she spent so much of her time there—"

"She wasn't awfully well when she first got here," Nora explained. "Besides, her bedroom at least gets sun when there is sun."

"She didn't wish to have to come downstairs to the telephone," Patton said. "So, since she didn't intend to stay here permanently, she had only the one extension besides the telephone in the kitchen. She said it would be more convenient for me to have one there. Madam was very thoughtful about little things like that."

"Perhaps she realized she was very fortunate to have you here," Michael said pleasantly. "My wife and I have had trouble finding anyone who is willing to do a moderate amount of work about a seven-room house with every labor-saving device known to man. And this place is—how large?"

"Ten rooms, sir. But there are really only five to be looked after since, as Madam said, we are 'only camping out.' She meant to have a small apartment later, and I prefer doing for single ladies who are not too young. And I—I quite liked Madam."

"I see. May we have some coffee in an hour or so?"

What does he see? Nora wondered. Why Patton is working here?—if he thinks that needs explaining. Perhaps you would expect her to turn up her nose at a job like this, but she's as good as said she was looking ahead to what would be an easy berth—

"How many bedrooms upstairs?" Michael asked.

"Five, and one bathroom with a tin tub in a wooden frame," Nora, said, leading the way upstairs. "The big front bedroom was my grandmother's. When her father died, and Great-grandmother Gordon came here to live she was put into the blue room. That's sometimes called the 'shrine,'" she added, and told Michael why.

"My father and Uncle Stephen had these two back rooms as boys, and later Uncle Stephen was

promoted to this room across from the shrine."
Nora pointed out the doors as they paused at the
top of the stairway. "Lona took away his belongings when he died; that was one thing my grandmother couldn't stop her doing. There were a few
things of my father's packed away in his old room,
and Aunt Amalia asked me to look through them
Thursday afternoon."

"You said she'd begun turning out the place
Wednesday?" Michael said.

"Yes, she'd put it off until then. She particularly
hated going through things in the blue room.
She used to sit in there with Great-grandmother
Gordon when she was a child—especially Sunday afternoons when they'd read the Bible, and
Great-grandmother would tell her stories. Well,
when I left on Thursday she said she was going to
get at that room, and I suppose she did, because I
think some of the things she carried in here must
have belonged to Great-grandmother Gordon—"

Nora threw open the door of Amalia's bedroom
and put on the light. Michael whistled.

"Offhand I'd say this lacks the professional
touch. How can you be certain nothing was taken?"

"We can't," Roger said. "But if anything was
taken wouldn't you suppose it was something that
wasn't easily found? Nora says Amalia had no valuable jewelry—"

"She hadn't. These toilet articles are sterling," Nora said, stopping at the bureau. "Wouldn't any ordinary thief grab them at once? Of course they're initialed—"

"That doesn't mean they couldn't be disposed of," Michael said absently, still looking about the room. "Articles like solid silver picture frames are coveted by petty thieves. . . . What is it? Was a picture frame part of this set?"

"Yes. And it's gone. I hadn't noticed before. But why take just a picture frame—"

"Was there a picture in it?"

"Aunt Amalia and her husband, taken about ten years ago."

"And she hasn't been photographed since."

It was more an assertion than a question, but Nora nodded. "No. It was the best picture she'd ever had taken, she said. She'd thrown away the old ones."

"Well, suppose someone did grab a picture?" Roger said. "What is there about that to—"

"It was a good likeness of Mrs. Landreth and a fairly recent one. These"—Michael pointed to the old photographs stacked beside Amalia's desk—"apparently haven't been disturbed, but you'll probably find nothing of Mrs. Landreth taken after 1908 among them. And I intended telling you before I leave that the authorities will want not only a description of her and what she was wearing but, if possible, a good photograph."

"You can't recognize a person from a description that is just a catalogue of her physical characteristics," Roger admitted. "That kind of thing doesn't make any impression; no one knows that better than a writer—"

"The police know it, Mr. Keith. And that even a really good likeness printed in the newspapers doesn't mean people who have seen that person will remember having done so. I can't help thinking someone has looked ahead to the time when the newspapers will be asking if anyone saw Mrs. Landreth after four forty-five this afternoon—and where. And that by destroying the one good photograph of her, someone has helped to make it difficult for any stranger to say that he did see her."

Roger was frowning now, chewing on the stem of an unlighted pipe. Nora's face looked pinched and waxy white, but Michael went on:

"Besides, you've asked how a thief was able to get into this house, but the simplest way for anyone to do that doesn't seem to have occurred to you."

"The simplest way? What's that?" Roger said.

"By using the key to the front door, that Mrs. Landreth must have carried in her purse."

VI

For an instant the shrewish ticking of the old marble clock was as distinct and cheerless a sound as that of water dropping on cold stone. Then Nora began:

"But if anyone had that key—or her purse—"

"Of course someone could have her keys," Roger said quickly, "and she could still be alive."

"But held in duress vile?" Michael said unpleasantly. "Kidnaping involves ransom, and ransom calls for cash—"

He was at the desk and had Amalia's checkbook in his hand before either of them could object. "A balance of a little more than fifteen hundred dollars in a New York bank, according to her check stubs."

"See here, you haven't any right to do that," Roger said.

"No? She ordered clothes to the amount of nearly three hundred dollars at the shop this morning. Though she struck me as a lavish person I hardly think she would have run up so large a bill if this money was all she had or expected to have."

"Well—in an indiscreet moment Edwin Lacey told me she'd converted what Landreth left into cash," Roger said. "So what else could she have except what little Aunt Alice left and what she'd get from selling this house?"

"Aunt Alice? That's what you called Mrs. Land-reth's mother—Nora's grandmother?"

"Yes. But she wasn't my aunt. I never bothered to get the relationship straight. You might be able to work it out by referring to that." Roger point-ed to the big family Bible. "The center section is devoted to births, marriages and deaths. However, my father and Edwin's mother were Keiths, cous-ins of some sort to Amalia's father. None of the Keiths were well to do; it was Gordon money Aunt Alice brought into the family when she married David Keith. The only important point is that if Amalia had anything to leave, only Nora has any claim on it."

"I see. Mrs. Landreth seems to have seen so few people since she returned here I can't help being curious about Edwin Lacey. His name keeps crop-ping up, you know."

"Well: Profile of Edwin Lacey. Copyright 1939 by Roger Keith. All rights reserved. Edwin, better known as the Boy Wonder—"

"That's not fair!" Nora said.

"Leonora, darling, the Keiths are apt to be pre-cocious. We don't improve with age any more than a souffle does. I had my first book published at nineteen—and I prefer not to go on from there. To resume: Edwin was born here in 1899. Join-ing the army in '17 kept him out of college for a while, but he graduated in due time, loaded down with honors. His record in law school was also brilliant.

"But Coolidge prosperity got Edwin. Got him a job with a building and loan company at a fancy salary. He should put in a lean year or two establishing his own law practice or even be a junior partner when the pickings elsewhere were so easy! Well, in '31 the company folded—permanently. Edwin lost his job, his investments—bought on margin, of course—and in time, his wife."

"He married Dolly Chartos," Nora said. "She expected to be maintained in style. So she went to Reno and then married a man named Gerard. Now she's divorced from him, but he pays a nice fat alimony."

"Either he does not pay it promptly, or it isn't fat enough to meet Mrs. Gerard's demands on it," Michael said. "I never contemplate her account with any great pleasure."

"Oh, you know her? What is she like?"

"She is a beautiful woman and, I imagine, a bitch from the word 'go.'"

"Well, Edwin picked up the pieces and went back to law," Roger said. "But he started late and at a bad time, so it's been tough sledding. Wills, trusts and so on are his line. Oh yes: footnote.

You don't call him 'Ed.' And I don't imagine people ever call you 'Mike.'"

"People have tried," Michael said imperturbably. "Was Lacey old Mrs. Keith's lawyer?"

"He made her last will. Before that he'd never had anything to do with Aunt Alice."

"Why? He was a male and a Keith of sorts, and I gathered from Nora that her grandmother may have had a weakness for that particular article."

"She had Son Stephen till '25. Oh, she'd seen Edwin now and then, but he lived down South from about 1901 until he came up here to college. That, and his being ten years older than I am, is why I didn't know him when we were younger. And Aunt Alice didn't approve of Edwin's mother, Edwina Lacey. She didn't approve of my father either, even if he was a male Keith."

"Well?" Nora said suggestively.

"Do you think you're paying me back for calling you a snob? You aren't. I can see why your grandmother wouldn't think highly of my father though I've kept an open mind on the subject. Because while my mother was a terrifically good woman she was a most dismal person to live with."

Michael was on the point of asking Roger what his father's peccadillos had been, but he thought he could guess from Roger's description of his mother. He thought, besides, that possibly his time might be better employed just now. Still, Nora's and Roger's constant references to Edwin Lacey and Lona Keith hadn't much meaning unless you knew something about them. . . .

He smiled bleakly. He was not often self-deceived, and he could diagnose his own symptoms. They all pointed to the recurrence of a malady that hadn't attacked him for more than a year—a determination to meddle in something that was none of his business.

For an instant he considered telling Nora to count him out. It wasn't his liking for her that stopped him: it was the memory of Amalia Landreth smiling at him across his desk while even the ridiculous half bird on her ridiculous hat seemed to quiver with excitement.

He could have drawn Amalia out to confide in him; that was the hell of it. She'd said she had never been a bargainer, and he was afraid that today she'd made the last of her bad bargains. She was no poker player, and without knowing it she'd already drawn aces and eights: dead man's hand. . . .

"A terrifically good woman is more than a woman. She is an institution," he said hastily, seeing that Roger was watching him curiously. "And an institution is a chilly bedfellow. When did old Mrs. Keith begin to cultivate Lacey?"

"He took charge of her affairs in '36, because she was bedridden two years before she died. But she'd asked him to come to see her before that. I don't know just when. I don't suppose she approved of his divorce either. Her viewpoint hadn't changed any since 1900, but she was apt to forgive a man, if not a woman, in such cases."

"Edwin notified Grandmother when his parents died so close together," Nora said. "Wasn't that about four years ago?"

"I guess so. Edwin's folks went on living in the South; Lacey always had. He was well off once, but by the time he and Edwin's mother died there wasn't anything for them to leave Edwin," Roger said. "None of our parents or relatives have ever left us anything that could be called money. There's Lona, for instance—"

"She was eighteen when Stephen married her—she says. I'd guess she was at least twenty. Anyway, as he was thirty-seven she must have thought she was making a good match. But all she got was the bum's rush from Aunt Alice, and what Stephen had managed to save from the allowance he got for staying home with Mamma."

"I've seen Lona Keith," Michael said.

"Yeah? What did you think of her?"

"Oh—Brunhilde as Rossetti would have painted her."

"That's very good. She has one of those bee-stung Rossetti mouths. And come to think of it, there's a sort of Blessed-Damozel flavor about Lona."

"'Her hair that lay along her back was yellow like ripe corn'?"

"Yes—and also: 'less sad of speech than mild,'" Roger said, grinning. "You have to talk with Lona to appreciate her."

"I appreciate her work. Her weaving," Michael said, as Roger looked rather blank. "I saw her at an exhibition of hand-woven materials. Is she of Scandinavian descent? The Scandinavians have a natural aptitude for that sort of work. And does she make her living by it?"

"Yes, but not too good a one," Nora said. "I don't know anything about her family except that they lived in the San Joaquin Valley. Farmers, I think. Michael, this isn't getting us anywhere! Why don't you—"

"*Do* something," Roger finished for her. "It may not be getting us anywhere, my sweet. But it might all be very useful to Dundas and his friend Sullivan later on. They could get off to a running start with the suspects all lined up and classified. I suggest you look through these pictures and see if you can find one of Amalia that might be worth handing over to the police. And, by the way, where is your soul mate?"

"If you mean Neil, say so," Nora said coldly, sitting down on the floor beside the photographs. "It's only—well, it is past ten-thirty, but he may have fallen asleep reading. Oh, it will take hours to go through these!"

"But it might be a good idea if you did," Michael said.

He had turned back to the desk and stood looking at its jumbled contents: stamps, envelopes, ink, a fountain pen, railroad timetables, Amalia's checkbook, a flattened tube of glue, playing cards, an overturned box of calling cards, a penny box of matches, several opened letters with New York postmarks and the glass letterweight Nora coveted.

"Looking for anything particular?" Roger asked.

"For a letter Mrs. Landreth was carrying in her purse this morning. It had a foreign stamp: Italian, possibly."

"If it was in her purse this morning she probably never took it out," Nora said. "She carried everything under the sun in her purses."

"And that fact deserves some consideration."

"Why, Michael?"

"Because of a remark Fanchon Weiss made to me. Also, the overstuffed state of her purse made Mrs. Landreth think of her grandmother's work-bags—"

"Why not? I'm certain those two on the table belonged to my great-grandmother. What do you think—"

"One thing at a time, if you don't mind."

"The letter?" Roger said. "Why do you want just that one? Aren't you interested in these opened ones in the desk?"

"I imagine you'd feel you must object if I asked to read those—now. But I believe Mrs. Landreth had made some notes on the envelope I referred to. She looked at it before she copied that name or address from the telephone directory. I gave her a sheet of paper, and she remarked that men always have notebooks. Then she said that notes scribbled on old envelopes are not very impressive when you want to refer to them impressively. And that it does not impress people if you have trouble deciphering them."

"You think those notes may have had something to do with this 'bargaining' she was looking forward to?"

"Perhaps. It had occurred to me that, after saying what she did about the notes, she might have made a fair copy of them before she left here this afternoon. She would put that in her purse, and then there would be no reason to return the envelope to it—"

"Hey, do you feel dizzy, Nora?" Roger said anxiously. "Maybe that crack on your head is worse than we thought—"

Nora opened her eyes, started to get up and then gestured helplessly toward her lapful of photograph albums.

"Over there," she said. "In the pocket of that quilted robe over the rocking chair. Patton spoke as if Aunt Amalia wore it this afternoon. I pulled it around me in the closet, but I was so woozy I forgot about feeling a letter in its pocket. . . . Is it the one?"

"I think so," Michael said.

He came over and knelt down beside her, holding the envelope so that both she and Roger could see it. Its back was covered with penciled, closely written notes. Amalia's handwriting was fine, spiky and difficult to read. That, and the fact she had obviously written hurriedly and used the baldest of abbreviations throughout, made the notes as indecipherable as she had pronounced them.

"T. R.—5-30—$3500," she had written. "Bald.—20-51—2500; C. M. & T.—5-49—2500; 10-49—3000; Dub.—5 & 10-50—1200 & 1500 (49s ?); Kell.—50-55—1500; F. D. K. Ings.—3500 (4); 50s 5000 & 4000; M. & C.—5-49—2500; J. S. O.—5 & 10—2000 & 3000; Pac.—5-49—

2000; 10–49—3000; W. M. & C.—10–52—2000; 20–55 ditto—"

A line was drawn under the last notation, and below that she had written: "Acc. C. S.—C. M. & T. 10—3000 (1908); Dub. 10—3900 (29); M. & C. 5—7900 (29); W. M. & C. 20—7000 (29)."

VII

Roger read the notes through a second time, his lips moving, as if he hoped sound would help where sight did not. Then he stood erect, shaking his head.

"The only thing it reminds me of at all is the stock market reports, and I never could make sense out of those."

"She put the dollar sign before thirty-five hundred in the first item," Michael said. "It doesn't appear after that, but if you're adding a column of prices you very seldom bother writing the dollar sign before every one of them."

"Then if all the large figures—the thousands—are that many thousand dollars—" Nora began.

"There's money involved," Roger said. "Let's see. . . . Hell, if those figures stand for dollars it comes to more than fifty grand. And that's without allowing for what she's written after 'acc. C. S.'

It looks to me like she repeated some items there and at higher prices. What the devil are 'ings'?"

"You know we don't know," Nora said irritably. "And I don't see any sense to all those five-dash-thirties and twenty-dash-fifty ones. It might as well be a code—"

"Ah, now we have it! Amalia is an espionage agent, and this is her cipher," Roger said flippantly. "She has gone out to sell the plans of the latest bomber. . . . Well, don't glare at me, Leonora. I'm only trying to furnish a little comic relief. What other point hits you in the eye, Dundas?"

"She has, in the second section of these notes, written one figure I think must be a date—1908 in parentheses. Therefore, the three '29s also in parentheses may also be dates

"Yes, she might have gone back to abbreviations and meant those for 1929s. But what of it?"

"Just that if she wrote her abbreviated dates without an apostrophe some of the figures in the first section of her notes might be dates. I don't know where that gets us," Michael admitted. "Except that it's interesting that the number forty-nine occurs so often—"

"Why?" Nora said wearily.

"Didn't you tell me this morning that the Gordons and Keiths were forty-niners? And your great-grandmother Gordon did seem rather to be in Mrs. Landreth's mind this morning. She spoke of her grandmother's workbags; said they reminded her of her own purses—"

Nora nodded toward the table to one side of her. "See for yourself what was in Great-grandmother's workbags. I'm certain those were hers and so was the glove box."

"Well, let it go. And this cipher for the time being. Though you'll notice that except for the first item—'T. R.—5–30—$3500'—the others are listed alphabetically. That may mean something—or nothing."

Michael put the envelope in his pocket. Roger grinned but offered no objection.

"I'll say Great-grandmother Gordon kept everything but the kitchen stove in her workbags," he said, inspecting them and their scattered contents. "But there's nothing valuable here, though Aunt Alice's motto was 'everything just as dear Mother left it.' Have you finished recalling interesting items from your conversation with Amalia?"

Michael nodded. And at the moment he had honestly forgotten Amalia's saying: "But I don't think chains are attached to pencils in public places to keep just women from walking away with them. . . ." Neither did he think of her: "I've lived so many years in Europe I didn't even know the laws of the United States—"

"What luck, Nora?" he asked. "Shall we help you?"

"You'd better. No luck at all." Nora closed the third and last of the plush albums. "There's none of Aunt Amalia in these that was taken after she was nine or ten."

Michael took one stack of photographs over to the bed. Roger sat on the floor and dug into another.

"This was probably taken just before she went to Europe," he said finally. "She looks about nineteen and quite Gibson girlish."

The photograph showed Amalia in a high-necked, excessively tucked and shirred dress. Her blonde pompadour drooped fashionably, her waist was waspish, and she filled out the space above it satisfactorily. To one who knew her this was Amalia, but as a picture to show a stranger you hoped might recognize her by it it was hopeless material.

"There's a lot of people I don't recognize, besides your father and Stephen all the way from lounging nonchalantly in large seashells through short dresses, sailor suits . . . wasn't that the doorbell?"

"I wasn't listening," Nora said. "There's nothing more recent than the one you have of Aunt Amalia in my lot, Roger."

"Nor in this," Michael said.

He made the pictures he had examined into a neat stack without—apparently—arranging them in any particular order. But he saw to it that two group pictures in which he was interested topped the stack. They raised a question in his mind that Nora might or might not be able to answer. Very likely she could not, and it would be as well not to give her anything more to think of just now.

He was not surprised when she put her head down in her arms and began to cry. "I c-can't help it. Getting hit over the h-head is no fun, and I am fond of Aunt Amalia," she said disjointedly. "And we haven't done one thing—"

Roger's hand hovered over her coppery head in a gesture that was complete self-betrayal. Then he said, without having touched her:

"Come on, snap out of it. There's no use—"

"I beg pardon," Patton said from the hall, "but Mr. Lacey, Mrs. Keith and Mr. Sturtevant are downstairs. And the coffee has been ready some time—"

"We'll come down. The whole damn gang," Roger said disgustedly. He helped Nora to her feet and added by way of comfort: "Your slip shows, youngster. Hike it up and come along. You don't have to explain everything again. I'll do the talking. Coming, Dundas?"

Michael made a sound that might have been "yes" or "no." His actions proved it to be "no." He trailed them to the door and a step or two into the hall, then turned and went quickly back into the bedroom.

The photographs he wanted were too large to go into a pocket, and he finally thrust them under his belt and buttoned his vest over them. They were no more hard and flat than his waist line, so their addition to it only made him appear a trifle rigid.

For an instant he hesitated; then turned to the desk and glanced quickly through the opened letters in it. None of them was long, but all of them gave the impression their writers knew Amalia Landreth was no longer even moderately well off.

A woman who signed herself Marianne urged Amalia to "come back here where you have friends. After all, you haven't lived in San Francisco for thirty years. You can stay with me as long as you want, and there's no use saying 'something will turn up,' because from your last letter there's apparently no chance anything will. You admit even if you sell that house there won't be enough for you to live on the rest of your life even if you were very economical—"

VIII

Though it was not more than ten minutes after Nora and Roger had gone downstairs that Michael entered the living room, Edwin Lacey seemed already to have the most important facts at his finger tips. Michael thought he understood why after listening to Edwin's final incisive questions and noting his pleasant but very drastic way of suppressing Roger's tendency toward volubility.

Roger's slight grin suggested he noted it too and found it amusing. There was a marked resemblance between him and Edwin in features and coloring. Both had slate-gray eyes, but Edwin's were more deeply set, more reflective than inquisitive. They suggested that, instead of being forever alert for new information, he preferred to ponder what he had.

Both were tall, long-armed and long-legged, but Edwin gave an effect of having been more carefully assembled and more securely welded together than Roger. His smile was usually an act of courtesy; Roger's was so frequent as to be sometimes meaningless. And though Edwin's hair was the same dark brown as Roger's, it remained unadventurously wherever he combed it.

"Well," he said when Nora had rather defiantly introduced Michael, "I wouldn't be too much alarmed if it wasn't for your description of the state of Amalia's bedroom. Yet I can't imagine what it was that anyone was looking for that was so well hidden he had to tear the room to pieces to find it."

"If Nora had told me about that I would have been alarmed then and gotten in touch with you earlier," Lona Keith said with a sweetly reproachful glance at Nora.

"She didn't want to upset you," Cornelius said from where he was stationed behind Nora's chair. He patted her shoulder again, and she smiled at him gratefully, though very many of what he considered tender love taps would soon leave one black and blue.

"I'm sorry I wasn't home when you called," he went on. "But I left early, decided it was too early to come get you and stopped in to get a beer. Met a guy I knew and couldn't get away from him, or I wouldn't have been so late getting here."

"I wouldn't have been home if Lona had called me very much earlier," Edwin said. "But if my client hadn't been rather unreasonable so that I couldn't get away from her early, I would have come by here. Since I was drafting a will tonight, it reminded me Amalia wanted to make one—"

"Why? When did she speak of it?" Roger said.

"Friday noon. I've been keeping an eye out for a buyer for this house. I thought I had one Friday morning and drove out here to talk to Amalia about it. And while it is true Nora is undeniably Amalia's next of kin, you can't expect a lawyer to advise anyone not to make a will, any more than a throat specialist will advise your keeping your tonsils."

"I suppose not. Did your prospective buyer run out on you?"

Edwin smiled ruefully. "A really good salesman got him in his clutches and didn't let go. He—his name is Ross—did take one look at the place from the outside and didn't think he cared to examine the interior."

"You can hardly blame him. But I'd have been inclined to ask Amalia just what she had to make a will with—"

"Oh, you are always so refreshingly outspoken, Roger," Lona said. "But Edwin wouldn't say that—"

"I did ask her if she had any special bequests to make."

"And, I suppose, whether she was going to disinherit me?" Nora said stiffly.

"I knew she had no intention of doing that, my dear. But if she was leaving everything to you and had no special bequests to make, I wouldn't have expected her to bother with a will. But she said she would like to remember everyone."

"She was perfectly cheerful on Friday?" Michael said.

"Why, yes. I was glad that she was: I thought she might as well be as long as she could. Because—" Edwin hesitated, then: "I suppose you might as well hear this too, Mr. Dundas," he said. "So far as I know, she had not quite two thousand dollars in a New York bank when she arrived here."

Roger grinned at Michael from behind Edwin's back, and Michael guessed that Roger hadn't yet described their activities or discoveries in Amalia's bedroom. As he was fairly certain Edwin would not approve of his reading Amalia's letters and examining her checkbook and wouldn't willingly allow anyone to carry anything from her bedroom, Michael prepared for a quick exit. He wouldn't care to be searched, and there was no knowing when Roger or Nora might mention the notes on the back of the envelope in his pocket. But until they did. . . .

"I thought I'd made it clear in my letters to Amalia that her mother's estate would amount to very little, but I'm afraid she arrived here thinking I was merely being conservative—or pessimistic," Edwin went on. "She naturally thought of this house as still being a substantial family mansion and a valuable piece of property. She didn't realize it's a drug on the market and almost impossible to rent."

"I think she had realized that by Thursday," Nora said. "And then by Friday morning she was cheerful again. Both you and Roger say so. And this morning she bought several hundred dollars' worth of clothes. Even Aunt Amalia wouldn't do that unless she was expecting to come into more money—"

"Are you sure of that, dear?" Lona said. "Amalia's idea of economy wouldn't be yours or mine. For one thing, she could have found a servant for half the wages she pays Patton. People who have always been used to money are apt to say, 'It's economy to buy the best—'"

She smiled at Michael to show she was paying him and Gisele's a compliment. "But they don't stop to ask, as I've always had to do, whether it's necessary to buy at all. You know Amalia is so delightfully impetuous. I can imagine her thinking: 'I'll get some new clothes; that will cheer me up.'"

"So can I," Cornelius said. "She's very—very nice, but she struck me as being—erratic—"

"So are a lot of 'nice' people," Nora said. "But she isn't erratic enough to stay out after eleven o'clock when she asked me to dinner, along with someone else. All of you say you weren't the other one who was to be here—"

"Oh, but that must have been one of her sudden inspirations, from what Patton tells us," Lona said. "That is one thing that makes Amalia so interesting. She does things on the spur of the moment, instead of planning ahead so she won't inconvenience anyone—as stodgy people like me feel we must do."

She smiled at Michael again because he was regarding her rather fixedly and—she probably thought—with admiration. Actually he was thinking Roger had been wise in not attempting to describe Lona. Her remarks regarding Amalia's ideas of economy proved she didn't lack shrewdness, and also—along with nearly everything else she had said—that she was an expert at the verbal backhanded slap.

"And since Amalia hadn't gotten in touch with any of her girlhood friends yet, mightn't she have done so this afternoon?" she suggested. "And been persuaded to stay to dinner with them instead of coming home?"

"And what was to be keeping her from a telephone then?" Nora said angrily.

"Darling, I love to hear you talk like that. You sound so like your mother. Her mother had the most charming brogue," Lona told Michael. "She never could quite lose it."

"You damned cat!" Roger said deliberately.

"Why, Roger! I only said—"

"I heard what you said, and I know what you meant. I always do; just remember that. And Nora is a goop to be sensitive about the fact her mother once scrubbed floors here, but she is, and you know it—so lay off. Well, what do you think, Edwin?"

"If Inspector Sullivan promised Mr. Dundas to keep his eyes open unofficially and to notify him if—if anything turns up, isn't that as much as can be done tonight?"

"And suppose Amalia does walk in tomorrow morning?" Roger said. "And that in the meantime some bright reporter sees on the police blotter—if that's what you call it—that she's reported missing and decides it will make a good story for the morning papers? I still say it might be embarrassing for her—"

"I don't think she'd blame us," Nora said stubbornly. "And how are we going to trace her movements if she isn't reported missing in the newspapers? I'm right about that, aren't I, Michael?"

"I think so. Have you told Mr. Lacey she may have been in the Phelan Building sometime after twelve-thirty?"

"They told me. I was at lunch then, and if she had asked for me, the secretary would have told me—"

"You don't have to go into that central office to get into yours," Roger remarked. "Your private office has a door into the hall too."

"That door hasn't my name on it," Edwin said sharply. "Three of us share a suite of four rooms and a secretary, Mr. Dundas. The door of her office is marked with our names, and she acts as receptionist."

"I see." Michael was beginning to feel he had put in an unreasonably long day. He was tired of standing, but thought it best not to try to sit down while he was corseted with photographs. "I think I'll go home. What are you going to do, Nora?"

"I'll take her home," Cornelius said quickly.

"Naturally. But is she going home?"

"No. I'm going to stay here."

"But I don't like you doing that, even if Patton is here too."

"I'm sorry, Neil. I'm going to stay."

"But of course I'll stay too," Lona said. "I wouldn't even mind spending the night all alone here, but I realize a large old house like this is apt to be depressing to high-strung people like Nora."

"I still don't like it," Cornelius said with his usual placid stubbornness. "You're just three women and—"

"And a match for any four men," Lona said smilingly.

"You're fighting a losing battle," Michael told Cornelius. "I'll leave you to it. But I was thinking, when you pronounced Mrs. Landreth erratic, that your uncle Cornelius was a bit on the eccentric side himself—"

"What's he got to do with it? I guess he was eccentric. I'd call anyone who spends his life buying and selling antiques kind of peculiar."

"I wasn't thinking of that. I believe he was quite a bon vivant and man about town in his younger days—"

"He got through a lot of money. But I didn't really know him till he was pretty old—"

"I thought Mrs. Landreth might have told you what he was like in his thirties when she talked to you," Michael said. Cornelius eyed him uneasily.

"I don't know what you're driving at. Oh, Mrs. Landreth did say she knew Uncle when she was a girl, but she knew so many people when she was young. I supposed she meant her folks had bought stuff from him."

"That," Michael said, glancing about the room, "is not just to your uncle. He was a man of taste, and I doubt if you ever found such objets d'art as grace this room in his shop. It seems he must at least have been counted a friend of the family. And that perhaps your other inheritance from him—Martha Ferris—can straighten out that point. Good night. . . ."

IX

Patton, coming through the hall with a coffee tray, put it down on a table and hurried to open the front door for Michael.

"I've been thinking about Madam's choosing to walk this afternoon, sir," she said, her voice discreetly lowered. "And you mightn't know that when she said she was going to walk, and that it wasn't 'too far,' she wouldn't mean what someone else might by 'too far.'"

"She wasn't up to walking any great distance?"

"No sir. She didn't quite limp but she did—did favor one leg. And of course she walked slowly."

"It's a good point," Michael said. "And did you stay at this door long enough to see in what direction she went?"

"Yes sir, being a bit surprised she did walk. And she turned to the right—"

"Away from Larkin and Polk streets?"

"Yes sir. But I couldn't see as far as the next corner, so I didn't see if she turned off this street there."

"Since you've been so helpful already, I wonder if you would mind answering a few more questions?"

"Well—" Patton glanced back toward the living-room door, not apprehensively, but thoughtfully. "No sir. I don't think there would be any harm in that."

"Well then: how did Mrs. Landreth spend last Thursday?"

"She went on turning out the rooms where there were articles stored that must be disposed of, sir. She'd begun that Wednesday with the boxes and trunks in the basement, and a horrid mess they were," Patton said distastefully. "What with the place being so damp, and that not keeping the moths out neither. It was mainly old clothing we found down there, and a fair waste of time that was, for there was nothing worth keeping."

"But she found that a rather depressing task?"

"No doubt, sir. But I would say Madam was rather depressed before that. She got chilled working in the basement, and Thursday morning I quite thought she was sickening for something. But she began on the upstairs and said I couldn't help her there; that she was the only one who could judge what to do with what was there."

"Where did she begin?"

"With the back bedrooms. Then a middle room I understand Mrs. Stephen Keith and her husband once shared that had come to be something of a catchall for odds and ends, including old photographs and letters. Well, Mrs. Landreth was so altogether unlike herself—being ordinarily a very cheerful lady, you know—that I own I was thankful Miss Nora came in for tea that afternoon. No one else came in that day—"

"And Mrs. Landreth was more cheerful after Miss Keith left?" Michael suggested.

"I can't say she was, sir. I persuaded her to take a lie-down before dinner, but she still had no appetite. I hoped she would retire early, but about half after nine when I went into the living room to see to the fire she said not to bother with it, that she was going to turn out her grandmother's room and have done with it. That's the blue room, sir. And Madam sometimes jokingly called it 'the shrine.'"

"I know. And did she turn it out that night?"

"Yes sir. When I came upstairs an hour or so later and looked in to see if there was anything I could do, she just—just waved me away, so to speak."

"What was she doing?" Michael asked.

"Sitting on the bed with all sorts of things about her. Her face was that flushed and her eyes

so bright I thought she might be running a fever. But she told me to go to bed in such a way I
daren't oppose her. Well, she took no harm from it
and was quite herself the next morning."

"But she'd carried a number of things from that
room into her own bedroom?"

"Yes sir, besides the letters and photographs
she'd already put by to look through. There were
some workbags—"

"And a glove box painted with a spray of violets?"

Patton frowned. "I don't seem to recall seeing
that at any time, sir. And I dust very thoroughly."

"I'm sure you do. And would you mind telling
me why you decided to answer my questions?"

"Well, one learns who it's safe to talk to, sir.
And if I may say so, there is usually one person in
any group you feel is the one to cope with matters, so to speak. Besides"—Patton flushed faintly
and smoothed her hair—"I thought that if—if it
should come about that Mrs. Landreth won't be—
be requiring my service, and you are looking for a
competent maid—"

"Oh? I thought you preferred doing for single
ladies."

"Rather than for the average young American
couple. But I rather think. . . . It isn't that one's
employers demand too much of one in service, but
they have no standards in a manner of speaking.

And they won't let a body keep herself to herself if you know what I mean? Mrs. Landreth had lived so much in England that she quite understood—"

"And kept her place?" Michael said, smiling. "You and my wife would want to inspect each other, and I don't know if we could live up to you, and we won't promise not to have children. But you'd find my wife divinely laissez-faire. Only I think I should warn you that I am 'in trade.'"

"I know, sir. Madam spoke most enthusiastically of your—your work this afternoon."

"Why not? If I were English I might hope to catch royalty's eye and even be knighted for my labors," Mr. Dundas said immodestly. And with sudden nervous vehemence: "I'd gladly design Mrs. Landreth a complete and original winter wardrobe for no more payment than knowing she would wear it— Well, one more question. Did she go anywhere through Friday until this morning?"

"Saturday afternoon she called a cab about two and, as I remember, returned home after five o'clock. She had a few small parcels: hosiery and gloves. That was really the only time she had free, sir."

"Because her relatives were unusually devoted over this week end?"

"We-ell. But they have all dropped by frequently from the beginning, sir. And," Patton said conservatively, "they seem to be very pleasant persons."

Pleasant persons—and civilized persons, Michael thought, stepping out into the warm, windless night. But was any one of them even passably contented? Considering their histories and present circumstances—and not excluding Cornelius—it seemed to him that any or all of them might be nursing the canker frustration. "Hope deferred maketh the heart sick—" And how often you heard the frustrated and unsuccessful say: "Oh, but it would be different if I only had enough money. . . ."

X

Michael's exit did not, as Nora had hoped, bring down the curtain. She blamed Roger and Edwin equally for that: Roger for describing in detail What had taken place in Amalia's bedroom while they were there with Michael, and Edwin because he condemned those proceedings with unusual vigor.

"Short of gagging Nora when she started telephoning him or opposing his entrance by force, what could I do?" Roger said calmly. "I've no official standing here."

"Who has when we don't know what has happened to Amalia? Oh, I'm not blaming you and Nora," Edwin said more pleasantly. "For consulting

Dundas, that is. But you didn't need to take him upstairs, and I still cannot understand why you allowed him to walk away with that envelope."

"He put it in his pocket. Nora didn't object."

"I wasn't watching him, and I don't care anyway. We couldn't make anything from those notes, but he might."

Edwin looked at Nora as if she were a fractious child up long past her regular bedtime, shrugged and said nothing.

"Why," Lona offered brightly, "didn't you simply say to him, Roger: 'I'm afraid you'd better put that envelope back where you found it'? Politely, of course, and—"

"Firmly? Some time I hope to have the pleasure of seeing you be polite and firm with Mr. Dundas."

"Well, but I'm sure he is very courteous and—"

"Yeah, a kind of continental courtesy which does not mean one damn thing. I believe he's half Spanish—"

"Argentinian," Nora said mechanically. "His father was American, and his grandfather born in Scotland."

"I have a hunch Grandpop lives again in Mr. Dundas' jaw. Anyway, though Lona won't believe me, the Latins are realists and the Scotch canny— but often secret sentimentalists. However, that last is a digression—"

"If you are trying to tell me that Dundas is clever and intelligent you can save your breath," Edwin said. "I know more than you probably do about some of his past activities. You can't say crime is his hobby, but he's been concerned in two murder cases. That affair over on Gough Street in which his wife—who wasn't his wife then—was involved. And over a year ago, the Armstrong kidnaping case—"

"Oh, but a sheriff named Allan from some mountain county solved that case," Lona said.

"Michael was with him all that time, and the Allans are his and Valerie's best friends, so why wouldn't I think he was a good person to consult?" Nora said.

She twitched her shoulder impatiently away from Cornelius' heavy hand. It occurred to her that he was not being at all helpful. She didn't expect him to shine conversationally, but he might at least express some concern for Amalia or say something in Michael's defense. . . .

"I'm quite certain Dundas won't talk," Edwin said. "I object on principle to his highhanded methods. You know quite well he talked to Patton a long time, or the coffee"—he nodded toward the tray on a table near the fireplace—"wouldn't have been lukewarm."

"You'd better stress that 'on principle,'" Roger remarked. "Or someone might think you had a special interest in those notes, as well as not wanting Dundas to pump the admirable Patton."

"But naturally Edwin has a very special interest in those notes," Lona said. "We all have. But I think it's a mistake to go on talking when we are tired and worried. We might"—she smiled forgivingly at Roger—"say things we don't mean and will regret. I'm going to put Nora to bed at once."

She was too tired, Nora decided, to try to oppose Lona in a managing mood. She answered Cornelius' final: "I wish you wouldn't stay here" with a shake of her head that set it aching again and let Lona steer her out of the room.

But she was not too tired to grin when Patton interrupted Lona's suggestions with a calm: "I've attended to everything, Mrs. Keith. I've made up the room across from the blue room for you and the other back bedroom for Miss Nora. And laid out two of my own nightdresses—if you do not object to cotton—since you ladies are quite tall and wouldn't be comfortable in anything of Madam's."

"Polite and firm," Nora murmured. Lona ignored her.

"That will do very well, Patton," she said graciously. "And I think we must have some hot milk—"

"I've just put some to heat over a low flame."

"I hate milk," Nora said pettishly.

"But you must have something to quiet your nerves, dear. You won't find it too disagreeable this once."

"There is a tin of very good malted milk, miss," Patton said. "Would you prefer that?"

"Yes, I would. Put in quite a bit so it won't still taste insipid and like milk."

"Yes, do that, Patton." Lona drew Nora's arm protectively through hers. "Now, we'll just tuck you in—"

"Are you going to see that I wash behind my ears too?" Nora said ungratefully. "I'll use the bathroom first—"

When she was in the bathroom she stood for an instant, apparently staring with aversion at the painted walls that were so depressingly bluer than indigo. Actually she was remembering herself saying they couldn't hope to trace Amalia's movements unless her disappearance was given some publicity.

Michael had agreed with her, but the others seemed to have decided no further action was to be taken until morning. That meant the story wouldn't make the final morning editions but the early afternoon newspapers. Yet it was the morning papers that were read most widely and thoroughly at thousands of breakfast tables. . . .

Nora looked out into the hall and found it empty. She turned on the water faucets over the

bathtub, closed the door on the sound and hurried
down to Amalia's bedroom.

Anxious as she was not to be caught at the telephone it took her several minutes to decide whom
to call. She never thought of herself as a newspa-
per-woman, only as a superior sort of errand girl
or walking reference book on fashion's facts and
fancies. She sometimes looked enviously at those
who obviously found newspaper work the breath
of life. But its fascination hadn't touched her, and
she knew she was called standoffish.

She liked one of the cartoonists who approved
her drawings and the fat, genial dramatic critic
who gave her passes to the theaters now and then.
But neither of them seemed to fill her require-
ments just now. Then there was Jubal Hadley who
furnished her with football tickets when she'd
been sent to cover games from the fashion angle.
Jubal was a sports writer, but he was very definitely a newspaperman. Yes, Jubal would do. . . .

The conversation lasted longer than she had expected. When finally she thought she heard people talking in the lower hall, she broke through
Jubal's running fire of questions with a hasty:

"You know all you need to and far more than
I intended telling. I'll take the responsibility of
giving you the story, but I haven't energy enough
to face the others tonight if they know what I've
done. So I can't talk any longer—"

She put down the telephone and left the bedroom quickly. Leaning over the banisters she saw
Lona, looking the gracious hostess parting from
her guests, though Patton, standing at attention
by the front door, managed to suggest she still
considered herself Amalia's deputy in this house.

When the men had gone, with a last: "I'll call
you in the morning" from Roger, Patton picked
up the tray on which she had put a vacuum bottle
and glass and started for the stairway.

Nora dodged hastily back to the bathroom,
shut off the water in the tub and hurried into her
father's old bedroom. She slid out of her clothes
and was in bed before Patton came in, poured a
glassful of malted milk and put it on the bedside
table.

"I hope you'll like that and have a good night's
rest, miss," she said almost sympathetically. "Good
night—"

Nora eyed the drink unenthusiastically and
buried her face in a pillow. Patton had left the
light on; she was too tired to get up to put it out,
and besides, there was no use hoping Lona would
forget to say good night.

Lona didn't. She sat on the foot of the bed and
urged Nora, to "take your nice hot drink." She
even patted her shoulder encouragingly. Anything
was better than that; Lona, motherly, had the

same effect on Nora as a down comforter on a hot night. It might be soft and warm and silky, but you wanted to fling it off—violently.

She did fling off Lona's hand, sat up and gulped down the malted milk. But Lona was speaking admiringly of Cornelius now. He was "so dependable, so beautifully unexcitable. He doesn't say a great deal, so when he does talk one listens to him. He'll always want to look after you so carefully—"

As well as she knew Lona, it took Nora some time to realize she was contrasting Cornelius with Roger and pointing out that he would make a "high-strung" person like Nora a much better husband than Roger would. She scowled at Lona sleepily.

"I know what Neil is like. He may not be exciting, but he's safe and sane. That's why I'm marrying him. I didn't know you were interested in Roger—that way. He's younger than you are. If anyone, Edwin—"

She yawned. Then, to avoid listening to Lona rationalizing herself, she pulled the pillow over her head. I'll pretend to be asleep, she thought. Then she'll go away. . . .

It wasn't until she woke the next morning and saw the hands of her watch pointing to nine-thirty that she realized she hadn't been pretending to be asleep while Lona sat there. She'd already been drugged with sleep when she pulled that pillow over her head—

Drugged with sleep. She'd slept more than eight hours without once waking. And she was never a sound sleeper, especially if she was nervous or excited or even very tired when she went to bed.

Nora. turned on her side and lay staring at the bedside table. There was a dry chocolaty ring where the glass of malted milk had sat. But the glass itself was gone.

XI

By ten-thirty an energetic sun had mopped up the remains of a pea-soup fog that had spilled over on the city in the early morning. So they were still able to set off for the park before lunch: George Henry Tuttle, Senior and George Henry Tuttle, Junior.

George, Senior—Grampa—was in his sixties and George, Junior—Georgie—just over five. Georgie's legs and Grampa's breath were both short, so they walked well together, especially when they reached the last steep block on Taylor Street that bordered the park.

The park was only a reclaimed rock pile, and how much you admired that reclamation was apt to depend on what you thought of WPA projects in general. But there were paths winding down its several levels, a great many prickly bushes and a few fir trees. It was a good place to bring a small grandson to keep him and yourself from under Mamma's feet until lunch and the nap that followed it.

Having reached the park, Grampa seated himself on the nearest bench, panting a little. Georgie recovered more quickly, squatted down in the path and scooped up a handful of dirt. Three beautiful pebbles were safely interred in his sweater pocket before he stood up and said: "Play ball now."

The game was played according to their own rules, the important one being that not only must Georgie chase the ball when he didn't catch it, but also when he didn't throw it so Grampa could snag it without leaving the bench. As Georgie was no better a pitcher than catcher his fat legs were well exercised and Grampa's thin shaky ones no more than was good for him.

He could even indulge in a brief doze during Georgic's excursions away from the pitcher's mound. Georgie had an inquiring mind; wherever the ball rolled there was sure to be something he must investigate. During the last of these expeditions Grampa did quite definitely doze. He opened his eyes to find Georgie regarding him accusingly.

"Well, topper? Where's your ball?"

"The ball lost. It went in the bushes, and I crawled in and"—Georgie turned about and displayed a torn romper and part of a small pink paunch—"and the bushes scratched me," he said placidly. "And I saw a lady in there."

"Now, now! You know what happens to little boys that tell stories. Remember that bear you said was under your bed t'other night? There wasn't any bear—"

"I thought it would be nice if there was, so I 'magined one," Georgie explained. "But I didn't 'magine the lady. She's a little lady, and she don't say 'hello' or anything. She just lies there with her face down in the dirt. And a kitty round her neck," he added conscientiously.

Grampa had read the morning papers thoroughly. A little lady with a kitty—Georgie's word for a fur neckpiece—about her neck. A little lady who didn't say anything but lay still with her face in the dirt. . . .

Grampa got up and took Georgie's hand. "You show Gramp where you saw the lady, topper," he said.

"Right over here—"

Georgie led the way down the path that ended at the street and the entrance to the park. On the left some sort of enormous, low-growing shrub brushed the sidewalk, no more than its width from the street. There was one gap in the growth through which a small boy could burrow.

Grampa got laboriously down on his knees and thrust a long arm through the gap. In an instant he drew it back hastily and wiped his hand hard on his coat. What he had felt was a small, inert foot. He took Georgie's hand again. In another minute he was ringing the doorbell of the nearest house, asking if he might use the telephone to call the police. . . .

The neighborhood was a quiet one, but inevitably a crowd gathered. People moved back to the other side of the street, but they ignored commands to "move along." Also inevitably, one large, positive individual made himself the center of the group and dispensed conjecture with an air of infallibility that triumphed over his need of a shave and a clean shirt.

Attention was so well focused on him and the dumpy woman in a polo coat over blue pajamas who kept saying: "I just know I'll faint," that probably no one could have said when it was that a small man in mismated coat and trousers added himself to the group.

Anyone who had been looking down the street might have seen him walking slowly, head down.

And stopping as he saw the crowd, only to come on, drawn by the tentacles it put out of excitement and pleasurable horror.

No one would have been apt to look at him long at any time. He could have been any age from forty-five to sixty; his eyes were dark and his hair grayish. His hands—the hands that were finally to be of great interest to Inspector James Sullivan—were well shaped and well cared for, though heavily calloused. His face was thin and unaggressively melancholy.

Other latecomers joined the group, and the pontiff in its center hospitably summarized the situation. "Someone stuck a dead woman in those bushes over there. Some old fellow found her. I talked to him before he left, but he was in no shape to hang around—"

"Probably it's just a souse sleeping it off," said a skeptical voice from the rear rank.

"Souse, is it?" the chairman repeated indignantly. "Call me a liar? Do they call in the homicide squad for a drunk? That's Inspector Jim Sullivan over there. Know him well. Me and Jim was boys together—"

"Sure it wasn't while he was on the burglary detail you got so well acquainted?" the same irreverent voice inquired. This was ignored.

"And I know who that woman is, even if they do have to look things over careful before they take

DEATH OF A LUCKY LADY

her out. Guess you didn't read the newspapers this morning about the lady that ain't been home all night, name of Landreth. Only five feet, blonde, about fifty, wearing a blue suit and one of these fur pieces and a big pointed hat with a red-and-green bird on it— Hey, they're bringing her out!"

The crowd surged instinctively backward before someone cried: "Watch out, there! Catch her—"

But Blue Pajamas did not faint; she merely squawked. It was the small man in the blue trousers and gray coat who closed his eyes and swayed back on his heels. A young policeman promptly took him by the arm and led him away.

"You better get on home," he said kindly. "This is no place for you. Feel all right now?"

The man nodded. "Yes, thank you, Officer. You are quite right. I shouldn't be—here."

He walked away, stumbling a little. But young Healy was not watching him. He too was staring across the street. . . .

XII

For an instant after Fanchon Weiss came into the office Michael went on skimming through the classified advertising section.

"Batteries, beads, beans," he muttered. "Bearings, beauty shops—pages of those—Bibles, bicycles, boats, bottles, brokers . . . but none in the

Phelan Building. Too bad. She might have been thinking acquiring a broker. Burlap, burners, bus lines, cabinets—"

"Skipping a few, aren't you?" Fanchon said.

"Yes, but I've been through this without skipping. Cameras, canes, canning, carpets, caskets—"

"You make my blood run cold, the way you say that."

"Catering, chains, chemicals, chili, coal, coffee, coin machines, colonic irrigations, costumes, crackers, draperies, drums, dumb-waiters, Dy-Dee Wash . . . Oh, the hell with it!"

"That's what I say. What do we pay cops for?" Fanchon asked reasonably. "And I hope you aren't going to get mixed up in this and let your own work take care of itself."

"And I hope, Miss Weiss, that you will attend to your end of this business and allow me to remain a free soul."

"Sure, if you feel that way about it," Fanchon said meekly. "I didn't know. I mean, you don't even know Mrs. Landreth is dead."

"She hasn't returned home; it's nearly eleven now, so that's eighteen hours she's been gone."

"Did Nora Keith phone you?"

"Yes. And she's quite positive someone gave her a stiff dose of some sort of sleeping medicine last night. She says anyone could have drugged the malted milk she thinks she took the stuff in, but she suspects Lona Keith— But I wanted to ask you: just how heavy was Mrs. Landreth's purse? Unusually heavy for a very large purse stuffed to capacity?"

"Well, I guess not. Compacts and things are fairly heavy—"

"But you said the purse felt to you as if she were carrying lead weights in it. Why did 'lead weights' come into your mind?"

"Just because it was heavy, I guess," Fanchon said unsatisfactorily. "Gosh, I never pick and choose my words. But maybe it did seem to me her purse was heavier than you'd expect it to be."

"Did she seem to mind your handling it?"

"No, though all I did was hand it to her. And she didn't talk about anything but clothes. She might have gotten confidential to a fitter—they do, you know—but she just had her measurements taken. The models she chose had to be made up for her, she was so short. She never was out from under my eye. Now can I get to work?"

Michael nodded. An instant after Fanchon had gone someone knocked on the back door, and a husky feminine voice asked: "Can I come in? It's Martha Ferris—"

Michael glanced thoughtfully at the two photographs on his desk, then turned them face down
before he got up to unlock the door.

"You needn't have bothered to be polite," Martha said. "I could— Oh, was it locked?"

She crossed the room and sat confidently down
in the nearest chair, though it was a fragile gilt
article, and she weighed one hundred and seventy
pounds. She was tall and agile, her flesh was solid and well proportioned, but it still undeniably
added up to one hundred and seventy pounds.

To this she insisted she had long been resigned;
that she had made her choice between "starving to
death and still being plump, or eating and being
just plain fat" many years ago. In her late forties
she was, probably better looking, with her very
black eyes and very white hair and skin like that
of a soap-ad baby, than she had been in her 'teens.

"Well," she said now, producing her own cig-
arettes and lighting her own match, "what's this
about Amalia Landreth not coming home last
night?"

"I didn't know you knew Mrs. Landreth."

"You can answer my question whether I know
her or not, can't you?" Martha blew smoke out her
nostrils. "But Nora Keith brought her to the shop
about ten days ago. And of course Cornelius has
been running round in circles this morning."

"Really?"

"Well, mentally, if not physically. He's gone over to talk to Nora, damn it! There were some heavy boxes I wanted moved."

"It's nice you've found something about the shop Cornelius can be trusted to do," Michael said dryly. Martha looked at him sharply.

"I guess that's a dirty crack, and it's no sure thing he can even do that without dropping the box or falling into it. Talk about bulls in a china shop! I hold my breath every time he takes anything at all fragile into those hamlike objects at the ends of his arms."

This description of Cornelius' hands was accurate enough so that Michael grinned briefly and let it pass. He had intended remarking to Martha that it was odd Sturtevant's was no longer a very profitable business, and that she wasn't holding its oldest and most valuable customers.

But he decided now to postpone that—unless, of course, he had to try to bring her to heel by suggesting it would be an act of friendship on his part to point out to Cornelius that his late uncle's trusted manageress must know one can buy a deteriorating business more cheaply than a flourishing one.

"I suppose you've read this morning's papers—"

"Yes." Martha chuckled. "I guess everyone's hauling Nora over the coals for giving them the story. Cornelius says she acted too hastily. He says he doesn't like the publicity—for her. And himself because his name will be linked with hers."

She threw her cigarette on the floor and stamped on it. "If he'd get his name in the papers in the right way, like Mr. Sturtevant used to, it wouldn't hurt business. But even if Cornelius ever makes a go of this business he'll still just be a shopkeeper. His uncle was a connoisseur."

"And socially acceptable?" Michael said. "He knew the Keiths and Amalia Landreth before she married."

Martha shrugged. "Maybe. Yes, I think she did tell me she'd known Mr. Sturtevant—"

"She didn't need to tell you. Nor were you introduced to her for the first time ten days ago, as you implied. At least," Michael said, tapping one of the pictures under his hand, "I don't suppose you went picnicking with her and a large family group without first being introduced to them."

"H'm-m. You speak very positively, my fine-feathered friend. What have you got there?"

"A group picture taken in May of 1908. The names of those present are listed on its back. Among those present—"

"I know. You can't blame me for trying," Martha said philosophically. "Because there's publicity *and* publicity. And while I hope Amalia is alive, I strongly doubt it. Well, we went to the same school, and I had a terrific crush on her, but she was three years older than I, so you can guess how well I knew her."

"You look to be about sixteen in this picture," Michael said, without offering it to her.

"That's right. Amalia graduated from the seminary at the end of my first year there. I've forgotten how I came to get asked on that picnic. Of course Amalia was a kindhearted sort, but it might have been Mr. Sturtevant who was responsible for the invitation."

"Then you already knew him?"

"He was a friend of my father's. Father was something of an expert on old clocks and watches. We were genteelly hard up, but I was educated genteelly—with the idea that I'd marry young. Strangely enough, I could have. You'd never guess why I didn't."

"Not if it wasn't that you hankered for a career."

"That came later," Martha said. "You know I've always been fat? In the early nineteen hundreds you were called by God either to be fat or thin, and you didn't fly in the face of Providence by dieting. Men liked curves then, but mine were billows, and I can't remember ever being called even a 'fine figure of a woman.' But I had a proposal at eighteen in spite of my billows. And I refused the man, because I'd just made up my mind that I might have to be fat, but by God! I didn't have to be good natured."

Michael saw that she was quite serious and tried not to laugh. "I've always maintained, it's better to have others gratefully surprised when you are in a good humor than aggrieved and indignant any time that you aren't."

"Certainly. Only you don't know most people take it for granted a fat person is cheerful *because* he's fat. And that you'll be good natured and laugh at all jokes about your weight. And what does it get you?"

"It would have gotten you a husband at eighteen," Michael said, grinning.

"And for his bed and board I would have been expected to laugh, not just at his jokes, but at his jokes about me. No thanks. I could wait. And from then on, whenever anyone made me the butt of their jokes I stared at 'em in stony silence. If they didn't take that hint I told them off in no uncertain terms. People soon stopped saying Martha was such a good-natured gal.

"Then I did go to work, though the family fought it. Schoolteaching would have been refined and ladylike, but I hate children. I had a few odd jobs before Mr. Sturtevant took me on, and I never left. And after a pretty successful twenty-five years in the business world, people will still look at me and think: 'Oh, she's just a fat, easygoing slob.' Experience and a really good look teaches 'em better. Well, are you satisfied?"

"Why, yes. In fact, your connection with Mrs. Landreth seems so slight and harmless I wonder why you didn't want it known," Michael said.

"I suppose people have told you 'it isn't what you say but the way you say it'?" Martha remarked. "Well, as Cornelius pointed out, Amalia had seen so few people since she came back that all of them are bound to be questioned a lot. And what's your official standing?"

"I have none, as you must know. You don't have to answer my questions. You can, if it becomes necessary, answer the same questions—put to you by the police."

"One of the things I like about you, Dundas, is that your threats are always uttered so politely. It's a gift. Well, is that all?"

"If you don't mind, I'd like you to tell me what you can of Mr. Sturtevant's connection with the Keith family. You might be able to tell me something about various people in this photograph—"

The telephone rang. He answered it with the feeling that this was a call he had known was coming and promised to wait for.

"I'll come to your office," he said when he had heard what Inspector Sullivan had to say. "I have something for you. . . . Yes, I'll come at once."

He took the envelope on which Amalia had made her indecipherable notes out of a desk drawer, locked the photographs into it and put the key in his pocket.

"I'm sorry, Martha. I'll have to go."

"Did they—did they find her?" Martha said. "And—and is she—"

"Yes, they found her. And she is."

MRS. DUNDAS TO MR. DUNDAS
Hollywood, Monday night
November 20th

Michael Darling:

Mother is prostrated and has gone to bed in tears and her best nightgown. She accepts our proofs, but we didn't need to spend all that money to find out her "count" used to run a delicatessen in Brooklyn. The world and his wife could tell you that, but it seems they don't bother—down here. The idea is that any foolish woman with money is fair game.

I can add one interesting fact to those we already had. The "count" wears a black patch over one eye, not because it was shot out during the last war, but because he is cross-eyed. I have also dealt with him this evening. He made a pass at me, and I made one at him, and he took off his patch to see if his eye was swelling. It was.

Well, that's that, but I'm going to have to stick around for a few days. I can't help it, darling. I agree with you that if you don't like your relatives you've as much right to avoid them as any common acquaintance you don't like. And that I don't owe Mother much. But I haven't seen her for so long that if I left at once I'd arrive home feeling like a low-down dog.

Speaking of home reminds me: do you think we might have Lona Keith weave our drapes? She wouldn't charge any more than the Liebes concern and might do them more quickly. If you have time, get in touch with her. I'm putting an air-mail stamp on this and going out to mail it now. . . .

With all my love,
Valerie

P.S. I hate to tell you, but there are some library books on the bedside table that are already overdue. I mention this, because, while you'd think nothing of fifty dollars for books you want to own, you do object strenuously to fifty cents in fines for books you don't.

Mr. Dundas to Mrs. Dundas

San Francisco, Tuesday afternoon.

. . . so let your conscience be your guide, my dear. But ask yourself if you won't be more stricken should you return home to find your husband has taken to strong drink in your absence than if you left Mamma to recover her faith in human nature alone.

You will be surprised to learn that I welcome your suggestion that I interview Lona Keith regarding drapes—even while I am wondering if there is ever a time that our library books aren't overdue. I am going to explain, or I wouldn't have taken to the typewriter. I know that even in exile you manage to have your usual San Francisco newspaper.

You'll read in it that Nora Keith's aunt was found murdered this morning. This will save your wiring to ask for details—and if I'm allowing myself to be drawn into the affair. You won't need to ask that when you have read this.

So far all is sweet amity and accord between Sullivan and me, but he says rather uneasily that I "mustn't let my imagination run away with me." This because I insist the seed from which this murder sprouted may have lain in the old Keith house more than fifty years. (High-flown language, but Sullivan calls the whole idea "fantastic.")

You see, Amalia's grandparents, Mr. and Mrs. Gordon, came here in '48, newly married. And Mrs. Gordon was thrifty, because she'd come from a poor family, and it took time for her to become accustomed to there being so much money or convinced her husband would always be lucky. So Amalia told me, and, though Sullivan says that can't be important, I'm not so sure. Mrs. Gordon was certainly on Amalia's mind yesterday morning, and I think anything that was is apt to be important.

After being widowed Mrs. Gordon lived out the rest of her life quietly in her daughter's home, in her own room, surrounded by her pet possessions, much like a Louisa M. Alcott grandmother. Now that I think of it the situation has a strongly Alcottian flavor. When she died her room was preserved, unchanged, as she left it. Isn't that straight from an *Old-Fashioned Girl?*

Well, whatever her reasons, Mrs. Keith did preserve Mrs. Gordon's room as she left it. Amalia remarked that Alice Keith was a very stupid woman; that she hadn't read or learned anything new in the last forty years of her life. Perhaps that was only a remark in passing. But I wonder if she could have been thinking that Mrs. Gordon left something valuable among her possessions: something whose value Alice Keith wouldn't have had the wit or knowledge to recognize.

Because it was finally left to Amalia to clear out the house. She arrived here with less than two thousand dollars and the expectation that her mother's estate would be more valuable than her lawyer said. Or perhaps she merely had the feeling that seems to have been customary with her—that something would turn up, and that her luck wouldn't run out.

But by last Thursday it appears even her optimism was beaten down by hard fact, and she was as depressed as only a customarily cheerful person can be. This persisted from Wednesday through Thursday until rather late at night when her maid looked in on her while she was engaged in turning out Mrs. Gordon's old room.

Patton thought Amalia was running a fever, her face was that flushed and her eyes so bright. I think that, sitting there on her grandmother's bed with the old lady's possessions about her, Amalia had found something that excited her.

Because she was, from then on, unusually cheerful, even for her. And also excited, with a "I-know-something-I-won't-tell" air about her. Unfortunately, Nora didn't see her from Thursday to Monday, though everyone else concerned did and more than once.

On Saturday she left the house in the afternoon but probably only to do some shopping. She certainly went by taxi to the City of Paris, but if she took another when she came out of the store its driver hasn't yet been located.

Those are established facts. And it is pretty well established that before nine-fifteen Monday morning she had arranged to meet someone, somewhere, sometime after five o'clock that afternoon. And that that meeting was for the purpose of striking a bargain that was to assure her future financially. I could quote chapter and verse (the gospel according to Nora and Michael) for this supposition, but I don't care to pay extra postage on this screed.

She had also, sometime between Thursday night and Monday noon, made some hopelessly cryptic notes on an old envelope; notes she meant to refer to impressively during the process of bargaining. Those notes might as well be in cipher for all I've been able to make out of them.

But if one hunch I have is correct—that certain numbers should have the dollar sign before them—then her bargaining involved from fifty to seventy grand, and there you have motive for more than one murder.

But what in God's name did Grandmother Gordon leave in her room that could be worth even fifty grand? I'd give you a hundred to one that what Amalia had to dispose of came from that room. And you know, even as a figure of speech, I don't give such odds often.

What Amalia carried from Mrs. Gordon's room into her own was two workbags and an old glove box and perhaps some letters and photographs. Not helpful, is it? Patton can't remember having seen the glove box, and that does suggest to me that Amalia might have used it to keep her "valuables" in when she was at home—and of course kept the box hidden too.

Sullivan suggests old Mrs. Gordon might have hoarded gold. But then why those indecipherable notes of Amalia's? Gold is gold, and fifty thousand dollars in gold isn't easily carried about. You certainly couldn't hide it in a glove box. Nor could the person who tore Amalia's bedroom to pieces yesterday evening have carried away that much in gold.

After looking at the stacks of old letters in her bedroom Sullivan put one of his men to reading them and suggests Amalia was blackmailing someone with old letters she'd found. I don't think much of his idea. Still, I suppose her notes might be a list of letters with names, dates and the values she set on them discreetly abbreviated. Remembering some of your weird abbreviations I've tried to decipher on grocery lists, I can believe Amalia's might stand for almost anything.

Of course this summary includes very little that interests Sullivan most just now. She was killed—

strangled, throttled or what you will—between five and seven last night. The doctor is agreeable to that theory; we know when she left the house, and we take for granted the murderer used her keys after she was killed to enter the house. Patton looked into the bedroom at seven, and it hadn't been disturbed then, but after that she was in the kitchen.

No one on Sullivan's list of suspects has an alibi for all of those two hours. Then there is another period of time to be taken into account. At—probably—an hour when the streets are most deserted, Amalia's body was brought from somewhere and hidden in one of the bushes on the edge of that park at Taylor, just over and down the hill from where we live.

It's good to know various experts agree for various reasons that she wasn't killed there, though I would have taken for granted she wasn't without hearing their opinions. Of course a car is indicated. Lona and Roger Keith, Edwin Lacey, Martha Ferris and Cornelius all have cars of various makes and ages.

They are all tall and strongly built, while Amalia was a very small person. Well, you may imagine a car cruising along the street, its driver faced with the problem of disposing of a body. The park looms up, a deserted street, a large, low-growing bush only the width of the sidewalk away from the curb . . .

But though Sullivan is interested in what everyone Amalia knew was doing in the early hours of the morning, I'd rather know why her body had to be moved. There was no attempt made to destroy it. Why did the murderer feel he must take the risk of moving her from where she had been killed?

However, much as that interests me, I want first to know why she was killed. Sullivan, once he began to get a fair picture of Amalia, remarked very pertinently that "it sounds like she's the kind that 'd almost have to confide in someone."

Which is true, and offhand you'd suppose she'd go to Lacey for advice. But Roger Keith has a very active curiosity, no aversion to asking questions and, I imagine, a way with women Amalia's age. And Lona Keith would probably not only invite but actively solicit confidences. . . .

But if we knew what it was that Amalia had to tell it might be easier to decide whom she'd be most apt to tell it to. And until we know what she had to dispose of that might be worth fifty grand we can't say why she was killed. As it stands now, only Nora gains by her death.

What could the woman have found in that house so valuable someone killed her to gain possession of it? And why did she feel she mustn't talk about it at once?

Perhaps this hasn't been wasted effort, since it's made me remember Amalia's remarking: "I've lived so long in Europe I didn't even know the laws of the United States." She said "didn't," not "don't." Is it too farfetched to argue she did know the law by Monday—on whatever subject she was interested in? And that not knowing it on Thursday night or Friday morning made her proceed cautiously?

But it seems to have become six o'clock, and Sullivan suggested we have dinner together. His affability is almost overpowering. Is it due to his belief that I have told all or only an indication that he suspects I haven't? Good night, my love. Be a good little girl in wicked eight-o'clock Hollywood, and some day I'll write you a love letter.

Michael

PART TWO

"To what dost thou not compel the minds of mortals, thou accursed hunger for gold?"

I

A little before six o'clock Inspector Sullivan was looking gratefully across his desk at what experience had taught him was a rare specimen: an intelligent witness who was also inclined to speak disparagingly of the information she had to give.

"I'm not quite certain enough that this can't be important," she said. "I've been turning the matter over in my mind all morning since I read of Amalia Landreth's being missing. And when I saw in the afternoon papers that she'd been murdered I decided to come to you. I wouldn't ask you to come to me. My employers wouldn't like that. I'm with the legal firm of Pratt and Newman, secretary to Mr. Pratt."

Sullivan nodded. He would have guessed, from her quiet poise, the pleasant smile held a little in restraint, her conservative if not inexpensive clothing, that she held some such position.

"And you wouldn't welcome publicity," he said. "I understand that, Miss Wilson."

"Thank you. That's rather a relief—" She stopped to cough, having what was either a good beginning or the bad ending of a cold.

"I didn't feel I could come earlier, because I wasn't able to be at the office yesterday, so the work piled up," she explained. "It was because I wasn't well enough to go to the office that I—

"But I'm not doing justice to my legal training by beginning where I should. I have a small apartment on Jackson Street, Inspector. My telephone is a two-party one, but until about a month ago I didn't think there was any other party on the line. It often happens that way, you know."

"Yes, I know. What is your number?"

"Prospect 8940. And if Mrs. Landreth and I are not on the same line what I'm going to tell you means nothing. I didn't know if the telephone company would give that sort of information to just anyone—"

"They'll give it to us." Sullivan summoned Sergeant Cooley, told him what he wanted and turned back to Miss Wilson. "You might as well go on while he's doing that."

"I use my telephone very little and almost always at night. One night about three weeks ago, while I was talking to a friend, we noticed that clicking sound that means someone on the wire is taking up the receiver and then slamming it down again. So I rather wanted to know if there was someone on my line now," Miss Wilson said. "I stayed at the telephone and picked up the receiver several times, until I finally heard a woman's voice saying: 'Yes, this is Aunt Amalia, darling. How are you?'"

"That's all?"

"Yes, but Amalia is rather an unusual name. And the voice was very distinctive. I heard her laugh too. She had what we used to call a school-girl giggle. Not so inane as that; it was very attractive, and I would have thought from it that she was younger than fifty.

"Well, twice more before yesterday I heard her talking. Of course both times it was when I wanted to make a call of my own. I would rather have liked to listen in," Miss Wilson admitted with her reserved smile. "But I was brought up to consider anything like that ill bred."

"I wish you hadn't been," Sullivan said. "Didn't you hear anything at all?"

"I heard her call someone 'Nora.' When I read she had a niece named Nora Keith that helped me make up my mind. She was saying she wondered if any of the furniture or pictures in the house were worth keeping; that she didn't know enough about such things to be certain.

"The other time she was talking to a man called Roger, and a Roger Keith was mentioned in the newspapers too. That helped me remember that she asked what he had been doing that day, and he said he'd spent six hours writing six pages, all of which he had just thrown into the wastebasket."

"I guess there's no doubt you and Mrs. Landreth are on the same line," Sullivan said. "Roger Keith's a writer. Well, does that bring you up to—would it be yesterday morning?"

"Yes, at about ten minutes of nine. I'd caught this miserable cold, but I thought I'd be able to go to the office. I even had my coat on before I realized I was too shaky to do anything but go back to bed. So I picked up the telephone to notify the office, and the woman I'd come to think of as 'Amalia' was talking—"

"Just a minute." Sullivan opened his notebook. "Now, if you'll go on—"

"I think I can trust my memory, though I won't claim I can repeat every word that she said. But I believe she said: '. . . rather it were earlier, but the least one can do is to let him choose his own time. I won't be there before five-fifteen. And I don't mind dealing with eccentric people—'"

Sullivan groaned softly. "Then you stopped listening?"

"Yes. I didn't hear the voice of the person she was talking to. You'll say that was sheer bad luck, because I was very anxious to call the office, and in about five minutes I tried again. She was laughing then, and she said: 'Oh, even I am not indiscreet enough to tell you that over the telephone. I'm sure there's someone else on this line. But they're quite safe, and I'm not in the least afraid. I shan't bother to bring all of them with me; only the best—'

"And then," Miss Wilson said regretfully, "I stopped listening again, mostly because she'd said she thought there was someone else on the line. When I tried to get the line again in another five minutes she'd stopped talking.

"But of course when I read this morning that Mrs. Landreth was known to have gone out a little before five, presumably to keep an appointment, what I had overheard began to seem significant. Of course, it isn't much—"

"It's a step in the right direction," Sullivan said. "It may give us a lead. . . . Well, Cooley?"

"Yep," said Cooley. "Telephone company says they're on the same line."

II

"So now we know Mrs. Landreth did have an appointment to meet someone at five-fifteen," Sullivan concluded.

"Didn't you know that before your Miss Wilson told you?" Michael said.

Momentarily Sullivan ignored him, gazing lovingly at the steak the proprietor of Mary's Little Lamb just then slid in front of him. Mary's Little Lamb is on one of the dingier blocks of Kearney Street. One tablecloth per table per day is the allowance; the service is catch-as-catch-can and the food beyond criticism. Sullivan consumed his first three chunks of steak in respectful silence before he helped himself to French fried potatoes from the platter in the center of the table.

"Better have some of these. They're just cooked. Well, of course we guessed she must have made an appointment to go somewhere yesterday afternoon, and that it might have been arranged over the telephone. And we questioned the maid about telephone calls, because sometimes she must have answered the phone in the kitchen, and she could have listened in any time she wanted to. She says that's the last thing she'd ever do. What do you think about that—and her?"

"I think the odds are she told you the truth. And that she is exactly what she appears: a well-trained English servant. I'll admit that at first I thought she was almost too typical: the feminine equivalent of Jeeves, Bunter, Ruggles and any other famous gentlemen's gentlemen you'd like to name."

"You name 'em," Sullivan said. "I'm no reader. They speak very highly of Patton at the agency where she's been listed. She was with one elderly widow for seven years till the woman died. They said that since then she hadn't found any job that suited her for any length of time."

"I believe that. And she was looking ahead to a permanent berth with Mrs. Landreth in a small apartment. I imagine that, since she was used to English servants, she was the sort of mistress Patton's been searching for. I don't really think Patton was casing the joint for an outside accomplice."

"That kind of thing happens. And Mrs. Landreth was the sort you'd think must be pretty well to do, just meeting her. But I think Patton's O.K. And she couldn't have listened in on that particular telephone call yesterday morning. Seems she prefers to do the shopping in person—"

"She would," Michael said. "And I suppose she always did it early, since, according to Nora, Patton never woke Mrs. Landreth before ten o'clock. I imagine others besides Nora knew Amalia's schedule and Patton's habits."

"Probably they did. Patton says if she went out a little before nine she got back just in time to fix

Mrs. Landreth's breakfast. Of course that 'd be the safest time to call her if you didn't want Patton to hear your voice. And Patton was at her usual grocery store at the usual time yesterday morning. They know her there, so I guess she isn't keeping anything back."

"Or planning to blackmail the murderer?" Michael said. "You read too many detective stories, Inspector. The maid always knows something, she always tries to collect from the murderer and is killed for her pains. So it might be as well to protect Patton in case this murderer should be afraid she knows more than she's told."

"There are some things we do without you telling us," Sullivan said. "That's taken care of. She's at a small hotel on Larkin; respectable place, and the manager's a friend of hers. But, though you thought you pumped her dry last night—"

"No. I want to talk to her again. You had so many questions to ask her when we went over there this afternoon that I decided to wait."

"Oh. Well, while you were talking to Nora Keith I just happened to mention Friday night, and Patton looked as guilty as that dead pan of hers will let her. She said she'd quite forgotten she went to a show that night. Seems she hadn't taken time off before, but there was a picture at the

Alhambra she wanted to see, and Mrs. Landreth insisted she serve dinner early and go to it. It didn't begin till eight-forty—they print starting times in the newspapers—so she walked down to Polk Street about eight-twenty and was back a little after ten."

"Did Patton think Mrs. Landreth wanted to get her out of the house?"

"She 'couldn't say, sir.' But she doesn't really think so, and she said if Mrs. Landreth left the house she probably called a taxi. We checked on that, and apparently she didn't, so probably she stayed home. Well, what do you think of what Miss Wilson did overhear?"

Michael studied the typewritten copy of Sullivan's notes on Miss Wilson's evidence. "Of course it was always fairly evident Mrs. Landreth didn't walk out to meet one of her relatives—"

"And if you stick to it that she went out to make a bargain involving fifty grand it certainly wasn't one of them she was bargaining with."

"No. But this at least tells us the appointment was not arranged by Amalia directly with the person she was to see at five-fifteen but through a third person. That brings to mind another third person: the one who was to be at dinner last night but didn't appear—for dinner. I wonder if Amalia didn't suddenly decide to ask him to dinner as a mark of appreciation for arranging that appointment?"

"Maybe. Read what it says, will you?"

"'. . . rather it were earlier—' That's characteristic. Amalia was impatient to have the thing settled . . . 'but the least one can do is to let him choose his own time. I won't be there before fivefifteen. And I don't mind dealing with eccentric people—'"

Sullivan sighed. "Do you think she wouldn't have blackmailed anyone?"

"I don't insist she wouldn't have, in a ladylike way, and someone who could afford to pay. But I can't think those notes she made fit into that theory."

"No. Only her saying that the least one can do is let him pick his own time, does seem to fit in with the blackmail theory. But then the part about not minding dealing with eccentric people strikes a false note. On the other hand, she said: 'I shan't bother to bring all of them with me: only the best—' That could apply to letters, you know."

"Yes," Michael admitted. "And that tells you that whatever she had to—shall we say to sell?—was not a single article. Of course those notes would tell us that."

Sullivan soaked a French fry in the juice from his steak. "I wish you'd stop harping on those notes. Maybe they hadn't anything to do with it."

"I told you what she said to me about wanting to refer impressively to notes. If she hadn't at least consulted them yesterday afternoon they wouldn't have been in the pocket of her robe instead of her purse. The letter inside the envelope was certainly not important; a few commonplaces from an old friend in Italy."

"O.K.," Sullivan said soothingly. "Anyway, according to what Miss Wilson overheard, she did take at least some of her valuables with her when she left the house. And the fact she didn't take all of them accounts for her room being torn up. The murderer had to come back to the house to get what she'd left there before anyone called the police in."

"I wonder why he couldn't be content with the 'best' ones she carried with her? If they represented fifty to seventy thousand why not argue it had been a profitable enough murder and play safe?"

"A guy that kills for money is apt to want the whole hog," Sullivan pointed out. "Well, she didn't tell him where the rest of 'em were. He'd evidently asked her where she had them, and if they were safe. And she said: 'Oh, even I am not indiscreet enough to tell you that over the telephone.' So he had to hunt—"

"Until he found what he was looking for, despite the danger of being caught in her bedroom. I still can't see why he took that risk, unless there was some reason we haven't thought of that made it absolutely necessary."

"Just plain greed," Sullivan said again. "But it seems to me if she'd wanted to bring someone home to dinner with her that Patton knew she'd have mentioned them by name."

"It would have been more natural for her to have mentioned her second guest's name even if Patton had never met that person. The only way I can account for the omission is that she wanted to be able to say to that guest: 'See, I did keep a secret for once in my life. I didn't even tell Nora you'd be here tonight or what we've been doing—'"

"Not bad. Aren't you going to finish that steak?"

Michael shook his head and pushed the platter toward Sullivan. "It's too large. Do you want the rest of it?"

"You don't know what's good for you," Sullivan said disapprovingly. "You're the fussiest eater I ever saw. Well, not fussy exactly. You just don't take any interest in food, though somehow a person would expect you to know all about it—and wines and things."

"Have you ever eaten a fifteen- to twenty-five-cent dinner on Howard Street?"

"No, I guess not. I've heard they're filling."

"Oh, *sin duda*. So, the Chinese would tell you, is mud. A two-year course of meals on Howard Street, interspersed with coffee and boiled rice and beans is apt to make you lose interest in food for the rest of your life."

"Umm," said Sullivan tactfully. It was his opinion that, whatever else you might say about Michael, you couldn't claim he lacked guts. He would hate to toss his own son into a strange city at twenty with two dollars in his pocket. He wouldn't be too helpful that thirteen years later his yearly income would run legitimately to five figures. . . .

"Well, we're working on the Phelan Building angle," he said. "If we just had a good picture of Mrs. Landreth! We can't photograph her now, because that brush— Well, it's no subject for the dinner table. Between you and Nora Keith we got a better description than usual, especially of her clothes. Women might be apt to notice those, though hats are all so crazy this fall I don't suppose anyone would notice hers especially. Are you sure there was a bird on her hat?"

"Yes. Half a red-and-green bird to be exact."

"Well, there are some loose threads on the front of the hat that I guess it was sewed on with. It evidently came loose somehow, because it's missing. The hat looked like it 'd been stepped on. But a description never does much good—"

"Nora sketches rather well. She might be able to help us along that line," Michael said. "I suppose you are still stalking alibis?"

"They can't prove any. Which isn't necessarily suspicious in itself at this stage."

"What about Cornelius Sturtevant?"

"I don't just see why you keep counting him in. But the Ferris woman can't alibi him, he says. He says he was in the office, and she was in the front of the shop, and he left about five-thirty but used the back door, because it was nearer where he parked his car.

"Lacey says he was in his office till six, but the stenographer in the central office goes home at five. Roger Keith was home writing and Lona Keith home weaving. None of them can prove it. We gave all their cars the once-over too but didn't find anything suspicious.

"As to fingerprints, we didn't turn up any that shouldn't have been in that bedroom, but some places where there should have been some there weren't any. Well, if you don't want dessert, I'm through," Sullivan said. "Going to the Big Game Saturday?"

"If Valerie is home by then."

"Well, it's just a social event this year," Sullivan said, squirming out of his chair. "Cal's won two games and Stanford none, so it doesn't mean anything, whichever one wins."

"You tell that to the little Californias and Stanfords," Michael said. "If you think you can weather the resulting storm of oratory to the effect that, regardless of depression, earthquake, fire or flood, the Big Game is always the Big Game."

"I still say Santa Clara could lick 'em both the same afternoon. What are you doing now?"

"I have a perfectly legitimate excuse for calling on Lona Keith. So, if you don't mind—"

"Mind? Could I keep you from it?" Sullivan said jovially. "Go right ahead."

III

Lona Keith rented the upper half of a small frame house on a one-way street; a street that was little more than an alley and did not try to live up to its official designation of Montmorency Court. The house had a flat unadorned face and an outside stairway leading from the yard directly to Lona's front door.

With its glistening white paint that shamed the dilapidated flats across the court and because of the terraced rock garden in front of it, the place was not unattractive. And Lona's living room was very large, with two big front windows that meant light and sun. All of which she needed, Lona explained almost at once.

"The loom takes up so much room I must have space, and I hate to work by artificial light in the daytime. Besides, the loom does make some noise people above or below you in a lot of places would object to. But the old lady who owns this house— Miss Montmorency—is deaf and lives below me. So it has its advantages—"

"Don't apologize for your 'umble 'ome, dear," Roger said lazily. "You ought to realize it's a damn attractive room. You don't, because it's the result of contriving—"

His gesture included the hand-woven drapes, pillow and couch covers, the braided rugs and furniture Lona had painted or varnished herself.

"But you're tired of contriving," he finished. "Aren't we all? Only I hate to think what sort of furnishings you'd have if you could have your pick. Probably something very ornate that would fairly shriek its own expensiveness—and twice too much of it. Why don't you ask Mr. Dundas what he wants?"

"I never mind what Roger says, because I know he doesn't mean half of it," Lona said indulgently. "Don't you think clever people are often like that? They'd almost rather hurt others' feelings than not to say something clever—"

"I'm coming down, Davy Crockett," Roger said. "We get the idea, which is that I'm not clever, and you are very charitable."

"Oh, you don't have to be careful what you say to me, Roger. We've been chums too long for that. Of course neither of us is feeling very cheerful tonight."

"I know that," Michael said. "But you can't stop working indefinitely because of what happened last night. And—"

"I'm so glad someone does realize that. I'm afraid people think I'm heartless when I'm only practical. I had to keep on weaving today to finish some drapes by tomorrow, or the woman who ordered them might refuse to take them. And you can't let other people down simply because something's gone wrong with your own affairs."

"What she means is that Nora threw up her job this afternoon," Roger said. "She said it would be damned unpleasant being around the newspaper office right now."

"I hardly blame her for feeling like that. But I've been trying to tell Mrs. Keith I had a letter from my wife asking me to speak to her about drapes for our new house. I could show you the letter," Michael said, glancing briefly at Roger. "But I won't."

Roger grinned. "I'm still not convinced," he murmured, stretching out more comfortably on a couch. But whether or not he became convinced

Michael had a legitimate excuse for being there he was soon very obviously bored.

His eyelids drooped sleepily as Lona dragged a chest to the center of the floor and displayed samples of her work, while the talk ran on yarns, designs and colors. Michael's interest was genuine; he appreciated expert craftsmanship of any kind, and he considered that in this line Lona was an expert.

"But though I like the work I'm never paid what it's worth," she said finally. "It's that way with all handicrafts. People like to see how things are done—you remember the crowds around the Javanese batik- and metalworkers at the fair? But when it comes to buying they choose something that will 'give the same effect' at a quarter of the cost. They don't even want things to last too long."

She passed a hand over the length of fabric in her lap. The broad, close-fitting silver bracelet she wore on her right wrist shone dully against the dark blue of the material.

"I made a rather good thing of this business once. After my husband died, until after 1929. In those days I could get twenty-five dollars for a small purse. And I wove so many of these suit lengths to order from imported Scotch wools. Well, I'll want to measure your windows—"

"Shall we say the day after Thanksgiving, circumstances permitting? The house is in Russian Hill Place, off Vallejo. You can't miss it, since it's the only new one on a corner lot—"

"Look, Dundas—I'm convinced." Roger sat up, yawning. "And I wanted to ask you if you gave that envelope to Sullivan? Well, I supposed you would, so why hasn't there been anything about those notes in the newspapers?"

"I asked Sullivan that just before I left him. I do feel that if those notes were printed in the newspapers someone to whom they'd mean something might read them."

"Well, then why doesn't he give them to the newspapers?"

"He said very candidly that printing them so soon was an admission the police hadn't been able to make anything of them. He would prefer to decipher them first and then make them—and their meaning—public."

"Oh. Well, now let's have a nice, uplifting conversation about art and stuff. What did you think of *Elizabeth and Essex,* Lona?"

Michael wondered why Roger's gray eyes should twinkle when he asked this question, but Lona answered it unsuspiciously. She thought Errol Flynn was very attractive, especially in costume pictures, and Bette Davis was always very fine. But she did think it was a mistake to let Miss Davis play Queen Elizabeth as an elderly woman.

"But when she had her last little fling with Essex she was a hell of a lot older than Miss Davis portrays her, Lona."

"Oh well, if it's complete historical accuracy you want, Queen Elizabeth was really a man," Lona said scornfully.

"I beg your pardon!" Michael said.

"Yes, she was really a man. Or one of these—these borderline cases," Lona said delicately. "But of course it was always kept a secret, and no one was ever allowed to see her with all her clothes off."

Michael looked at Roger again. Roger returned the look with one of cheerful innocence, but his right eyelid drooped slightly. In the next twenty minutes, as the result of his skillful introduction and changing of subjects, they learned from Lona that Mrs. Harding had poisoned President Harding, that Jafsie really engineered the Lindbergh kidnaping, that football coaches receive larger salaries than the President of the United States, that a certain unmarried movie star had borne a certain newspaper publisher nine children, that most writers use pen names, that the Grand

Duchess Tatania is living in New York today and that Hitler is not Hitler but someone else.

"Well," Roger said, seeing Michael was beyond speech, "it doesn't matter a damn whether our Hitler is the original Adolf or a double. The results are the same."

"Some day we'll have a dictatorship here," Lona began. "They're only waiting their time to take over the army and the—"

"We'll never have a dictator named Adolf," Roger said, yawning again. "Americans would never think a guy with that name is anything but funny. And they'll have to get some substitute for the Nazi salute and goose step. Every time they show those on the screen the whole audience snickers. Trouble with the Germans is they've no sense of humor. Are you sure your people weren't German, Lona?"

"You know they were Swedish."

"No, I don't know anything about them. You've always avoided talking about them—"

"Avoided? I'm afraid you're letting your imagination run away with you," Lona said firmly. "You're inclined to do that, but of course you're a writer and out of touch with reality."

"Out of touch with— My God!" said Roger simply.

"Oh, but you are. However, I didn't have a happy childhood, and I'd rather forget it. My father thought children were given their parents to work for them. We were a large family, but there was plenty of work to go around," Lona said ruefully. "And I don't know what good working so hard did anyone. Because there's not many of us left. I was thinking of that when we were talking about Amalia and how few Keiths there are left."

"Well, Nora's father died young, and you and your Stephen and Amalia had no children. While the black sheep stray away and don't return. Every well-conducted family has a black sheep or two."

"We had one who strayed; the only one of my brothers I cared for," Lona said. "And I suppose I strayed too. At least, an elderly woman in Merced helped me get away; gave me money and letters to people here. Well, I do make good coffee, if that's a Swedish trait. And I'm going to make some now."

When she had gone into the kitchen Michael closed his eyes and groaned softly.

"I know," Roger said. "But you wouldn't have believed me if I'd just told you. I never knew anyone who collects misinformation more eagerly than Lona. And there is no use arguing with her."

"But she does seem quite practical even if she is inclined to say so too often."

"Oh, she is when it comes to everyday affairs. Don't get her wrong," Roger said. "You got the

whole dose at once, because I know all her pet
delusions. She's only gullible about things she
doesn't know anything about firsthand. She goes
in for the Sunday magazine sections, and she believes everything she reads until it's contradicted
by something else she reads. Then she believes the
most sensational account."

"Was Mrs. Landreth convinced of her practi-
cality?"

"Yes, I think Amalia would have considered
Lona a very practical and helpful person. She can
always tell you where to have your fur coat made
over, your gloves or clothes cleaned or broken
china mended. Or recommend a doctor, lawyer,
merchant, butcher, baker or tailor—whether she's
ever patronized them or not. You get the idea?
And why do you ask?"

"I was wondering if there was any chance Mrs.
Landreth would have confided in Mrs. Keith
when she had you and Mr. Lacey as possible con-
fidants—"

"It all depends on what she had to confide—"

"And, I should think, whom she happened to
see first."

Roger grimaced. "There is that. I got the idea
when we were all at the old homestead this afternoon that you think the whole thing began Thursday night when Amalia turned out the shrine. And
I saw Amalia Friday morning. However, Edwin is

her man of affairs, and I don't think Amalia considered me a particularly practical person."

"But you do ask questions?" Michael said.

"Why not? People are my stock in trade. Nothing ever happens to me," Roger said in an injured
voice. "I never hunted wild game anywhere, swam
the Hellespont, climbed the Matterhorn or lived in
the South Seas. Neither have I ever been a stoker,
bartender, prize fighter or anything picturesque.
I joined the navy once, partly for the free board
but also expecting to collect a wealth of material
about strange and glamorous foreign ports—"

"And you saw the world from a porthole?" Michael said, laughing. "'And what did I see? I saw
the sea!—'"

"And never got over being seasick or used to
sleeping in a hammock. It's like sleeping in a
frankfurter. Besides, I spent most of my time on
land at a typewriter copying records," Roger said.
"That's what I get for being one of the few living
writers who is an expert typist. But about Amalia:
of course I plied her with questions."

"Are you by any chance planning a 'family' novel
dealing with your own family?"

"That's it. Amalia was the missing link I always wanted. Besides, I'd only have made a mess
of it—"

"How do you know that?" Michael said curiously.

"Oh, there's a kind of indicator inside you that either says: 'I can do this' or, 'I'm not up to that,'" Roger said vaguely. "Anyway, it will probably take me more than a year to do the book the way I have it outlined in my head. I've done a lot of research on early California history, but I'm only about half finished. Meanwhile, what am I to use for money if I don't turn out my yearly 'sophisticated comedy for the discriminating reader'? See blurbs."

He got up as Lona came back into the room. "I'm going home. You make good coffee, but if I drink one cup I'll drink three and never get to sleep."

"Oh, do you have trouble sleeping?" Lona said. "I thought I was the one who is supposed to have an unlimited supply of sleeping medicines always with me."

"Tsk, tsk! That remark isn't worthy of you, my girl," Roger said, opening the door. "It hits you in the eye instead of circling gently about until it can stab you in the back. It's almost as forthright as Nora's accusations. But since Nora and the faithful Cornelius have just driven up I have a hunch he's persuaded her to apologize. Good night, Dundas. I'm certain it's not good-by."

IV

There were dark smudges under Nora's eyes, and
her clothes had more than their usual look of being uncertain they were on the right person. Cornelius had apparently been saying it with flowers.
There was a corsage pinned crookedly to her coat
lapel, its maidenhair fern brushing her cheek. She
unpinned it with an impatient gesture before she
began:

"Neil says I should apologize for accusing you
of putting something in that malted milk last
night. So I do apologize—"

"My dear, I knew you would when you had time
to think over what you'd said—"

"Because I'm sure you 'did it for my own good.'
I think it was damned officious of you, and you
knew I'd think so. That's why you took the glass
down to the kitchen, so Patton would wash it before I woke up. I don't see why you didn't admit
what you'd done—before we learned they'd found
Aunt Amalia. Of course, after that—"

"Nora!" Cornelius said forbiddingly. "You said
you'd—"

"I am apologizing, Neil. I was saying that
of course after they found Aunt Amalia, Lona
couldn't say she'd made sure I'd sleep last night. I
understand that," Nora said sweetly. "The police
might have thought she did it so I wouldn't catch

her sneaking out to get her car and go to collect Aunt Amalia's body from wherever she was killed. I'm sure you didn't do it for that reason, Lona, because no one with any sense would use that car of yours for a risky business like that."

"Well! Call that an apology!" For once Lona seemed overcome but she rallied swiftly. "Nora, how—how Irish of you."

"Oh, my mouth may be large, but my feet aren't," Nora said, glancing from her own narrow feet to Lona's broad Oxfords. "So I never have any trouble putting my foot in my mouth. There's my apology; take it or leave it."

"Oh, of course I'll take it. I realize what a strain you're under. So are we all, but even if you didn't see her any more—or quite as often as the rest of us did—Amalia was your aunt, so of course you think you feel more badly about this than any of us."

"I saw her as often as I could!"

"I know you did, dear. And I'm sure she realized you were very busy. But, Nora, simply because you slept soundly, and I took that glass downstairs with me to save Patton—"

"'To save Patton a few extra steps.' I know. Just because of that I shouldn't jump to the conclusion I was drugged," Nora said bitterly. "And you'd like to be reminding me again that people don't carry sleeping powders around with them in their purses or pockets. Because Edwin or Roger could have doctored that malted milk while Patton left it on the table in the hall. Or Patton could have done it in the kitchen. But I know Roger and Edwin take things to make them sleep sometimes—"

"Do I," Lona said superbly, "look as if I ever needed a doctor's care—or prescriptions?"

"Only when you sprain an ankle like you did in September," Nara retorted. "And any of you could have guessed I'd insist on staying all night over there and come prepared. I'll admit that for all I know someone wanted to get back into the house again—and did."

Lona shrugged pityingly and adjusted the wide silver bracelet on her wrist. "I'm sure this can't be very pleasant for Mr. Dundas—"

"I find it very interesting." Michael put down his coffee cup. "Why would no one with any sense use your car to carry a body in?"

Lona shivered. "It sounds terrible when you speak of it so—so bluntly. Why, I suppose Nora means . . . Will you open the door, Neil? That must be Edwin. . . . I suppose she means my car would be too easily identified. It's over fifteen years old."

She stopped to beckon Edwin toward the couch where she was sitting. "It was my husband's car and new in 1923. And a cream-and-black Pierce Arrow is very noticeable now. I didn't think I had to sell it at first, and then I couldn't get anything for it. And I need a car to make deliveries in sometimes. That's why I've kept it, but I don't use it any more than I have to. I'm never sure when I start out that I won't have to be towed home."

"Is it that bad?" Edwin said. "I told you you could take mine when you need to, and I thought Roger had given you the keys to his—"

Nora laughed hysterically. Edwin stared at her. "I hadn't realized I was a humorist."

"I'm sure you didn't. But I'm not so certain, Lona, that I don't take back that apology. Why are you here, Edwin?"

"I came to tell you that I have nothing to tell you. I drove by your place, Nora. The landlady said you'd come here. I rather thought Roger might be here too. I've been in touch with Sullivan again, and he had no information for me. He seems to have chosen me to represent the family.

"Not," Edwin added dryly, "that he hasn't checked every statement I've made. They even got in touch with the man—Mr. Ross—that I hoped might buy the house. And Patton admitted overhearing Amalia talking to me about a will. This is more or less a warning to the rest of you not to think anything you've said is going to be overlooked."

"Did Sullivan ask you if Mrs. Landreth had ever consulted you regarding any specific law of the United States that she might have forgotten in thirty years away from this country or that might have been new to her?" Michael asked, knowing quite well that Sullivan hadn't because he hadn't been told of Amalia's saying ". . . I didn't even know the laws of the United States—"

"I imagine you choose your words deliberately to mean exactly what you want them to mean, so I don't think you are asking me, as Sullivan did, if Amalia ever consulted me on 'legal matters.' The answer to that was 'yes,' and to your question—'no.' The matter of a will or inheritance involved state law."

"I see. I asked you because, as Mr. Keith says, you were Mrs. Landreth's man of affairs," Michael said innocently. "And she would be most apt to confide in you or to go to you for advice."

"And did he mention that she preferred his company to mine—" Edwin stopped and smiled apologetically. "I suppose I've said just what you and Roger expected. Roger is amusing; Amalia wasn't the only one who thinks so. But there are times when I prefer him in small doses. He says whatever comes into his mind— You don't agree with me?"

"You know him better than I do," Michael said. "And certainly he does talk a good deal. But I can't help thinking he may believe language is given us to conceal our thoughts."

"That maxim wouldn't be one of yours too?" Edwin said. "Perhaps you're right about Roger, but some-one must tell him not to rattle on at his usual rate to the police. They might take him too seriously."

"Do you think they would?" Cornelius said. "I mean, people expect writers to be kind of—of queer. Of course he talks too much. I never pay any attention to him."

"There's no need to be complacent about that," Nora muttered.

She shrugged impatiently when he asked what she had said. To show he had forgiven her he had moved behind her chair and folded his arms over its back. She wished he would go away. Did the broad leather belt about his solid waist always creak every time he drew a deep breath?

The sound irritated her; she wondered if you could be in love with a man one day and out of love the next. Of course she had always known he admired Lona. He thought she was "sort of calm and restful and never gets mad at anybody." There was no use trying to tell a man the truth about another woman. . . .

"I'm going home," Nora said abruptly. "I don't want to talk any more about anything. Michael, I didn't see your car parked in the street."

"Strange as it will seem to you, I walked. It isn't far, but I'd be very grateful if you'd take me home. I'll call you Friday morning if I don't see you before, Mrs. Keith. Good night. . . . Nora, do you think you could manage several rough sketches of Mrs. Landreth, as she was dressed yesterday? See what you can do, at any rate—"

V

Cornelius stopped his car where Vallejo appears to come to an end at Jones Street with a stone wall topped by an ornamental balustrade. However, thus guarded from spilling into Jones, the street proceeds over the hill past another protective barrier at Taylor and slides down into the Italian quarter.

Cornelius glanced toward Russian Hill Place, one of Vallejo's two tributaries above the barrier. "The house on the corner up there is yours, isn't it?" he said. "What is it, English?"

"Modern Anne Hathaway," Michael said. "It will have to wait for the years to make it picturesque and quaint, but depend on Valerie to discover a lot off the beaten track. I wasn't too enthusiastic about becoming a householder, but building our own house was at least guarantee Valerie wouldn't coax me into some ramshackle nest hanging over a cliff or some 'perfectly adorable quaint cottage' in a cul-de-sac like Montmorency Court."

"Uh-huh," Cornelius said inattentively. "Look: I've been thinking—"

"You can't take a patent out on that," Nora said.

"You better take a grip on yourself and try not to be so snappy," Cornelius remarked mildly. "I know this is hard on you, but you don't want to let it get you down."

"I should be brave and resolute—like Lona?"

"I don't see what you've got against Lona. I think she's a darned nice woman. But I was thinking about my own business. And what you said, Michael. That it didn't seem to you Uncle's death should make such a difference in it when Martha's still there and all the old customers have known her for years."

"Yes?"

"Yes," Cornelius said stolidly. "So I've been wondering if she's trying to spoil the business for me. Maybe she thought Uncle would leave it to her, she'd been with him so long and practically ran it the last ten years."

Michael got out of the car and lighted a cigarette. "I suppose it would be only natural for her to hope he might decide she might as well carry on."

"Yes, she does have a kind of—of possessive attitude about the shop. But Uncle wanted it to pass on to another Sturtevant. And I thought Martha was really trying to help me learn the business. But she'd better not try any funny stuff because she can't fool me on figures," Cornelius said grimly. "Only I got to thinking how she always waits on the really important customers

"Well, she knows what they're talking about, and I don't. That's all right, only it's funny how many times she says: 'Oh, we didn't have what they wanted.' How do I know if we did or didn't? Or that she wouldn't sort of hint the stock isn't what it should be since I own the place, but it would be different if it was hers? Do you think she'd do anything like that?"

"Oh," Michael said evasively, "you'd better practice what you've evidently been preaching to Nora tonight and not accuse anyone rashly— especially Martha. She is quite capable of raising merry hell if you tread too heavily on her toes."

"She steps on other people's. Anyway, I don't like the setup. Sure, I own a business, but by the time I pay expenses and Martha's salary I'd have a better income if I had a good job."

Nora put her head repentantly against his arm and Cornelius patted her shoulder absently before he went on:

"Sell the stock, and you haven't got a business. And probably not too much capital if you had to sell the whole lot to the highest bidders And I haven't heard of anyone that wants to buy an antique business and pay for the good will too—unless Martha does. The only thing is, I don't know what she'd use for money unless she knows someone that 'd put it up as a silent partner."

"But hasn't she drawn a good salary for years?" Nora asked. "And she has only herself to spend it on—"

"She's kind of like Uncle. She's made good money and spent it. She lives better than I do right now. But if she will leave her bills and bank statements around the office I can't help seeing the bills are overdue a lot of the time, and her bank balance isn't much."

"Since we've been talking about Sturtevant's—when Mrs. Landreth visited the shop, did she by any chance suggest either you or Martha might cast an expert eye over the furnishings of the old homestead?" Michael said.

"Hunh? Oh, you mean see if there was anything that was worth anything in her house before she sold it? She didn't say anything to me—"

"But she did, Neil. When I brought you to see her at the house the first time and told her what your business was, she waved a hand about the living room and said that perhaps you could tell her if there was anything in it that could be sold to anything but a junk dealer."

"Oh. I remember now. I guess I told her I didn't know any more about it than she did—"

"And mentioned Martha as the expert of the firm?" Michael suggested.

"I don't know. I might have."

"She talked to Martha that day we were at Sturtevant's. But I didn't listen," Nora said. "I was prowling around the place like I always do. But Aunt Amalia mentioned that matter more than once. She spoke of it over the telephone one evening too. But does it matter, Michael?"

"Perhaps it doesn't. I won't keep you any longer—"

"You aren't keeping us. If we're keeping you, why not just say so?"

"You'd better go home and try to sleep, my child," Michael said, walking away from them. "I agree with Cornelius your temper might be improved on. Don't forget to see if you can manage a fair likeness of your aunt. . . ."

Arrived in his own living room, he scowled at its desolate neatness. No one had ever called Valerie a perfect housekeeper: she threw newspapers and magazines on the floor as she finished reading them and considered dust a necessary evil. But she had put the room in order Sunday night, and he hadn't sat in it since then. Or, he thought, going on into the bedroom, had more than six hours' sleep after he had given up trying to make anything out of Amalia's "cipher" after he had left the Keith house last night.

He took the library books Valerie had mentioned from the bedside table and put them on the bureau where he would see them in the morning. Then he sat down on the bed and dialed Martha Ferris' number. Martha was not cordial toward his suggestion that she come over to his office at ten-thirty the next morning.

"I've got something to do besides helping along your unofficial inquiries," she said. "And while I didn't say anything this morning I wouldn't say again, I still don't know what you were driving at. I like to know what's on the other fellow's mind before I commit myself. Or anyone else, because I'm not just thinking of myself."

"Your solicitude for Cornelius does you great credit. I suppose it is Cornelius you are referring to? And I was just talking to him—about you. He asked me if I thought you were trying to spoil the business for him, turning away old customers by damning your wares with faint praise and suggesting it would all be oh! so different if you owned Sturtevant's—"

"Why, that—that dumb Dutchman! Did he think that up for himself, or did you suggest it to him?"

"You know that though Cornelius' mental processes may be a trifle slow they are exceeding sure. And I advised him tonight not to be too hasty. You do appreciate that, don't you? And this little warning? Because Cornelius is apt to take an idea to his bosom and cherish it there."

"You just try to prove anything, either of you!" Martha snapped. "And if you'd mind your own business—"

"But it almost minds itself, and I become bored with it. And I would like to know the reason for your excessive caution. I can't see why you are so determined not to talk at all unless— Where were you last Friday night between eight-thirty and ten, Martha? Answer yes or no."

"Friday between . . . I was snuggled up with a good book. What do you think I was doing?"

"What do you think I thought you were doing?"

"Oh, I get it. The iron hand in the velvet glove. I'll come over to your office tomorrow, but those pictures you've got are the only thing I'm talking about," Martha said. "And I hope you choke!"

"Pleasant dreams to you too," Michael said.

He put down the telephone, went to bed and slept soundly, while not a dozen blocks away a

small man with dark melancholy eyes paced back
and forth across the linoleum of a kitchen floor.

Sometimes he stopped to look again at an oil-
cloth-covered table where a faintly perfumed,
initialed handkerchief lay beside two bedraggled
feathers, red and green. At last, though it was
nearly one o'clock, he dropped into an old rocker
and sat there, staring unseeingly at the floor until
he heard quick footsteps on the walk outside.

He started up then and looked about for a place
to hide the articles on the table before he opened
the door. He did not have to unlock it. He knew
that, and he meant to open it even though death
should enter when he did.

VI

The photograph dated May 1908 had been taken
outdoors. There were large oaks for shade and a
grassy slope on which the gentlemen had flung
themselves in studiedly careless attitudes. However, the first Cornelius Sturtevant had remained
on his feet, a spare elegant figure whom his large
square nephew in no way resembled.

Martha Ferris had stood next to him, her ruffled dress brushing his feet, her flowered hat tilt-
ed over her eyes. Amalia was unmistakable among
the women seated on rough benches in a frenzy

of millinery. Except for Martha, all the women were older than Amalia. There were six men on the grass and one well-scrubbed small boy.

"That's Edwin Lacey," Martha said. "His folks must have been visiting here that spring. Here's Lacey, the oldest of the men on the grass. And Roger's father, but Roger wasn't born yet. However, if you look closely at his mother—"

Her forefinger moved from the slight, smiling man on the grass to the tall, sour-visaged woman on the bench.

"You'll see Roger was definitely on his way," she finished. "I guess I remember that so well because girls weren't supposed to recognize a woman in a certain condition in those days, and I thought I was pretty smart when I did.

"These two best-looking men are the Keith boys: Stephen and Hubert—Nora's father. He's the one with some chin. And these other two young fellows I don't recognize—"

"They are listed as Charles Falconer and Willie Bernard," Michael said.

"Oh, they were beaux of Amalia's. I think they were from families the Keiths had known for years. Yes, and Amalia was about half engaged to Willie Bernard before she went to Europe. I remember now: the older women talking about it and little Martha trying to listen in. I don't know what became of those boys, though I have a vague idea Willie Bernard was killed in the war."

"I think you're right about their being members of families the Keiths had always known," Michael said, offering her another photograph. "This was taken in 1899, apparently in the same spot."

"It was somewhere outside the city as the city was then," Martha said vaguely. "I think they always went there on picnics. Well, you see I'm not in this group, so you didn't keep it on that account."

"But Mr. Sturtevant is."

"So what? He's dead, and Cornelius couldn't have met Amalia until Nora introduced him to her. Even if he was more than twenty-nine, you know he was raised up North in Fort Bragg. Mr. Sturtevant never even saw Cornelius' family for years—or Cornelius until he came down to Berkeley to college," Martha said resentfully. "As for me, I was only about seven when this picture was taken—"

"I know. I kept it because it proves Mr. Sturtevant did know the Keiths fairly well for at least nine years. But I honestly don't know if that's important," Michael admitted.

"Then why bother about it?"

"Of course your being in that 1908 picture did interest me, Martha. That was more surprising than

Mr. Sturtevant's being in it. I already knew Mrs. Landreth had told Cornelius she had known his uncle. But their initials happen to be the same—"

"Amazing," Martha said sarcastically. "Did you get me in here to tell me men with the same names have the same initials?"

"No. But those initials have turned up in a rather peculiar—document," Michael said, thinking of that section of Amalia's notes which began: "Acc. C. S.—"

"Well, there are lots of 'C. S.s' in the world. About this picture: I see what you mean about it showing the Keith children had always known the Falconer and Bernard boys. This looks like a regular nursery tea."

"Not exactly the sort of function I would have expected Mr. Sturtevant to attend at the age of twenty-five or so."

Martha snorted and indicated the one young woman in the group, a swanlike creature holding a flirtatious parasol.

"Maybe this was the attraction—Beatrice Palmer. Never heard her name, but I have heard Mr. Sturtevant never married because he was in love with some girl who died. Though that might be just a romantic story someone made up. Well, here's Amalia's mother: the sourpuss in the middle pretending to be Queen Victoria with Mr. Keith behind her. He was dead by 1908 when that other picture was taken—"

"And his widow was still shunning the world?"

"N-no, I think she was out of mourning by 1908. I don't know why she wasn't on that picnic. If she had been there she'd have disapproved of Roger Keith's mother being out of the house in her delicate condition. Lord, when I think how women used to be expected to hole in from about the third month on—but still wear their corsets!"

Martha glanced approvingly down her own comfortably girdled bulk. "And now you fool fashion designers try to bring back the wasp waist. Pity they wouldn't lace the lot of you into hour-glass corsets and make you wear 'em a day or two. Oh, I know the new ones aren't quite cast iron like ours were, but they're bad enough.

"Well, about this picture. I suppose you've picked out the same ones as in the other, only nine years younger. The Keith boys, the Bernard and Falconer boys, Roger Keith's father, Amalia—about ten years old, she is. I don't know who this young man in the yachting cap named Beaumont was. Maybe he was Mr. Sturtevant's rival for the affections of the beauteous Beatrice Palmer. They look to be all about the same age. I guess Amalia's mother didn't mind the young folks courtin' around her till her own boys came of courtin' age. Who's this other middle-aged couple?"

"Mr. and Mrs. George Falconer, I believe."

"Charlie Falconer's parents, I suppose. Yes, they must have known the Keiths fairly well—"

Martha threw the photograph on the desk. "I don't know why you should bother with these things, and that's the best I can do for you. And about Mr. Sturtevant. I think it was Amalia's father he was friendly with. I seem to remember Mr. Keith used to dabble around at painting.

"But I don't think Mr. Sturtevant saw much of the Keiths after Amalia's father died. I doubt if he liked old Mrs. Keith though he did like Amalia. By that time he was a sort of stand-by with each new crop of debs. I don't imagine he ever saw anything of the Keiths after Amalia went to Europe and married there."

"That seems reasonable enough," Michael said. "From all accounts most of the gaiety went out of the family with Amalia— Come in!"

"The Harris girl is here," Fanchon said. "She wants to know—"

"No! Go away. Tell her to— Oh, tell her I am giving her damn trousseau my personal attention and am in a trance and can't be disturbed. Tell her anything, but don't let her in here. I want, if possible, to have a vague, impressionistic memory of her when I tackle her problem."

"Schlemiel!" said Fanchon and withdrew. Martha chuckled.

"It 'll take all her money and your artistry to gild a pill like Miss Harris," she observed. "Isn't she marrying young Hopkins? I've heard he's a young rip. Well, 'change the name but not the letter; change for worse and not for better.'"

Michael looked at her thoughtfully. "Did you ever marry, Martha?"

"Me? What gave you that idea? I told you—"

"You told me you could have married at eighteen but 'no thanks: you could wait.'"

"And you think that implies I did marry eventually. Pretty farfetched. And it's hard enough for a woman to get anywhere in the business world even when she puts getting ahead before everything—if she can. It's usually the women of a family, if they're earners, that get stuck with the responsibility for any lame ducks that happen to be floating around.

"Not," Martha added hastily, "that I ever let family feeling or what some people call a sense of duty hold me back. And I've always been Miss Ferris."

"You did take a sabbatical in Europe during Coolidge prosperity, didn't you?" Michael said. "And business women keep their maiden names in business. However, it's not my affair."

"You've got something there. Well, I must get back to the shop. Cornelius wants to go somewhere this morning. He isn't saying where, but he wasn't keen on waiting till I get back. Oh, don't get up. I'm perfectly capable of opening a door for myself."

She paused with her hand on the doorknob, watching Michael put the photographs back in a desk drawer and lock it again.

"Not going to look at the pretty pictures any more?" she said jeeringly. "Going to give some attention to your own business for a while?"

"The answer to both your questions is 'no.'"

Michael put the key to the desk drawer in his pocket simply because that was where he always carried it. At the moment he was inclined to think Martha's mockery was justified.

"I'm going to talk to Mrs. Landreth's maid again after lunch," he said. "I want, among other things, to hear more about last Friday night when she left Mrs. Landreth alone for several hours. I think Patton is helping Nora look through Mrs. Landreth's belongings this morning. Perhaps Nora asked Cornelius to be there too."

"In that case there's no reason why he shouldn't say so. Look here: what made you think I might have been married? Is it because you think I'm not a virgin?"

"Since you ask—yes. That is—no, I don't."

Martha grinned. "Says he without turning a hair. I'd like to know how men guess. But at my age—I'm flattered."

VII

Michael glanced about the hotel manageress' private parlor and guessed that she also must be English. The royal family, past and present, was assembled in force on the room's walls, and on a fumed-oak sideboard a portrait of Edward of Windsor was not quite displayed and not quite hidden by a violently pink-and-green tea service.

"'Oh, my fur and whiskers, where's the Duchess?'" Michael said, and very nearly sent the conversation off to a bad start.

But though she adequately expressed her scorn of the former Wallis Simpson in two words—"that woman!"—Patton had lost some of her stiffness, like a mold of gelatine a short time removed from the refrigerator. She didn't "mind owning it was distressing to look over Mrs. Landreth's things and try to advise Miss Nora what to do with them. And I feel I was very remiss, sir, not to tell you I left Mrs. Landreth alone for two hours Friday night. But with all else there was to think of Monday night it simply didn't come to my mind."

"Which means, I imagine, that it didn't occur to you at the time or later, that Mrs. Landreth was anxious you should be out of the house for a few hours that night?"

"Oh no, sir. She didn't press me to go. It was all quite—quite extemporaneous. And she would have had to dress to go out that night as she was wearing a house coat for warmth when I left. When I went to turn down the bed after I returned there were no signs in her bedroom that she had dressed, and there would have been, I'm sure."

"Oh, I don't think she went out," Michael said. "But did she ever tell you what she meant to do with the furnishings of the house? Did she plan taking anything with her when she moved, or did she intend selling the house as it stood, minus personal family heirlooms?"

"I think she did mean to sell the house as was, sir. She always spoke of a furnished apartment. She said once she didn't believe any of the ornaments or pictures were worth keeping, but she wasn't certain—"

"How long ago was that?"

"Why, several weeks ago, I think. But you remind me that Saturday she brought several things into the dining room and said—" Patton frowned. "Yes, she said: 'It seems these are worth keeping.' I pointed them out to Miss Nora today. There was a jug Madam said was old luster and a pair of what she said were genuine Chelsea candlesticks. Very pretty they are, and she showed me how the candle piece is removable, and I remembered we had some like that in my old home, though nothing so fine."

"Was that all she'd—decided was valuable?"

"No, there was a sort of openwork fruit basket she said was Leeds ware. And a Sheffield candelabra and a sort of Chinese jar she said was better porcelain than she had supposed. She wondered if some old Chinaman hadn't given it to her grandfather or grandmother. She thought the other things must have been in the family a long time. Then there is a sort of Italian cabinet in the library, but she always intended keeping that."

"So she didn't need an expert opinion to know it was worth keeping? Tell me, did you ever have the impression, after Thursday night, that Mrs. Landreth might be hiding something in her bedroom?"

"Well—if you could be a bit more definite, sir?"

"She must have had something hidden there or the room wouldn't have been torn to pieces. You said you had noticed the workbags she carried from her grandmother's room into her own, but not the glove box—"

"And I'm quite certain that was never on the table where the workbags were—before Madam left the house for the last time. But after Mr. Keith and I found Miss Nora in that closet and saw the state the room was in, of course I saw the box on the floor, seeming as if it had been stepped on. And now I can't be certain that box wasn't on the table when I went up to tidy the bedroom after seeing Mrs. Landreth walk away. It seems like I can see it there, and then again, I think I must be mistaken. Because it wasn't as if I did more than hang up her robe and so on before I left the room again."

"I think it's probable you did see the box on the table at a quarter of five," Michael said. "I had a notion Mrs. Landreth might have kept her—well, we'll call them 'valuables'—in that box. My wife insists on putting any unusually large amount of money under her pillow at night in spite of my telling her that only means a burglar would have to reach under . . . Well?"

"Why, I was just recalling that when I brought Madam's breakfast tray to her Saturday, I started to adjust her pillows for her. And she told me quite sharply not to bother. And that brings to mind another time when she spoke rather curtly, which wasn't at all her way. You know the hat-boxes, sir?"

"The hatboxes? Oh, they were on the closet floor Monday evening, weren't they? I suppose they should have been on the shelf above?"

"Oh yes, sir! But they were on the floor and every which way with the shoes. So we thought they had been searched too. Well, when Madam returned from her shopping trip Monday, she laid down for a while. I came up to her after a few minutes, and that was when she asked if I could manage dinner for three instead of only two.

"She'd flung off her things the way she had, and I put her suit on its hanger and hung up her fur. And then took her hat to put it in its box, sir. And one of the hatboxes was quite crooked and not pushed well back on the shelf. I reached up to straighten it, and Madam said, quite sharp: 'Not that box!'"

"Oh. You are fairly tall, but she was very short," Michael said. "She'd find it easier to get the box down than to put it back on the ledge— Go on."

"Oh, I presumed she meant that hat didn't belong in that particular box, sir. I told her I was only putting the box in its place. Then she laughed and said that I was 'too fussy.' And not to bother to put the hat into its box because she would wear it when she went out again."

"I see. Well, there's a woman's idea of a good hiding place for you. 'Quite safe.' Still, since the person who searched her bedroom apparently had to tear it to pieces to find what he wanted, her hiding place was a good one after all. And you're certain she said nothing that would help you guess who the second person she was asking to dinner might be?"

"No sir. I've puzzled over that a good bit. I'll own I was surprised she mentioned no name, but it wasn't my place to ask questions. Nor she didn't question me about the menu, sir. But then it was like she had other things on her mind. She said she would lie down because she was tired. I wanted to make fast the feather ornament on that hat when she said she would wear it again. I noticed the threads were quite loose. But she told me not to bother with that either. Then she said she'd try to sleep though she knew she couldn't; that she had what her grandmother used to call 'the fidgets.'"

"Oh, I think that fact is pretty well established," Michael said, tearing himself from the arms of an old-fashioned Morris chair. "If I don't see you before, when my wife returns, I will present her for your approval. Don't be deceived by her girlish look. She has an excellent disposition—and a will of her own. And, Patton: be careful."

"I quite understand, sir," Patton said calmly. "Someone might think I know more than I do. I bolt and lock my door at night besides putting a chair under the knob. As well as taking a large ice pick to bed with me in case I should be called on to defend myself."

"An excellent weapon," Michael said approvingly. "And I'm sure you'd handle it very efficiently. . . ."

And no doubt she'll handle us very efficiently, he thought, getting into his car and heading down Larkin. But she must be an improvement on any or all of the four—or is it five?—maids we've sampled since September. If she will keep her place she'll find we'll most gratefully keep ours. . . .

He realized he was too far across Sutter Street to turn toward Gisele's, shrugged and continued on toward Civic Center as the library books on the seat beside him caught his attention by spilling off it. It was only three o'clock, he might as well return the books and at the same time refresh his memory of some of the plates in *Costumes Historiques de la France.*

He parked beside the square overlooked by the city hall, that pretentious madam chairman presiding over a committee of earnest public buildings. In the center of the square privileged pigeons were scornful of dingy, voracious sea gulls. Flowers were yellow and orange, crimson and purple in their beds, while black acacia trees purred softly under a gentle breeze, and the sun dreamed of summer.

Michael went up the broad front steps of the library and on to the second floor where he parted—grudgingly—with twenty-eight cents in fines. The book he wanted to consult was on reference, and he went to look up its call number in the card catalogue before going into the reference room at the front of the library.

He found the drawer of cards he wanted; carried it over to one of the stands between the two sections of files; reached into his breast pocket for a pencil. And then stood staring at the pencils on the writing stands: stubby, almost pointless pencils but each one attached protectively to a chain that disappeared into a small slot in the wood.

He remembered Amalia Landreth saying: "I don't think chains are attached to pencils in public places to keep just women from walking away with them—" and promptly forgot *Costumes Historiques de la France*. For an instant he looked irresolutely toward the plump, pleasant-faced woman at the information desk in the center of the room.

But in the end he decided not to try to wrest information from civil servants. He went down to the first floor and spoke urgently to James Sullivan over the telephone.

VIII

Nora was lying across her bed when the telephone rang at a little past three o'clock. Martha Ferris wanted to know if "you've got any idea where Cornelius is. I haven't had any lunch, and I'm so hollow inside I feel like the Grand Canyon."

"I don't know where he is," Nora said. "He took me over to the old house about eleven, you know."

"I didn't. But aren't you through over there? I take it the police turned the place back to you?"

"Yes. Inspector Sullivan said he didn't think it was necessary even to leave a guard there any longer."

Martha grunted. "There still might be one hiding out somewhere. Did you do that sketch of Amalia I just saw in one of the afternoon papers?"

"Yes. It isn't very good—"

"You managed to make it look like Amalia. Well, if Cornelius isn't with you—"

"He hasn't been for quite a while. He took me to the house, came back there about one and took me to lunch—"

"Trust him not to miss his lunch," Martha said angrily. "Didn't he stick around with you after that?"

"Since you seem to think it's important—he did ask if I wanted to bring anything from the house over here in his car. But I left things as they were.

I couldn't bear having any of Aunt Amalia's things around me now. The other things can stay in the house for a while too. No one seems in a hurry to buy it. I saw Neil was bored, waiting for me to be through, so I told him to go on, and he did."

"Well, I'm going to put the 'out to lunch' sign on the door," Martha said. "There's no business anyway, the afternoon before a holiday. Sorry if I woke you up."

"Oh, I wasn't sleeping," Nora said. But for an hour or so she had achieved a state of mental and physical languor that was better than sleep. If you slept, you dreamed—

She might have lain here for hours more if Martha hadn't called. Now it seemed important again that there wasn't even coffee in her tiny kitchenette. She must have bread, butter, eggs— yes, and soap powder if she was going to wash stockings tonight. . . .

She said: "Damn!" staring guiltily at a ringless finger, remembering that when she washed her hands just before she left the old Keith house, she had removed Cornelius' ring. And of course left it on the washstand when Lona called to her as she was drying her hands.

Well, she would have to get it because Neil would frown over her carelessness—even if it wasn't

officially an engagement ring but an old opal that
had belonged to his mother. Nora had been born
in October, so the old superstition about opals
didn't apply to her.

It would do, Cornelius said, until he could afford
to buy her a "real humdinger of a diamond." The
opal satisfied Nora, and she thought, slipping into
a light coat, that it might be difficult to admire the
engagement ring of Cornelius' choice. It would
probably be pretty ostentatious. He'd once remarked disparagingly that he didn't see why Michael
hadn't given Valerie something that "looks like more
money than that star sapphire of hers . . ."

On this warm and sunny afternoon the old house
was still damply cold, and there was no more than
the half-light of dusk in the lower hall. Nora had
stood a full minute at the front door before she
unlocked it, but once in the house she went swiftly upstairs and on to the indigo-blue bathroom.

The opal was there. With the relief that came
from having it safely on her finger again she felt
herself equal to going on to Amalia's bedroom instead of hurrying out of the house at once.

What she wanted from the bedroom was the
glass letterweight that enclosed Little Red Ridinghood and her dog. She not only had a childish liking for the thing; it had belonged to her

father. And she had been remembering that Lona
had remarked this morning that the letterweight
was "cunning," and she would like to have it.

It was certainly legally her own, Nora thought,
but it would save argument to take it now. She
knew where it was, on top of a pile of papers on
Amalia's desk. She had only to walk straight to it
and out again; she needn't look about the room.

She opened the bedroom door. This room was
light enough with its big windows higher than
the tops of the trees in the front yard. It was so
brightly washed in sunshine that Nora closed her
eyes for an instant.

What she saw when she opened them was a small
thing to make her mouth go dry and her hair cling
moistly to her temples. Nothing more than a last
flake or two of snow fluttering down over Little
Red Ridinghood in the glass letterweight—

But it meant that not a minute ago someone
had inverted the glass ball, releasing the white
particles in its base. The last white flake had fall-
en: Little Red Ridinghood and her dog were completely covered with snow that would settle slowly
to the base again. You had to turn the ball upside
down or shake it to produce a snowstorm. Someone had; someone who must still be in this room,
hiding in the closet or under the bed. . . .

She mustn't look toward either one. Just turn
and walk out, not too quickly, but before someone

understood what she'd been looking at, and that she knew what it meant.

She turned, she walked to the door; she even forced herself to close it without haste. In the bedroom she thought she heard another door open or close. She ran then, but the old hall carpet was a quagmire that sucked eagerly at her feet.

Yet she must be running because she heard her own footsteps. Her own—or others behind her as she felt the stair railing under her hand an instant before she fell forward into darkness. . . .

Her next thought was that she must be choking to death. But it was only brandy trickling down her throat. There was a great deal more of it on her face and dress, and someone had been begging her to open her eyes. When she did open them there was only Roger grinning down at her and saying:

"It's a good thing you have a hard head, Leonora. You've a fine bump on your forehead to match the one in back."

Nora closed her eyes again. "Oh, it was you then?" she said wearily. "How did you get in front of me?"

"What do you mean? No one hit you; you caught your foot where the stair carpet's ripped and pitched downstairs."

"Do you say so? And how did you get in the house?"

"You left the front door open. What do you think happened to you if you don't think you fell downstairs?"

Nora told him. "Though perhaps I did just trip and fall," she admitted. "If it's a bump on my fore-head I have, I must have. I know there is a rip in the stair carpet. But I wasn't mistaken about the other! The snow was still falling over Little Red Riding-hood in that letterweight. And it wouldn't have been unless—"

"Oh, I know how the thing works. Afraid to be alone while I look in the bedroom? I'll be right back. . . ."

Returning, he reported: "Nothing out of order that I can see. Except—"

"Well?" Nora put her head back against the banisters.

"I looked the letterweight over in that strong light. Fingerprints show up plainly on glass like that, but it just looks to be in a fine state of polish."

"It shouldn't be. We were all handling it this morning. Didn't you yourself, when you came in on us to ask could you do anything to help?"

"Hum? Yes, I guess I did. The things are sort of fascinating. There's a lot of snow in that one too; takes longer for it to settle down again than it does in some. Well, I guess Sullivan told the truth when he said he wasn't going to keep the place under observation—in the daytime, at least. The papers the letterweight was sitting on don't seem to have been disturbed—or to be anything important—"

"Just letters and bills. Maybe someone had just lifted the letterweight to look at them when I came along. And wasn't it a lucky chance you just happened by the house and saw the door was open?" Nora said politely.

"I was out for a stroll. You know I do resort to walking sometimes when sitting doesn't produce the right word in the right place."

"You can keep on writing in spite of what's happened?"

"What's so shocking about that? As our Lona says, life must go on. That doesn't mean I haven't been emotionally disturbed," Roger said. "I have. That doesn't keep me from writing; it may even drive me to it as an escape. What time did you get here?"

"Oh, about three-thirty, I suppose."

"Well, it's ten of four now, so you must have been out for about ten minutes. I'm going to take you home. Up you come!"

He slid his long arms under her knees and shoulders and carried her down the stairs. "I was afraid to move you until you'd come to. I was even afraid you'd broken your silly neck."

"You wouldn't want to be the cause of me doing that, would you? I don't really think you would. Put me down."

Roger shook his head. "Unfinished business," he said, kissed her and caught her hand when she tried to slap him. "You should learn to accept these little attentions in the same spirit in which they're offered—"

"I am. You don't love me—"

"'No, no, my darling love, I did not love you!' But I did, absurd as you were at nineteen, foolish as you are at twenty-four. Well—" He put her on her feet and kissed her again. There was nothing unfinished about that kiss.

"Remember that the next time your Old Dutch pats you passionately on the shoulder," he said. "Or when you're married to him. I can't believe you'll be fool enough to go through with it, though I know you haven't guts enough to marry me. And that's a proposal, not a proposition."

"I will too marry him!" Nora said. "He's dependable and—and kind and—"

"What a feeble set of reasons for marrying anyone."

"At any rate, I have no intention of marrying you! For one thing, I don't think I left the front door open. I wouldn't risk finding I'd married a murderer—"

"Good," Roger said calmly. "Don't risk it."

"You don't mean Cornelius? Why, that's ridiculous! How can you say—"

"I can't say there's any reason to suspect he's involved in this affair. But I don't think Mr. Dundas has counted him out. And if Amalia was killed because she had something that spelled money, it hasn't escaped my notice, if it has yours, that your Neil would like above all things to have money and plenty of it. Oh, don't cry!"

"I'm c-crying because you make me so mad! And you bruised my arm and my h-head aches—"

"And as usual, you've no handkerchief. Your slip shows too. Here—"

Roger yanked a handkerchief from his coat pocket and gave it to her. Something small and bright fell to the floor. He stooped and picked it up, but not quickly enough to keep her from seeing it was a razor blade.

"Were you thinking of dropping in here to shave yourself perhaps?" Nora said, feebly sarcastic.

"You might find anything in my pockets," Roger said briefly. He put the blade back in his pocket. "Come on, I'm seeing you home. . . ."

IX

"I think you're trying to make a lot out of nothing much," Sullivan said disgustedly. He was out of breath after rushing up the library steps. "Just because Mrs. Landreth mentioned pencils attached to chains in public places—"

"In what other public places are pencils attached to chains?"

"Well— But after I got started I thought: what if she did go to the library Saturday afternoon? Oh, it's got to be checked on," Sullivan admitted. "But suppose she just wanted to get some books to read?"

"She would have to acquire a library card before she could take books home. You didn't find any library books in the house, did you? I saw none in her bedroom—"

"Oh, all right." Sullivan fanned himself with the newspaper he was carrying. "Shall we start with the woman in there at the information desk?"

"I'd try the reference room first."

"Why?"

"I don't believe she would have noticed those pencils unless she used one. You almost never do use those writing stands unless you are consulting the card catalogues. If you want fiction you usually simply walk into the reading room to see what's on the shelves. But you must look up the call numbers of nonfiction, and they get the books for you from the stacks.

"Since she couldn't take books from the library, if she found something that answered her purpose labeled 'reference room' she might as well go down there. Besides," Michael said wearily, "almost all the best reference works are in that room, not to be taken out. You really should make use of your civic institutions."

"I told you I'm no reader. All right, we'll try your reference room first. . . ."

The reference room was presided over by a slim pale-haired woman who had herself the informative, authoritative and slightly disused look of a rare reference work. She glanced disinterestedly at Sullivan's badge and the newspaper reproduction of Nora's sketch of Amalia Landreth.

"Yes, that woman was in here recently. I remember her dimples when she smiled. And I think she wasn't very familiar with the reference room. What is her name? Oh, that woman?"

"I take it you don't read about murder cases?"

Sullivan spoke in his normal voice, which was neither soft nor low, though an excellent thing for dressing down subordinates. Instantly four earnest seekers after information at tables near the desk raised their heads and glared at him. Sullivan reddened, with the guilty look of one who has laughed aloud in church, and continued in a creaky whisper:

"Well, some people don't, and this is the first good likeness of her that's been in the papers. You wouldn't have any reason to remember one name out of hundreds. But if you could remember what she wanted, Miss—uh?"

"Miss Galbraith. Do you know what day last week she was here? I'm certain it was last week—"

"Saturday afternoon, probably about this time."

From somewhere underneath the desk Miss Galbraith brought out a stack of small yellowish slips of paper.

"You sign your name and address on these along with the call numbers of your books," she explained. "We keep them for quite a while because so often people come back wanting a book they've had before and whose name they've forgotten. That helps us to help them—"

She was running rapidly through the slips as she spoke. Without looking up she smiled briefly.

"And at times we need these to engage in detective work of our own. People will mistreat books; they will even carry them away. . . . Yes, here it is. I put down the call numbers. I think she had them written on one of the forms they use at the main call desk. But of course she signed it."

"That's it: Amalia Landreth, on Union Street. And the books she wanted?" Sullivan said anxiously. "Can you tell the titles from the letters and figures—"

"You mean the call numbers?" Miss Galbraith said precisely. "We'll find the same books for you. Let me see: 737 R21, copy five. Oh yes, I know that book. It's one we keep here—"

She turned and took a thin purplish volume from a shelf behind her chair. "*Raymond's Standard Catalogue of United States Coins and Currency,*" she said in her pleasant remote voice. "Does that help you?"

"Does that—*Válgame Dios!*" Michael had the book in his hands before Sullivan could reach for it. "And here stand two of the world's worst num-skulls—"

"Sh-h!" Sullivan said.

Michael opened the book and stalked abstract-edly toward the door. Miss Galbraith watched him doubtfully.

"Do you think—"

"Oh, it's safe. I'll see he brings it back," Sullivan said. "But about that other call number—"

"I think it must also be a book dealing with coins and currency," Miss Galbraith said. "But I'll have to get it for you from the stacks. If you'll excuse me?"

Sullivan followed her from the room and found Michael just outside it. He was halfway through the catalogue now, flipping its pages over rapidly, muttering: "Not enough, none of them are, or even begin to be—"

"Not enough what?" Sullivan asked.

"Money. The prices aren't high enough. Besides, nothing I've seen so far fits any of her abbreviations—" He turned another page. "Have you ever," he inquired then, "actually heard anyone shout 'aha!'?"

"I don't know. And hold that so I can see it."

"Well, I'm saying 'aha!' now. Read it for yourself," Michael said, and then read it for him. "'Private Gold Coins, Georgia, Templeton Reid, Lumpkin County, Georgia 1830.' Amalia's grandmother, Mrs. Gordon, came from Georgia. And Amalia's notes begin: 'T. R.—5–30—$3500.' T. R. not for Teddy Roosevelt but for Templeton Reid. And a Templeton Reid five dollars of 1830 is listed here as being worth thirty-five hundred dollars."

"Holy mother! You don't mean even a gold coin like the one in the picture there would ever be worth that much money?"

"Evidently Mr. Raymond thinks so, and he compiles catalogues. I know nothing whatever about coins. Let's see what else we have here. There are four Templeton Reids listed but Amalia only noted down one—"

"North Carolina, Christopher Bechtler, 1831–1842," Sullivan read. "Three pages of 'em, running

from ten to twelve hundred dollars. Was there anything like that in her notes? You seem to 've learned
them by heart."

"I did. No, the Bechtlers are out along with
the Colorado firms and the Utah Mormon coins. I
imagine California is what we want. . . . Yes, here
is California, beginning with Baldwin and Company."

"That was in her notes, wasn't it?"

"'Bald.—20–51—2500.' You see that a Baldwin
and Company twenty dollars of 1851 is listed here
at twenty-five hundred dollars."

"I'm like the old farmer at the fair that looked
at the giraffe and told his wife, 'There ain't any
such animal,'" Sullivan said. "What a lot of trouble she'd have saved us if she hadn't abbreviated.
Evidently she put down the firm first, then the
denomination of the coin without bothering with
the dollar sign, then the year it was coined without
even an apostrophe before it and then the price."

"Yes. Her next item was 'C. M. & T.—5–49—
2500; 10–49—3000.' That would stand for the
Cincinnati Mining and Trading Company issues
of 1849, five and ten dollar pieces, listed at twenty-five hundred and three thousand. But we needn't
go through the whole thing like this," Michael
said. "They are listed alphabetically according to
the firms that issued the coins. That explains why

her notes had an alphabetical sequence that I tried to explain in every way but the simplest one."

"Wasn't there something about 'ings.' in her notes? I still don't know what an 'ing.' is."

"An ingot. They were stamped from gold bars and precede the fifty dollar slugs. The six issued by F. D. Kohler, containing varying amounts of gold, seem to be worth a little matter of twenty-three grand."

"I don't believe it," Sullivan said flatly.

Michael grinned. "Neither do I—really."

"Well—we can buy this catalogue, can't we?"

"From any coin dealer, I imagine. And I think a telephone book is the next—"

"I beg your pardon," Miss Galbraith said. "Here is the other book. I must get back to the desk. Will you come in there if you need my help in any other way?"

"Yes, we will. Thank you." Sullivan put the thin volume she handed him under his arm. "You mean that address Mrs. Landreth looked up in the telephone book that you thought must be someone in the Phelan Building? You think it was a coin dealer?"

"Don't you? I doubt if there are very many of them in the city. You know she remarked one would think there would be more. Besides, we need to talk to some expert. This catalogue is useful but I

can think of a dozen questions no one but an expert can answer."

"I can think of a few myself," Sullivan said.
"And maybe Mrs. Landreth did too, even if it was
evidently this catalogue she took notes on. Sa-ay!"

"Yes," Michael said, "that had just occurred to
me. The second section of her notes: 'Acc. C. S.—'
Let's see that book. It couldn't be—"

"But it is," Sullivan said. "*Private Gold Coinage in California* by Cornelius Sturtevant. Printed
here in 1930. And he wishes to acknowledge the
help he had from Miss Martha Ferris in compiling
and writing the article."

X

"Well," Sullivan said finally, "I suppose even I'd
have to cut through a lot of red tape to take this
book out of the library—"

"Why bother? Undoubtedly Martha has a copy
of this book and probably old Sturtevant gave one
to Cornelius too. And to all his cronies. I have
noticed that anyone who writes a learned article
and pays himself to have it printed is always very
generous in its distribution."

"That's an idea. Look: I'm not much good at
skimming things quickly. I'll go down to the telephone, and you glance through the article and see

if it gives you any ideas. There's a few calls I'd better make while I'm at it. . . ."

Returning ten minutes later he found Michael just glancing down the final page of the book. "Well?" he said.

"It's written more for the amateur than I'd hoped," Michael said. "Though he evidently had a very good collection of his own. And he does devote a paragraph to prices and says that in 1908 a Cincinnati Mining and Trading Company ten dollars of 1849 sold for three thousand."

"That was the first item Mrs. Landreth put down after 'Acc. C. S.?' I suppose that stood for 'according to Cornelius Sturtevant'—to her."

"So long as her notes meant something to her they served their purpose. And Sturtevant also mentions three prices paid for coins in 1929; the three that are also in the second section of Amalia's notes. Her 'Dub. 10—3900 (29)' stands for a Dubosq and Company ten dollars. I suppose an 1850 issue. Because Mr. Sturtevant has several very interesting paragraphs regarding Dubosq. But I'd prefer not to discuss that until we find our expert."

"There's a coin dealer named Henry J. Conklin in the Phelan Building. I called the office and tried to find out how he was missed," Sullivan said grimly. "I didn't. But if he was just skipped over, I will! I think we'd best see him first, and then maybe we can talk to young Sturtevant and the Ferris woman with more authority."

"If you don't mind, I'd like to ask Miss Galbraith a few more questions while we are here."

"I don't mind. Better you than me. I don't like to have to talk in a stage whisper."

Miss Galbraith was reading the newspaper Sullivan had left on the desk. She pushed it away hastily as they approached; then smiled, apologetically.

"One can't help being interested—now," she said. "And one should keep in touch even with happenings of this sort. But with so much else to be read— Did the books help?"

"Immeasurably," Michael said. "Haven't you a great many books on early California history in this room?"

"Oh yes. All of the best and most rare."

"And no doubt you get to know those who do any great amount of work in here?"

"Y-yes. I—I see that Roger Keith is mentioned as one of this Mrs. Landreth's relatives. And I do know him by sight and have talked to him often and helped him find the books he wanted—"

"I know he's planning a novel with an early California setting," Michael said as she hesitated. "And that he has a great deal of research to do."

Miss Galbraith nodded. "Yes, Mr. Keith will come in every day for perhaps a month or two. Then we may not see him for several months more."

"He hasn't been coming in regularly lately?" Michael suggested. "He's working on his yearly comedy of manners now, I think."

"They're good enough of their sort, but I do think he is capable of doing something really worthwhile and—"

"Yes, but was he in here last week?" Sullivan said impatiently. "Friday, Saturday or Sunday? Are you on duty at night?"

"No." With a look of distaste Miss Galbraith began running through call slips again. "Here is one signed by Mr. Keith on Friday night. He consulted *Bartlett's Familiar Quotations*."

"Oh. That's the only one? Are there any signed by an Edwin Lacey. Or by—"

"Probably only Roger is known here, so only Roger would have to sign his own name," Michael said. "Suppose, Miss Galbraith, that you knew me as well as you do Mr. Keith. And that I asked for Bartlett and made out a slip in the usual fashion. And then returned Bartlett to the desk and said casually: 'I'd like that coin catalogue.' Mightn't you simply hand it over and not bother to make a record of it on the slip I'd already signed?"

"I might," Miss Galbraith said reluctantly. "If I was quite busy. But Mr. Keith didn't come in this last weekend while I was on duty. Miss Blessing comes on at six; you'll have to see her."

"But she knows Mr. Keith too?"

"Yes, she does. We've discussed his—work quite often."

They left Miss Galbraith looking as if she had come down from her shelf for a glance at the world and didn't care overmuch for what she saw. "You follow my car," Sullivan said. "Then you won't have any trouble parking on Market. I'll take care of the traffic squad or any tags you get. I want to see this fellow Conklin right now. . . ."

Henry J. Conklin was a small, attractively rabbity man who appeared to be on leave from a woodland drawing by Disney. And Mr. Conklin was gently reproachful.

"If I'd been asked if a woman answering Mrs. Landreth's description had been here Monday I would have remembered the incident at once," he told them. "I gave it a good deal of thought. But she didn't tell me her name. I knew a woman named Landreth had been murdered but that meant nothing to me and I'm afraid I never read accounts of murder cases in the newspapers."

"This country needs more people who do," Sullivan said.

"But when I saw the sketch of Mrs. Landreth in my afternoon paper I recognized her instantly," Mr. Conklin said proudly. "I was going to get in touch with the police tonight, though I had no idea how to go about that. I'm very grateful you've come to me."

"I'd be grateful to know how the men I've had making inquires in this building missed you."

"I wasn't here yesterday afternoon, and the girl who looks after the place when I'm out isn't very intelligent, I fear. I don't open the place until eleven so perhaps your men simply missed me and meant to come back."

"Oh, more than likely. Well, what was this incident you thought so much about?"

"Will you come in here and sit down?" Mr. Conklin lifted a hinged section in the counter that shut off his desk, safe and several filing cabinets from the rest of the small room. "Well, on Monday at about one o'clock, the door opened and the woman who seems to have been Mrs. Landreth came in—"

Amalia had walked up to the counter, asked if Mr. Conklin dealt in coins and whether he was "an expert." He said modestly that he hoped he might be so called and that he did deal in coins. Whereupon Amalia opened her purse, fished about in it and put down on the counter what Mr. Conklin recognized as a Templeton Reid five dollars of 1830; a specimen that could not quite be called uncirculated but certainly very fine.

"Is that worth thirty-five hundred dollars?" Amalia demanded.

Mr. Conklin replied cautiously that Raymond's last catalogue did list the coin at that figure.

"The Templeton Reid issues were the first private gold coins to be struck in the United States. Might I ask how you came by this?"

"I can only guess," Amalia said. "How it came into the family, I mean. But my grandmother came from Georgia. She was married there in '47, and then she and my grandfather started for California. Well, her mother might have given her this coin so she'd have some money of her own, or she'd been given it as a child and never spent it. And she never needed to after she was married."

"I see. That is indeed very interesting."

"I've read the catalogue you speak of," Amalia continued. "And an article by a Cornelius Sturtevant—"

"A very competent discussion of private gold coinage."

"In California," Amalia qualified. "He barely mentioned the Templeton Reid coins, which is one reason I wanted to show this one to you. And perhaps you would like to look at this. . . ."

"And then," Mr. Conklin said impressively, "she threw down a coin I have never seen. In fact, so far as I know, no one has ever seen one—"

"Dubosq and Company—1849?" Michael said.

"Why, yes. Dubosq was a jeweler who brought machinery for striking private gold coins to San Francisco. His name is mentioned in that connection in 1849, and since there was a great need for coins that year it is probable that he did strike them then. There are two-fifty and five dollar trial pieces in existence with his name and the date 1849 but no gold coins. He did strike off five and ten dollar gold pieces in 1850 and they are valuable enough.

"But a Dubosq gold coin of 1849! So far as I know, that coin she tossed down so carelessly on that very counter is unique. Unique means that only one specimen is known to exist. The Moffatt and Company nine dollar and forty-three cent ingot, for instance, is so classified. Raymond does not even list any Dubosq issues of 1849."

"That's why, in her notes, Mrs. Landreth had a question mark after '49s' following the Dubosq items she listed," Michael said to Sullivan. "And I suppose it is a question what an unique specimen like that would sell for?"

Mr. Conklin said that Mr. Dundas was quite right, and he had said to Mrs. Landreth that it was impossible for him to put a price on the coin. But he didn't mind saying that any serious collector of private gold coins would be very anxious to acquire the only known 1849 Dubosq, and that a wealthy collector would pay a very high price for it.

"You said your grandparents started for California in 1847?" he had asked. "I suppose they arrived here by 1848? And that you know that as the population grew so rapidly after gold was discovered, something had to be done about a medium of exchange. Gold dust wouldn't always do."

Amalia laughed. "I'm afraid I didn't know that, though I knew they used gold dust for money. But I can see that my grandfather might even have known this Dubosq."

"That's quite possible. Of course other firms struck off many more specimens than Dubosq. Moffatt and Company, for instance. Between 1849 and 1853 they struck off twenty-six specimens, many of them not too difficult to come by."

"I know," Amalia said. "I have three of those, but they're only worth seventy-five dollars or so. I didn't copy any prices from the catalogue unless they were more than a thousand dollars."

"Unless they were— Oh, my goodness," Mr. Conklin said inadequately. "You mean you have more than the Templeton Reid and the Dubosq and some Moffatt and Company issues?"

"Oh yes. More than thirty altogether, but only about twenty that are very valuable. Grandmother couldn't know, ninety years ago, what coins were going to be valuable now. Naturally she kept some like your Moffatt and Company specimens that you say are still not too hard to come by."

"But—but how— That is, why—"

"Why did she keep them? I have to guess at that too. I don't think there's any harm in telling you—at this hour. My grandmother came from a poor family but everything my grandfather touched turned to gold, here in California. He was very generous; I imagine he often tossed her a handful of gold pieces to do as she liked with. I'm just as certain she had only what he chose to give her. Women expected that in those days. I suppose Grandmother did what many women did; put by a little money now and then. Just in case, you know; a sort of private savings account against possible disaster—or matrimonial disagreements."

"Y-yes. And then?" Mr. Conklin said.

"Oh, Grandfather's luck never ran out, and she never had to spend her hoard. I don't know why she kept it; perhaps the gold pieces came to have sentimental associations. And as she grew older she clung to old belongings. Most of the coins I found in her workbags; a few in an old glove box. If she ever thought of them she didn't mention them to me, and she and my mother weren't congenial. My mother didn't even go through her belongings when she died. That's how they were left for me to find."

XI

"Well, that's one for Ripley," Sullivan. said. "But she must have been telling the truth. You believed her?"

"I was amazed at the unusually large number of fine specimens she said she had, but given the circumstances as she stated them her story was quite believable. It happens; hoards of coins being discovered, that is. There are any number of instances—"

"Yeah? Well, just one will do us for a sample."

Mr. Conklin sighed. "Well, a man named Aaron White hoarded specie during the Civil War. He put it away in boxes that after his death were taken to the garret of a warehouse and not discovered for years. That's the sort of thing I mean."

"And since you believed Mrs. Landreth's story, you would have believed anyone else who came to you with the same sort of story to account for his having those coins?" Michael said.

"Oh yes. Of course you know it would be very difficult to sell a rare coin stolen from any known collection. Any competent dealer knows the whereabouts of rare specimens. But we expect new specimens of private gold coinage to come to light. The gold rush days were not so long ago.

"For example: a member of a pioneer family here was looking through trunks for old jewelry, anything to be sold as old gold. One of his uncles had kept an F. D. Kohler ingot as a lucky piece for years. Kohler was state assayer in 1850, you know. Well, this young man thought at first only of selling the ingot as old gold."

Mr. Conklin shuddered delicately. "Fortunately he showed it to me. One of my customers had given me a standing order for that particular ingot. He paid five thousand dollars for it. You see, there was another collector who would have paid that if he hadn't. So it was a very satisfactory transaction for all of us."

"I should say so," Sullivan said. "Well, did you offer to handle the coins for Mrs. Landreth; get a buyer or whatever you do? Or did she ask you to?"

"No," Mr. Conklin said regretfully. "Of course there was no question of my buying the entire lot outright. I haven't a great deal of capital and can't buy expensive items I'm not certain of selling. I don't collect private gold coins; they're beyond my means. But I've made myself thoroughly familiar with the subject since I have two customers—Mr.

Jaloff and Mr. Leroy—who have very good collections. So did the late Cornelius Sturtevant. I also
had dealings with him.

"But I would have done my best to find buyers for her. I knew both Mr. Jaloff and Mr. Leroy
would be very anxious to acquire that 1849 Dubosq and would—uh—bid against each other. But
she said . . ."

Amalia had said contritely: "I shouldn't have
consulted you without telling you first that someone has—well, an option on these coins. But there's
so much that we don't know about this business
that I wanted to consult someone like you. I've
been out of the United States so long that, though
I knew it's illegal to hoard gold, I wasn't certain
coins like these would be an exception."

"Oh certainly. Gold coins in collections—"

"I know that now. But I didn't mean to give
them up even if it wasn't legal to keep them,"
Amalia said cheerfully. "So I had to be discreet
in my inquiries. Under the circumstances, it's an
imposition, but there are still some questions I'd
like to ask you."

"Anything at all, Miss—Mrs—?"

"My name doesn't matter. Is this Raymond's
catalogue reliable?"

"Oh yes. It's a standard and much used. It is
especially useful to one who isn't an advanced

collector," Mr. Conklin explained. "Advanced collectors have records of auction sales that they also use as a basis for their judgment of prices."

"I see. Well, Mr. Sturtevant mentioned four prices paid for coins, one in 1908 and the other three in 1929. The 1929 prices were so much higher than the ones in Raymond's catalogue—"

"The prices paid in 1929 were exceptionally high," Conklin said. "Very high indeed. Are you thinking of the Massachusetts and California five dollars of 1849 that sold for seventy-nine hundred dollars in 1929? And the Dubosq ten of 1850 which sold for thirty-nine hundred and the Wass, Molitor and Company twenty dollars of 1855— large head— that brought seven thousand dollars in 1929?"

Amalia nodded. "And you say I'd better disregard those prices?"

"I'm afraid so."

"Well, if I do disregard them and simply go by Raymond's—excluding the Dubosq you say is unique—the lot comes to fifty-five thousand two hundred dollars," Amalia said. "Should I get that much for them?"

"That depends," Mr. Conklin said cautiously. "It always does depend on scarcity and condition. But the coins you showed me are very fine. You know if a coin is carried in one's pocket for even a day it can no longer be called uncirculated."

"Uncirculated fetch the highest prices? And what do you mean by scarcity?"

"Naturally it goes hand in hand with demand. If two wealthy buyers at an auction want the same coin the price may go to record-breaking heights. If no one is interested in that coin it may sell for a ridiculously low figure. So, you see, a coin might sell for much less than the price listed in Raymond's catalogue or you might get quite a bit more than that for it."

"Um-m," Amalia said thoughtfully. "Well, I'm not interested in auctions, but is that how collectors usually get their collections?"

"That is one way. There are sales of coins, and a collector buys directly from dealers—and at times directly from individuals who want to dispose of their collections."

Amalia nodded again as if—Mr. Conklin thought—his answer pleased her. "There aren't many dealers in San Francisco, are there?"

"Not a great many, but there are many reliable ones in the United States. A good deal of purchasing and selling is done by mail. That has its disadvantages, but it's often necessary. But, my dear lady, I would like to give you a word of advice—"

"Thank you. I wish you would."

"Then—be patient. That is one thing success-ful and advanced collectors learn, to be patient in selling as well as buying. Dealers are often as anxious to buy as to sell. We have trouble locating items our wealthy clients want. If I were fortunate enough to have stumbled onto so large and valu-able a hoard as you have, I wouldn't put them all on the market at once. It would be better not to glut it, so to speak."

"Ye-es, I can see that if I disposed of the coins a few at a time and only when I was sure I'd found the person who'd pay the highest price for each one, they might bring me a larger amount of money. But I've never been at all patient. I know my own failings. If I sold the coins in driblets, and the money came in the same way, I'd think it wasn't enough to invest and just spend it," Amalia said.

"Oh. You mean you want a lump sum?"

"Yes, I'll probably have very little else to live on the rest of my life. I want to try for once to live on my income even if it will be smaller than I've ever been used to. It frightens you when you realize you're fifty years old, haven't any income and don't know how to earn a living. That's why I must drive a hard bargain with the buyer of these coins even if I can't take your advice not to sell them all at once.

"That's why I decided this morning I should talk to someone like you. What you've told me will help me in bargaining along with the notes I took on Raymond's catalogue and Mr. Sturtevant's article. I think I will be satisfied with sixty thousand dollars even including the 1849 Dubosq gold piece. I'll throw it in as makeweight," Amalia said thoughtfully. "Or dangle it before his eyes as bait. An unique specimen should be good bait, don't you think?"

"Yes indeed," Mr. Conklin said rather feebly. "Do you mean you've found a buyer who will take the lot?"

"I think so. That's luck, isn't it? Especially since I'm impatient and anxious to have the matter settled. It's been a relief to talk to you, Mr. Conklin. The facts that I have may help me in bargaining as well as what you've told me. I can always threaten to put myself in your hands if I can't get my price elsewhere. But I really shouldn't have come to you, so you won't repeat what I've said to anyone, will you?"

"Not until you say I may," Conklin promised. "It is a very interesting story, though, and I think must be in time well known to numismatists."

"Yes, I imagine it will be." Amalia drew on her gloves. "But I had my own reasons for being secretive at first and now— Well, collectors are rather eccentric animals, aren't they . . . ?"

"And," Mr. Conklin told Sullivan mournfully, "I could not deny they sometimes are. I supposed she meant the person she hoped would buy those coins had asked her not to make the story of her finding them public until they were his. Then the story would be his, too, a—uh—toothsome morsel to pass on to his friends. Besides, some persons are most secretive until they've actually acquired a collector's item they want very badly. That's sometimes to prevent other collectors from bidding against them, but now and then it's only eccentricity."

"'And I don't mind dealing with eccentric people,'" Michael said.

"Hunh? Oh, quoting Miss Wilson's account of that telephone conversation?"

"Yes, Inspector. I imagine it wasn't too difficult to convince Amalia that anyone who might pay sixty grand for those coins must be a trifle eccentric. But was that the end of your conversation with her, Mr. Conklin? Didn't you wonder whom she'd found that would take all the coins? Of course we are fairly certain there was no

prospective buyer; that she was only made to believe there was, and that she was going to meet
and deal with him Monday."

Conklin spatted his hands together in a small
gesture of distress. "I had—misgivings. Though
only that she might be cheated. I wanted to ask
her more about the buyer she thought she was so
lucky to have found. I was certain it could be no
one I knew. But now and then some wealthy man
will wish to acquire what I call a ready-made collection. He never knows the real joy of acquiring
a collection piece by piece, with a bit of luck here,
a good bargain there—

"Well, I thought she had contacted such a person. For all she said it might be someone in another city. I couldn't persist in offering to serve
her without her thinking I was interested in my
own gain. I did ask her quite severely if she was
carrying the coins in her purse. She said: 'Only
the really valuable ones.' She was a—a very light-
hearted lady."

"Yes, she was," Michael said. "Did she go then?"

"She said I had been so kind that she would
come in to see me again and tell me anything I
might like to know. And that if she couldn't get
'her price' she would consult me again. She said,
laughing so one couldn't resent it: 'I'd have to pay

you a commission, wouldn't I? I've been fortunate too to know someone who was lucky enough to locate a buyer for me in a short time.'"

"That clinches it," Sullivan said. "It's additional proof that some second person arranged her appointment with a third person, who, as Michael says, probably didn't even exist. You have a good memory, Mr. Conklin."

"Yes, an excellent memory," Mr. Conklin said modestly.

"And you've told us a lot more than just things we didn't know about coins. Now we can reconstruct—"

"Do," Michael said. "Mr. Conklin deserves that much."

"She found the coins Thursday night. She kept still until she found out it wasn't illegal to have them—"

"More than likely she consulted someone on Friday," Michael objected. "Perhaps he told her to say nothing more until he found out if they would be considered hoarded gold. Even if he realized their value at once and knew the law, that would give him a day's grace."

"Am I doing this, or are you? But it could have happened that way. Then he said he'd find a buyer for her. But that she still mustn't talk because the buyer was an eccentric old duffer who didn't want any publicity—or maybe to have to bid against anyone else."

"And the murderer made his first error when he gambled on Amalia's obeying orders," Michael said. "She was convinced she shouldn't talk, and she rather liked the idea of surprising everyone with the story of her amazing good luck when she had her money. But her idea of perfect discretion was to tell people that she must and was being discreet. That being the case, I can't see why she wasn't killed before Monday."

"Stick to one line of thought, will you? But you're right about her idea of discretion, and she wanted to do some investigating for herself besides. So Saturday she went to the library, read that catalogue and article about coins and took notes on 'em. Apparently she just waited, Sunday. But getting more impatient all the time. Monday morning the murderer called her and said she was to meet the guy who'd buy the coins somewhere at five-fifteen."

"Where?" said Michael, with somewhat the effect of the raven croaking, "Nevermore!"

"Never mind that now! She was so excited about it that she threw out a lot more hints and called attention to the fact that she expected her financial situation to be changed for the better. She bought a lot of clothes, came here to see Conklin, went home and maybe made a fair copy of those notes, decided to bring the person she thought was helping her back with her to dinner and after a while went out early to keep her appointment."

Sullivan would have stopped there. He frowned uneasily when Michael went on:

"Which notes the murderer missed because they were in the pocket of her dressing gown. He may have thought the copy we suppose she had in her purse was the only one. But he did know she had hidden the less valuable coins somewhere in her room. She had told him that over the telephone, but not where they were. He must have been furious with her when she said she wouldn't carry all of them with her."

"Indeed?" said Mr. Conklin. "May I ask why?"

"Because that meant he must return to the house and remove those other coins from it. Now I understood why he took that risk. It wasn't because he considered them worth it from a monetary standpoint, but simply that he didn't dare let them be found there. If we found those we might guess that Amalia had had others—much more valuable—to sell."

"It seems to me," Mr. Conklin said with unexpected shrewdness, "that this murderer is not going to profit by his murder. I can see how he hoped to, originally. If no one had ever known

Mrs. Landreth had found those coins, he could have quite easily disposed of them. Over a period of time, perhaps, quietly and to a number of dealers all over the country."

"You've already implied no reputable dealer would buy a rare coin without first making certain it wasn't missing from any known collection. But after that, if the person who offered the coin for sale told a plausible story to account for his having the coin or coins, I suppose the dealer would accept the story and buy if he wanted the coin?"

"Oh yes. Who could say such-and-such a coin was rightfully the property of a Mrs. Landreth when no one knew Mrs. Landreth had ever discovered a hoard of private gold coins? You must see she had to be killed before anyone did know that. I think," Mr. Conklin said gratefully, "that she must have been killed before she could tell anyone she had talked to me."

"And lucky for you she was," Sullivan said.

"But the murderer must have realized when he knew we'd found Amalia's notes that his murder was apt to be profitless," Michael said. "He couldn't hope we wouldn't decipher them eventually. I don't see why he waited until Monday to kill her. . . . But I take it that when it is generally known murder was done to acquire those coins, very few dealers would touch them?"

"I hope none would. But I suppose there are rascals in this business as well as any other," Conklin said. "However, I don't see how anyone would dare risk handling them."

"Then I imagine the murderer is probably anxious to get rid of them by now, if he hasn't already done so. Unless he is someone who has—fantastic ideas of what a collector will do to add to his collections. We've called the murderer 'he' for convenience but—"

Michael did not finish his sentence. Mr. Conklin said uncomprehendingly:

"Some people do have odd ideas about collectors. They believe most collectors will shut their eyes to anything; that any of them would buy an old master stolen from an art gallery and be content with possession and private showings to trusted friends. Those cases are the exception rather than the rule."

"But those who read the Sunday supplements religiously are apt not to believe that? And while the general public has become more or less stamp conscious, numismatics hasn't yet become a popular science. Did the elder Cornelius Sturtevant sell his collection?"

"Eh? Yes, in 1931. His business, like all others, had suffered after 1929. He valued his collection, but he said anyone he left it to would sell it after his death. He was not well then, though he didn't die until last year. He said he would rather sell it himself than to pinch pennies during the remaining years of his life. The collection didn't bring as much as it should have, but he disposed of it not too hastily and didn't really sacrifice any item."

"Did you always deal directly with him?" Michael said.

"Sometimes he would send his assistant, Miss Ferris, to me. She knew quite as much as he did about private gold coins and was a shrewd bargainer. But she had no feeling for coins—as collector's items."

"And did you ever meet Mr. Sturtevant's nephew?"

"No, I'm sure I never did. But—of course I've read the newspaper thoroughly since I recognized Mrs. Landreth's picture—I did buy some coins from a Mrs. Stephen Keith in . . . I believe it was in 1930."

"Hunh? Lona Keith had some coins to sell?" Sullivan said. "What kind? Were they—"

"They weren't at all valuable, Inspector. Just a boy's collection of quarter dollars and half dollars. At least, she said her husband had made the collection as a boy. I believe I gave her twenty-five dollars for the lot."

"Oh. Do you remember if she seemed to know anything about coins?"

"My impression is that she didn't, though she wanted more than I would pay her for them. A tall, blonde woman, isn't she? A bit robust, some might say, but a fine-looking woman, I thought."

"That sounds like Lona Keith, so I guess that memory of yours hasn't let you down. It's interesting: Mrs. Landreth might have remembered her brother Stephen collected coins when he was a boy," Sullivan said. "And spoken to her sister-in-law about it. We'll have to see her. Well, you've been a great help to us, but we'll have to be getting along—"

"I wonder," Mr. Conklin said as Sullivan got to his feet, "if you'll satisfy my curiosity on one more point? Just what coins did Mrs. Landreth have?"

"Can you, Michael? I'd like a complete translation of that cipher of hers myself."

"If you can give me a copy of Raymond's catalogue, I believe I can . . . Thank you. Templeton Reid, five dollars of 1830, thirty-five hundred dollars," Michael said. He flipped over a number of pages and continued:

"Baldwin and Company, twenty dollars of 1851, twenty-five hundred dollars; Cincinnati Mining and Trading Company, five dollars of 1849, price twenty-five hundred; ten-dollar piece, same date, three thousand. The Dubosq and Company five and ten dollars of 1850 at twelve and fifteen hundred respectively and '49s' in parentheses with a question mark, referring to her unique specimen.

"Then Kellogg and Company's fifty dollars of 1855, listed at fifteen hundred; F. D. Kohler's six ingots of varying weights, four of them worth thirty-five hundred each and the fifty-dollar and the fifty-four-dollar-and-nine-cent ingots at five and four thousand. Those two she listed as '50s' in her notes.

"The Massachusetts and California five dollars of 1849 at twenty-five hundred; J. S. Ormsby's five- and ten-dollar pieces of no date at two and three thousand each; the Pacific Company's five and ten dollars of 1849 at two and three thousand; Wass, Molitor and Company's ten dollars of 1852 at two thousand and their twenty dollars of 1855 at the same price. She then repeats four items with the higher prices Sturtevant quoted. That's all."

"All! Dear me," Mr. Conklin said reverently. "My goodness gracious."

XII

"Stop at three," Sullivan said to the elevator man. And to Michael: "Isn't Sturtevant's open till six? And if we don't catch 'em there we'll get them where they live. I haven't got their addresses in mind—"

"They have small downtown apartments. Martha's is on Post Street and Cornelius lives on Bush."

"Are you married or do you live on Bush Street? That's what they used to say when I was a boy—"

Sullivan stepped out of the elevator and led the way down the hall to a door on which was lettered the names Samuel L. Jones, Edwin B. Lacey and Franklin C. Bartlett, all attorneys-at-law. He indicated the first door to the left.

"That's Lacey's. Almost anyone would go in at the center door and ask the stenographer to see him. I don't think Mrs. Landreth did try to see him after she'd talked to Conklin, and he certainly was out to lunch between one and two. But it's important that he can get in and out of his own office without anybody knowing it. And as long as we're here we might as well talk to him—"

There was no stenographer in the central office this afternoon, but a tubby young man was yawning over a magazine at her desk. He swiveled his chair about and regarded Sullivan with a queasy smile.

"Hello, Bartlett," the inspector said affably. "Did you let the help go early today?"

"S-she wanted to go home over Thanksgiving," Mr. Bartlett said. "We could get along without her this afternoon. Things are dull: I'm going home myself in a few minutes. Have to get in trim for turkey tomorrow."

"I'll be lucky if I get a turkey sandwich, the way things are going. Is Lacey in?"

"Y-yes. B-but there's someone with him," Mr. Bartlett said unhappily. "I'll t-tell him—"

"Don't bother." Sullivan rapped perfunctorily on the door of Edwin's office and pushed it open. "Oh, excuse me! I didn't know you were busy," he said and glanced questioningly at Michael.

Michael grinned briefly. The cause of Mr. Bartlett's uneasiness was facing Edwin across his desk: a dark, spectacularly beautiful woman—Dolly Chartos Lacey Gerard. Edwin's mouth, as he looked at Sullivan, was a thin angry line but his ex-wife gave the inspector her standard smile that was always quite acceptable and Michael the de luxe model that had everything.

"It's a police inspector, isn't it?" she said. "But I am thrilled! And I'd heard Mr. Dundas is one of these frightfully fascinating amateur detectives, but it's quite impossible to make him admit it. When he will give you his personal attention he's too impersonal. He makes you feel you have quite as much allure as one of these old-time dress forms blown up to the correct measurements."

"It hasn't escaped my attention that the measurements are admirable," Michael said. "And I'm sure the finished product has never suggested I consider you lacking in allure."

He did not add that when he looked at her he was always reminded of a small, sleek black panther. Holding that thought he had designed several sensationally successful gowns for her. And as she swirled about the vortex of café society he considered they had been an excellent advertisement for Gisele's.

"Why, I do believe you have paid me a compliment," she said. "I never quite know, when I do drag a few words from you, whether I shouldn't resent them. That's what's really too intriguing."

Sullivan was grinning now. Edwin was not. "If Sullivan will excuse me while I take you to the elevator—" he began.

"Edwin, you are really too stuffy. He doesn't think it's quite the thing for us to be seen together," Dolly Gerard said to Sullivan. "I'm sure we've been divorced long enough for it to be quite safe for us to see each other now and then."

"Uh—well, yes," Sullivan said doubtfully.

"But Edwin is a Puritan at heart. And he's too tiresome about some things. Do you think he will ever let me falsify my income tax report even a tiny little bit?"

"He's giving you good advice there. You may think you've put it over on 'em, but sooner or later they get you for any evasion."

"So Edwin says. And I say that if the government has nothing better to do than to compare my reports with Mr. Gerard's—he pays me a lovely alimony—why then something should be done about the government. As to its being dishonest, why, precious heaven! they'd never miss my few little dollars. But someone must look after things like that for me, and I always depend on Edwin to do it, even if he will insist on being honest."

"It's kind of early to be thinking about your income tax," Sullivan suggested.

"She wasn't," Edwin said shortly. He pushed a checkbook and several large brown envelopes across the desk. "I've corrected the balance in your checkbook, and here are your bank statements."

"I'm always hoping it will be the bank that is wrong," Dolly Gerard said. "Thank you, darling."

She laid one hand quickly over his. Edwin remained motionless for long enough so that it could not be said he jerked away from her. Then he drew his hand back, very definitely and quietly —but there were telltale streaks of white along his nostrils. Dolly smiled slowly.

"And if I follow your plan I can pay up my bills in three months," she went on. "I'm sure it's a very sensible plan but so tiresome. Though I must pay Mr. Dundas something on account because I'm in rags, and his manageress was positively glacial the last time I was in Gisele's."

"Something on account would be appreciated," Michael said. "As well as being a very pleasant surprise."

"Oh, I did hope you wouldn't say that."

"'A man named MacTavish is seldom lavish—'"

"But your name isn't— Oh, Dundas is a Scotch name too. Well, Edwin"—Dolly glanced down at the desk and his fingers drumming against it—"Edwin is called on to straighten out my accounts ever so often. But I chose today for him to do it because I am too intrigued by the family murder mystery—"

"Dolly!"

"But I am, Edwin. And it's foolish not to admit it," Dolly said reasonably. "I didn't know Mrs. Landreth. So do go ahead, Inspector, and don't mind me."

"Sorry, ma'am. I can't do that."

"Oh, I'd be very hush-hush— You won't? But suppose I won't go?"

"Then I guess we'll have to go," Sullivan said.

"I do think you're too stuffy for words." But Dolly collected her various belongings and stood up. Michael was swiftly on his feet, opening the door for her.

"I'll see you to the elevator—"

"I'll do that myself," Edwin said sharply. "As you barged in here without knocking the least you can do—"

"We're in a hurry," Sullivan said. "Michael has heard what I have to tell you. It will take time so, we'll save it by letting him see Mrs. Gerard out. . . ."

In the hall Dolly Gerard promptly put her arm through Michael's. "You did want to talk to me, didn't you?"

"Yes. If you are still fond of Lacey, you'd better guard your tongue. If you want to make trouble for him—"

"But, precious heaven! of course I'm fond of Edwin. I care as much for him as I can for any man. I've always said when he ever makes enough money again to live in even a moderately civilized fashion, we'll remarry. I never intended staying married to Gerard," Dolly said candidly. "But of course his alimony stops if I marry again or even misbehave too conspicuously. And I don't love anyone, not even myself, when I have to live on bread and cheese."

"It's bread and cheese and kisses, isn't it?"

"The kisses don't make up for the bread and cheese. Not in some hideous little apartment with no maid. Of course Edwin thinks it's in very bad taste to say so, but he'd marry me again if he could meet my terms. So you see, I'm really more than fond of him, and how could I make trouble for him?"

"Simply by existing," Michael said, stopping at the elevators. "And by talking to everyone as you have to me. If it should happen that Lacey went on trial for murder, and you were called as a witness by the prosecution, any respectable jury would take one look at you and think: 'She's motive enough for six murders.'"

"Oh, the prosecution? The defense wouldn't call me? Because I'm sure I'd be sensational on the witness stand, and at least two of my best friends would be quite mad with envy. Oh, I don't mean I want Edwin to be arrested. Will you tell me one thing? Was Mrs. Landreth killed for money?"

"For hope of financial gain."

"Isn't it the same thing? And I think it's too provoking. When I heard she'd come home I naturally thought she would be simply rolling. After all, she'd been a countess and lived in Europe or New York for years."

"And you hoped Lacey might be remembered in her will?"

"Why not? Why should that frumpy little Nora Keith get everything? Now you say she was killed for money, and of course Nora will get everything.

I do think it's sickening that it's always old people who have no real use for it that have money—or get it. Roger Keith thinks so too. Or he used to. We really thought a lot more alike than Edwin and I ever did."

"I didn't know you knew Mr. Keith," Michael said.

"Oh, we saw him quite often when Edwin and I were beginning not to have any money and before I went to Reno. Roger's only a little younger than I am. I almost never see him now. He's fonder of Edwin than you might think, and he thinks I should either marry him again or keep hands off. You've no idea what Roger called me the last time I did talk to him!"

"I think I have a very good idea." Michael jabbed at the elevator button. "However extensive one's vocabulary, there is a strictly limited number of words that will adequately describe a certain type of woman." As the elevator door slid open and before she could answer, he added: "Your limousine, *señora*," turned and went back to Edwin's office.

XIII

When he entered the room, Edwin was saying: "Of course the whole story is fantastic but you must believe it. I don't know why it didn't occur to anyone that rare coins would fit all specifications. You did wonder if Amalia's grandmother might have hoarded gold—"

"And it seems that she did, after all," Michael said. "I stated flatly and positively that gold is gold and fifty thousand dollars in gold couldn't be easily carried about. If I had stopped to consider if gold could be something besides gold in the usual sense—"

"You didn't know thirty or so gold coins could be worth that much money," Sullivan said. "I was born here and my father before me, and I never heard of private gold coinage. Did you, Lacey?"

"I always thought of gold dust as being the medium of exchange in the gold-rush days, and you won't find I've ever collected coins," Edwin said. "I was interested in stamps at one time, mainly because my father was. But those notes of Amalia's wouldn't fit in with the theory that she might have found some valuable stamps on some of those old letters."

"No, I suppose not. Well, Lacey?"

Edwin raised his shoulders wearily. "I know. Did Amalia ask me if she would be breaking the law if she kept the hoard she'd discovered? She did not, Inspector. I know you must think that with a lawyer in the family she would naturally consult him on that point."

"I'd be more certain she did if she hadn't told Conklin she meant to keep those coins regardless and had to be careful making inquiries about the law. And after some of the things Mrs. Gerard said . . . Did you and Mrs. Landreth ever disagree about anything like income-tax evasions?"

Edwin smiled wryly. "It's odd how few women consider it is dishonest to cheat the Federal Government. No, Amalia and I never discussed her income tax. But Nora, Roger and Lona may remember an evening when Amalia made a very good story of the way in which she smuggled a number of articles through the customs when she returned from Europe. She took my disapproval very light-heartedly."

"Well, do any of the others know anything about coins?"

"If I refuse to answer you'll think I'm protecting someone. Don't people who have hobbies almost always talk about them? And neither Roger nor Lona could afford such a costly hobby. Mr. Dundas probably realizes Roger is the sort of person who accumulates a large amount of miscellaneous information on all sorts of subjects. He's interested in early San Francisco history and talks of it very entertainingly, but I have never heard him mention private gold coinage. You know your own business, Inspector, so I needn't suggest that from what you've told me, Miss Ferris and young Sturtevant—"

"I know. We have Conklin's word for it that Martha Ferris knows all about private gold coins. And after she read old Sturtevant's article Mrs. Landreth would know Ferris helped him write it. And might think his nephew must have known a lot about the old man's hobby too. But you were right here in the building, so I thought I'd save time by talking to you on the way out."

"I'm glad you did. Because I have something to tell you," Edwin said. "Nora telephoned me a little while ago. It seems she had to go back to the old house . . ."

He told them what had happened to Nora in the old Keith home and, forestalling Sullivan's question, added:

"Our stenographer wasn't here this afternoon. Neither has Jones been here, and Bartlett only came out to sit in the reception room an hour or so ago. So no one could say that I was not out of my office between three and four."

"And Roger Keith wouldn't have an alibi, and he just happened to be walking by the old home and noticed the door was open. Phooey!" said the inspector. "Probably Lona Keith will say she was weaving or whatever she does—"

"She does say that. Nora called her and asked her what she had been doing this afternoon." Edwin sighed. "Nora is rather difficult at times. She says she has no idea where Cornelius may have been between three and four. I say between three and four to allow ample time each way—"

"That's always a good idea," Sullivan said.

"Well, Nora told me that Miss Ferris called her a little after three. Her excuse was that she wanted to locate Cornelius. At least, Nora says now she isn't certain it wasn't merely an excuse; that Miss Ferris seemed interested in what she'd been doing at the old house this morning. And that she found out from Nora that the police had presumably left the place unguarded, and that Nora thought she was through there for the day."

Sullivan grimaced. "Hell! there didn't seem to be any reason I should leave a man on guard there, and I haven't a small army at my disposal. I've got plenty working on routine checkups as it is. Well, I take it Miss Keith's idea was that Ferris could have gone over to the old Keith place right after she talked to her."

"Yes. She told Nora she was going out to get something to eat since Sturtevant hadn't been in the shop since morning. Nora said that another thing she told Miss Ferris was that she hadn't taken anything from the house."

"Oh. Well, I was considering putting a man on the house tonight. I suppose whoever broke in again figured I might. Or that he'd be able to spot anyone hanging around in the daytime and had better not wait. That is, if anyone really did break in. The girl is pretty jittery, and she did just trip and fall downstairs. All she has to go on is that letterweight—"

"Isn't that enough? And don't say it isn't important that someone found it necessary to return to that bedroom. It must be important because it doesn't make sense," Michael said irritably. "The additional coins Mrs. Landreth left hidden in her bedroom were certainly found and taken away Monday evening—"

"Yes," Sullivan agreed. "We tore the room apart ourselves and didn't find them."

"Oh, they were in one of her hatboxes," Michael said carelessly. "I'll tell you later what Patton told me. But if there was anything besides those coins that the murderer wanted badly, why didn't he take it Monday night? He did take the only good photograph of Mrs. Landreth to make your inquiries more difficult. What's happened since Monday to make him think of something else he had to have from that room? Something that probably has no direct connection with the coins. But what the bloody hell is there in that bedroom—"

"Take it easy," Sullivan advised. "Sorry to have bothered you, Lacey. We'll be getting along. . . . What," he asked Michael when they were in the hall, "did you get out of his ex-wife?"

Michael told him. "Um-m," said Sullivan. "She's a motive all right."

"Yes, poor devil. He has no illusions about her—and he still wants her."

"Yeah. I was thinking, listening to her talk— and you talk to her—that your business must have its angles. As well as its curves. Haw-haw!"

Michael eyed him with unconcealed dislike. "You are not amusing," he said.

"I think I am," Sullivan grinned. "Now I know one reason you make such a good thing of Gisele's. It's because you're too intriguing to dames like Mrs. Gerard."

Michael entered one neat mark against Sullivan's name in his mental "accounts outstanding." It is Sullivan's misfortune not to have realized that though Mr. Dundas is often ill-tempered he almost never loses his temper. Therefore he considered the incident closed—merely a stimulating conversational exchange—when Michael suggested:

"We'll save time if we use just one car."

"I'll ride with you. You're a better driver in traffic than I am," Sullivan said, stepping into the elevator. "We should make it out to Sturtevant's before six with about a minute to spare."

"Yes, unless Martha has closed the place early on the afternoon before a holiday. . . ."

But the front door was not locked, and a bell tinkled somewhere in the rear as they stepped into the shop. Sullivan looked questioningly down the long, dimly lighted room.

"Where—" he was beginning when Michael's elbow made sharp contact with his ribs.

"Quiet is kin to learning. That's engraved on one of the library walls, Inspector. This way—"

He started toward the back of the shop, moving silently along the narrow aisle between large tables overloaded with glass and chinaware. But Martha's voice could be plainly heard before they were within ten feet of the office.

"All right, if that's the way you feel about it! You go asking questions that 'll make you the laughingstock of the trade till you find a crackpot who says what you want him to say—"

"Vandahl is no crackpot," Cornelius said. "He was a good enough friend of Uncle's to tell me the truth. That you've been cutting my throat ever since I inherited Sturtevant's, and that they're laying bets in what you call 'the trade' on how long it 'll be before you take over the place. I'm already a laughingstock."

"You can't prove anything!"

"No, you've just spent a year giving the place a bad name; making the important customers think it's running down and won't ever be the same again till you're in complete charge. I never did like you," Cornelius said calmly. "I don't like people who know it all, and I don't like any woman to tell me what to do. But as long as Uncle swore by you I didn't want to change things—"

"All right, you thickheaded fool! See how well you get along without me! I'm resigning. And I'll have a shop that will wipe you off the face of the earth—"

"You won't have Sturtevant's, and you're fired. I'll find someone who knows about antiques at half your salary and won't double-cross me. I guess you'll get another job, but I don't know where you think you'll get your own store. Vandahl said he'd heard you were scouting around for money to try to buy me out cheap. And that you couldn't put up more than five thousand yourself. Five thousand! That wouldn't— Say! The bell rang awhile ago. . . ."

XIV

For several minutes even Sullivan, who naturally assumed people must listen to him, felt he did not have the full attention of his audience. Martha, her face a rich plum color, ostentatiously dug her belongings out of various desk drawers. And as ostentatiously, Cornelius scrutinized every object she laid on the desk while even the creaking sound his belt made expressed righteous indignation.

It was when Sullivan said: "So on Saturday Mrs. Landreth went to the library and consulted Raymond's coin catalogue and an article old Mr. Sturtevant wrote about private gold coins—" that Martha pushed her chair abruptly back from the desk and Cornelius began polishing one red cheek with his knuckles. Sullivan smiled complacently and went on with his story.

"So that's why she was killed," he concluded. "And why her bedroom was torn up. And now you realize it would have been very natural for her to consult either or both of you about those coins—"

"But I don't know anything about coins," Cornelius began. "Why should I?"

"You may be dumb but you aren't deaf," Martha said. "Your uncle showed his collection to everyone and explained every item in it. He hadn't sold it when you started to college. You began making up to him then, and spent many a Sunday evening at his apartment. Don't tell me you didn't get to know that collection of his pretty well!"

"And the article on gold coinage that Mr. Sturtevant wrote?" Sullivan said insinuatingly.

"Of course he gave his dear nephew an auto-graphed copy. I saw to passing those books out to everyone he knew—"

"And you helped him write it. The inspector just said so. That don't prove I ever read the arti-cle," Cornelius said. "I didn't. I wasn't interested. It's silly to pay good money for things like those coins. What do you have to show for it? I never pay any attention to people when they talk about things that don't interest me. I never really lis-tened to what Uncle said about the coins."

"Don't tell me you didn't wake up whenever he mentioned the prices he paid for some of them," Martha said nastily. "If money talks that's one kind of conversation you always listen to closely. Anyway, Amalia Landreth might have expected you to be better informed than you say you are."

"She'd know you were well informed, or you couldn't have helped Uncle write the book," Cor-nelius retorted. "I guess it had been suggested to her I was a half-wit so far as antiques went. So why would she think I knew anything about any kind of collecting? You were the one—"

"Then why did she come here Saturday after-noon?"

"What's that?" Sullivan said. "She was here Sat-urday afternoon?"

"Yes. She must have come here from the library. It was a little before five, I guess. I was out front; she said she wanted to talk to Cornelius and came back here and did—privately."

"She talked to you privately too. I didn't hear what she said to you out front but I heard her come in, and she didn't come back here for quite a while."

"But what did she want to talk to you about?" Michael asked. "And why didn't you tell us she was here Saturday afternoon? You did appear very anxious to avoid seeing her in my office Monday morning—"

"I told you she made me feel kind of tired," Cornelius said. "And Martha advised me to keep still. She said we didn't want to get mixed up in this; that it wasn't important Mrs. Landreth was here Saturday. And what she said to me wasn't important—"

"Take a deep breath and count ten," Martha advised. "Somebody might—just might—have been near enough the office to hear something that was said."

"So you were listening? Why were you interested? All you could have heard was Mrs. Landreth ask me if I'd ever read that book my uncle wrote. And I said 'no.'"

Martha shrugged. "I admit that's all I heard. A customer came in just then. I guess you know that too."

"I couldn't even think what book Uncle had ever written." Cornelius addressed Sullivan pointedly.

"When I said 'no,' she changed the subject right away. I see why she did now. Then she asked if I knew any safe investments that would pay six per cent. I thought that was really what she came about—"

"Funny she consulted you instead of Edwin Lacey," Martha said, refusing to be ignored.

"I'm an expert accountant. Why are lawyers always supposed to know about investments? She said Edwin was very conservative. I said it was just being sensible to say there aren't any safe investments you can buy now at a price that will mean they pay you six per cent. We talked like that a while without really saying anything else. Then she said I must find this business very interesting, and weren't collectors peculiar? And I said they certainly are.

"You've told everything you can think of out of spite and I've got something to say now. I kept still because I guessed it wasn't important," Cornelius continued unhurriedly. "But you did go to Mrs. Landreth's house to see her sometime last week."

"You're crazy," Martha said. "I did not."

"Oh, come off it, Martha," Michael said impatiently. "If Mrs. Landreth didn't have an expert opinion how did she learn there were a few things in the family collection of dust catchers that were worth keeping? Until Saturday morning she'd always said she didn't know if anything in the house would interest anyone but a junk dealer. On Saturday she could tell Patton a jug was old luster, a pair of candlesticks genuine Chelsea—and point out the removable candle piece as partial proof they weren't merely copies. She could pronounce an openwork fruit basket Leeds ware. Yet I've heard you say baskets of that sort are sometimes confused with similar ones by Wedgwood, but that an expert has no trouble in distinguishing between them."

"Mrs. Landreth said she wanted one of us to look over things in the house," Cornelius chimed in. "And that day Nora brought her here to look at the shop, she said so again. And Martha said she'd be glad to drop in some night and look things over. And then when Mrs. Landreth was here Saturday afternoon, just before she left she said Martha had been very helpful. I asked about what, and she said: 'Oh, telling me there were some things in the house worth keeping, after all.'"

"All right, I did go over there Friday about eight-thirty. And I did pick out a few things I told her to keep. I didn't have to; she wouldn't have known what was good and what wasn't," Martha said virtuously. "And just try and make something of it!"

"How'd you come to pick the night the maid was out?" Sullivan said mildly. "Did Mrs. Landreth set that time?"

"No. I found myself with nothing to do Friday night, so I called up and asked if I could go over. She said to come along, so I went and was there until ten—and that was that. And I've thought of something else you might like to know. I gave Roger Keith a spare copy of that article of Mr. Sturtevant's about a year ago. I was cleaning out this office. He was browsing around the shop. I knew he was interested in early California history and thought he might be interested in that article."

"Did he know old Mr. Sturtevant—which according to you, would mean he'd be familiar with his coin collection?"

"Keith never mentioned it to me, but I'll bet he did know Uncle," Cornelius said. "He could have, Inspector, without me knowing he did."

"You mean you'd like to think Roger knew your uncle. If he had, he has brains enough to listen to what people say. But it won't do, my fine-feathered friend," Martha said. "I'm sure Roger never knew Mr. Sturtevant. He only came in here looking for information about the kind of glassware, china, lamps and so on they used in the eighties and nineties."

"But I'll bet he read Uncle's book if you gave him one," Cornelius persisted. "And remembered what it said if he's so brainy. Personally, I think he talks a lot of piffle—"

"And oh! but the grapes are sour," Martha jeered. Unwisely, Michael grinned and murmured to Sullivan:

"They interview themselves, Inspector, and leave nothing for you to do." Martha rounded on him instantly.

"And you! A fine mess you've stirred up. If you'd minded your own business and not put ideas in Cornelius' square head—"

"I thought things out for myself!"

"You'd like to think so. Don't tell me Dundas wasn't responsible for you starting to do anything as drastic as thinking. Did you know he warned me last night after he talked to you? Told me he'd advise you not to be too hasty if I'd tell him some things he wanted to know. You can't tell him anything about playing both ends against the middle," Martha ended venomously, yet with a certain accent of admiration.

"You should know, Martha. You're a pirate at heart yourself," Michael said. "It wasn't a very good bargain for either of us. Cornelius has proceeded on his way as irresistibly as a landslide. And apparently what you told me is not important—"

"Could I pass an opinion on that?" Sullivan said.

"Oh, he just had some old photographs he hoped to prove something by. That I'd known Amalia when I was sixteen; that Mr. Sturtevant knew the Keith family once. That's all—as far as I know."

Michael nodded. "She's right. At the time I didn't know the meaning of 'Acc. C. S.' in Mrs. Landreth's notes. But the initials caught my eye and so did Mr. Sturtevant in those pictures. I was groping for a possible connection."

"You shouldn't have done that," Cornelius said abruptly.

"What shouldn't I have done?"

"Warned Martha I was getting wise to her tricks. You were double-crossing me too. I don't like that."

"No? I didn't invite your confidence, Mr. Sturtevant. Nor did you exact any promise of silence from me. I probably wouldn't have given one. You seem inclined to ignore this murder except when one of its feelers reaches out and nips you. Then you wonder why the nasty old murder won't leave you alone."

"That's not so. I'd do anything I could to make things easier for Nora. What good is it for me to run around in circles saying how terrible it is—"

"Where were you between three and four this afternoon?" Sullivan said hastily.

"In a beer parlor out on Chestnut Street, waiting for it to be four o'clock. This fellow Vandahl— he's a retired antique dealer—said over the phone he wouldn't be home till then. He lives in the Marina. But he still keeps in touch," Cornelius said, frowning at Martha, "with what's going on in 'the trade,' I mean."

"They heard you mention Vandahl," Martha snapped. "And probably the whole damn conversation. I was collecting a couple of sandwiches and two bottles of coke from the drugstore at, about three-fifteen. I brought them back here. . . . What happened between three and four?"

"While you tell them I'm going over to my own office to see how many memos Fanchon has left on my desk," Michael said. "Come over there when you've finished grilling the witnesses. . . ."

When Sullivan joined him twenty minutes later he was rereading a telegram on whose envelope Fanchon had scrawled: "This came here. Couldn't raise you at home, thought you might remember you had an office and find it here. Ditto letter." He put telegram and letter in his pocket and eyed Sullivan unenthusiastically.

"Well?"

"Oh, you can't break down their stories. They don't think Lona Keith ever knew old Sturtevant. Well, she and Roger Keith are next on the list."

"For you, perhaps. Not for me."

"Quitting on me? Why?"

"You'll get nothing but denials and nothing resembling an alibi from them. I'm tired of routine."

"That's too bad," Sullivan said sarcastically. "It solves murder cases. And I've got to see the woman who'll be in charge of the reference room at the library tonight. And tomorrow I've got to interview all the coin dealers in town and those two—Jaloff and Leroy—that Conklin says have good coin collections. Just in case any of 'em has been approached. And you're the one that kept harping on 'what did she have that made it worthwhile to kill her.' Now that we know you don't seem interested any longer."

"I'm not. I don't think the coins—as coins—will lead you to the murderer."

"Then what will?"

"*Quién sabe?* Naturally you wonder where they are. I don't think—do you?—that anyone would risk hiring a safe-deposit box to hide them in. But you'll check on that. The murderer will always be very much on guard at the mere mention of coins. I don't believe he'll ever let his tongue slip on that subject."

"Oh, I agree with you, but I've got to go on with routine. Suppose you tell me what you got out of Ferris this morning—and Patton. Yes, and what happened when you called on Lona Keith last night."

Michael unlocked a desk drawer, took out the two photographs and gave them to Sullivan. He examined them perfunctorily and tossed them on the desk.

"They're no good to us, though I see how you had that 'Acc. C. S.' in mind and were feeling around for some connection with Cornelius Sturtevant. Do you still think they're important, locking them up again?"

"I always lock this drawer. There are papers in it that would make good reading for the writer of a gossip column. He might learn from them what gentlemen are paying whose bills. Well, Patton told me several things that help clear up various points, including the question of where Amalia hid the coins she didn't carry with her—"

"Just a minute," Sullivan said. "What are you planning to do this evening after you leave me?"

"I shall construct myself a sandwich and a highball at home. Then get into slippers and dressing gown and write a long letter to my wife. I found a letter from her here, written before she received mine," Michael explained with suspicious readiness. "And a telegram sent after she'd read my letter. If I don't write her promptly, air mail and special delivery, she's quite capable of chartering a plane to our doorstep."

MRS. DUNDAS TO MR. DUNDAS
Hollywood, Tuesday afternoon

Dearest Michael:

I suppose you wouldn't be gent enough to write until you've heard from me, so I won't have a letter before tomorrow. If I don't, I shall begin to pelt you with telegrams. Couldn't you send me one, telling me to return home at once? Everyone knows I'm a docile and obedient wife. But if you won't, I'm leaving Friday morning. I put it to Mother we couldn't be expected to sacrifice eight-eighty worth of Big Game tickets.

It's insufferably warm, and what I've seen of Hollywood glamour I could put in my eye. When I look down Hollywood and Vine I am reminded of Sacramento or any other sleepy country town. Naturally, I am not unprejudiced. San Francisco may be a "ghost town"—as I've been told no less than ten times by associate members of the L.A. Chamber of Commerce—but we have such lovely ghosts. They'll do to live with.

A few of Mother's dearest friends dropped in awhile ago to see how she is "taking it." Cats! I quoted you unexpurgated on the subject of women who wear slacks, shorts—or just plain pants. I was sensational if not exactly popular. However, the green number I put on to dazzle the natives was much admired. The wife of an assistant to an assistant director said you should come to Hollywood. Please, no! You are quite enough exposed to glamour girls as it is.

Mother and I lunched at the Brown Derby, putting up a brave front and holding our heads high, you know. We may have seen a third of the Ritz Brothers, but it might only have been a fourth of the Yacht Club Boys. Otherwise, no stars. A party of large ladies from Oshkosh stared at us all during lunch. On our way by their table I gathered they thought I might be Barbara Stanwyck, so they had waited around for Robert Taylor.

Do write or telephone or come after me. It isn't four o'clock; another two days and three whole nights to be gotten through— I don't know of anything lonelier than a whole big bed to yourself. And you probably aren't even missing me.

Valerie

Telegram—Mrs. Dundas to Mr. Dundas just received your letter stop know you're already up to your neck in that case stop if it isn't dangerous yet it probably will be stop the police usually get along very well without you and their widows get pensions stop if i don't have a very reassuring letter from you tomorrow will take plane home stop

Valerie

Mr. Dundas to Mrs. Dundas
San Francisco, Wednesday night

. . . and that's the story, up to a quarter of five on Monday afternoon. I said I wanted to know what Amalia had that was so valuable she was killed for its possession, and why she hadn't talked at once and even on Monday was still trying to be discreet. We know the answers to those questions, and they don't help us. So far as the coins are concerned their existence only proves what we already suspected: that she was killed for hope of financial gain.

Everyone concerned had opportunity. No one has been able to prove an alibi. Everyone had motive; an uncomplicated desire for money in Lona's and Roger Keith's cases— Well, I suppose Roger's ambition to turn out a solid, worth-while novel makes his motive not entirely uncomplicated. He can't give his full attention to his proposed masterpiece when he must keep the pot boiling. And Lona must feel she should have gained more financially than she did by her marriage to Stephen Keith.

Offhand, you'd say Edwin Lacey had the strongest inducement to kill Amalia—if you had ever seen his ex-wife and his reaction even to her hand laid over his. And he had his era of prosperity. People who have been well off sometimes never resign themselves—even resent—a changed standard of living.

And again offhand, you'd say Cornelius has nothing to complain of financially. But Sturtevant's hasn't brought him the income he expected and wants. A private income plus a certain prestige that goes with ownership of Sturtevant's—and which he fully appreciates—would suit him very well. And he would never have to answer questions regarding an increased income; he could simply say: "Business has picked up."

And Martha is nearing fifty and has saved very little. In her way, she's ambitious too. I imagine it was a body blow when old Sturtevant left the place to Cornelius. We know she hoped to buy it cheaply but hadn't the money to do it herself. Sixty grand would give her capital to set up her own establishment.

The crucial question may still be: "Whom did Amalia confide in?" But each one has some special qualification that might have made Amalia choose him—or her. As often as you incline toward one of them you realize you daren't ignore the others.

So all this gets you exactly nowhere. We know how and where Amalia found the coins; what really valuable specimens she had; why she didn't immediately broadcast the story. We know she confided in someone who convinced her he'd found a buyer for the coins; we can trace her movements (though not all the telephone calls she may have made) from Thursday night to a quarter of five on Monday.

We know why her bedroom was ransacked the first time, and we can even guess at her state of mind. Everything she said to Nora, to Patton, Conklin and myself—four witnesses above suspicion—falls neatly into place.

But! Do you remember the grandfather clock you bought because it was a great bargain and decorative—though it didn't run? You must remember; you make such a good story of my tearing it apart and putting it together again. Successfully but without being able to find a place for more than half its parts.

I've always meant to prove to you that I can construct another clock from those extra parts. You see what I'm driving at—or do I flatter myself? I'm wondering if without knowing it I've collected enough extra parts in talking to everyone concerned—even before we knew Amalia was dead—to make another clock.

Because now I'm interested in those coins only from one angle. The murderer wanted them, yes— and he had to get them before anyone else knew they were Amalia's property if he was to dispose of them later himself. But because of that setup he didn't have to risk killing her in her own home; didn't have to risk being seen there by Patton or arrange to break into the house at night.

Because Amalia was so anxious to sell the coins for a lump sum he was able to get her to leave her own home without telling anyone where she was going and carrying the really valuable coins with her. But where did she go? Well, we know that she thought she was going to meet an eccentric collector who would pay her sixty thousand dollars for those coins.

And that narrows the field considerably. She was not scatterbrained enough to accept a down-at-heels dwelling in a shabby neighborhood as the home of a wealthy man. If the murderer would not risk killing her in her own home, he would hardly invite her to his to meet the "collector." Besides, Lona and Roger Keith and Edwin Lacey live not more than ten minutes walking distance from the old homestead. While Martha and Cornelius live too far away for anyone to walk it in less than forty minutes.

So—where did the murderer find a place to answer the specifications? Apartment or house, it would need to be furnished. If he rented a place in which to meet Amalia, surely the person he rented it from would have come forward by now. Unless that person is an accomplice. . . . But when it's known where Amalia went to meet that nonexistent eccentric collector I think we may know why it was necessary to move her body to the park where it was found, regardless of the risk involved in that act.

Of course Sullivan is trying to find the answers to these questions, but his method is to look for someone who saw Amalia between quarter of five and five-fifteen Monday. He must realize that wherever she went was no great distance from her own home. She wasn't up to any very long walk and, though she expected to take half an hour for it, she would walk slowly.

Patton saw that she started down Union but not if or when she turned off it. I say turned off because if she continued very far down Union she would find herself in the Italian quarter. So would she in a very few blocks if she turned to the left off Union on any street that crosses it past the old Keith house. North Beach is an interesting and very respectable district, but finding herself in it might have raised inconvenient doubts in her mind.

I don't think she turned off Union as early as its intersection with Leavenworth. That street has nothing to recommend it from Clay to Vallejo and it wouldn't have taken her ten minutes to walk only as far as Vallejo where you begin to see a better class of apartment house or home.

That leaves Jones, Taylor and Mason—and I'm not forgetting the park where her body was found is on Taylor. I doubt if the murderer drove about any longer than he had to with her body in his car. Or that it's necessary to consider any street past Mason, since with the next one, Powell, you again find yourself more or less in Italy.

I wonder what became of the red-and-green bird that was on her hat when she left home? And why did the murderer choose five-fifteen as the time to meet her? It was still daylight; more people for Amalia to pass on the streets; more chance they would get a good look at her then than after dark. Still, he couldn't know she would walk and must have risked her taking a taxi. . . .

And considering the question of time, why in the name of common sense did he wait until Monday evening to kill her? He must have known every hour increased the danger she wouldn't keep her possession of those coins a secret. But he took that risk rather than the one of killing her in her own home. And what has happened that made it necessary for him to chance breaking into the Keith house again this afternoon?

Well, my darling, I hope you will find this letter reassuring. I don't hope you will find it at all enlightening. I provided myself with stamps enough to ensure its being delivered to you sometime tomorrow. I'll mail it now: perhaps fresh air will blow some of the fog from my brain.

Michael

Stay out of planes. I'll meet your train Friday evening.

PART THREE

"Nor is there any juster law than that the contrivers of death should perish by their own contrivance."

.

I

Michael closed Valerie's portable typewriter, put sixteen cents in stamps on her letter for air mail and special delivery, emptied an overflowing ash tray and opened the living-room windows.

Anyone who hadn't read that letter but knew he had only two blocks to walk to a mailbox would have wondered why he thought it necessary to change from a fairly light gray to a navy-blue suit before leaving the house. Or why he looked through his bureau drawers for a pair of thin, flexible gloves and then dug to the bottom of a red-and-gold Chinese chest to find an extremely efficient set of picklocks.

With these, a flashlight and the gloves in his pockets, he walked past more than one mailbox. When he finally dropped the letter into a box he was only a block away from the old Keith house.

He went on until he reached it, stopped and looked at his watch.

It was half past ten. He turned and set off down Union Street, trying to move slowly enough not to outdistance an imaginary Amalia walking beside him. That wasn't easy to do. He disliked any sort of physical exertion but that didn't keep him from being nervously quick in all his movements. If he mildly disliked walking he definitely detested strolling.

Still he took Union Street slowly enough until he turned right onto Taylor and faced what any sound San Franciscan would call a slight incline, and any visitor, "another of those damned hills." He went up it, passed Green Street steps and crossed the street; climbed that second steeper block and was at the entrance to the little park.

When he stopped to take breath he stood beside what the police had left of the bushes where Amalia's body was found. Across the street Vallejo was buttressed against descent into Taylor; his own home was just over that hill.

"I suppose," he muttered, "that I came up faster than Amalia could have. She must have had to stop to rest several times coming up the hill. I'll remember that—"

He went on, downhill now; found himself walking too rapidly and stopped at Pacific. He stood for an instant or two looking down toward the International Settlement's arch of green lights and the longer curve of yellow sparks dimmed by haze that was the Bay Bridge.

He glanced at his watch; found that nearly twenty minutes had passed since he had left the Keith home. Now he walked slowly enough, looking carefully at every building on both sides of the streets.

He dismissed one block as giving too strongly the impression of shabby gentility. The next would have pleased Amalia: there was more than one attractive apartment house on it. But those that wore vacancy signs also admitted to being unfurnished.

Besides, Michael thought, you'd need the luck of the devil to carry a body from an apartment house to your car without being seen. Unless the apartment was a front one on the ground floor He had hoped to stumble on some not-too-dilapidated flat with a sign on its door stating it was open for inspection between ten and five-thirty. It wouldn't be furnished: furnished places weren't left unlocked. Still the murderer might have risked that. Once Amalia reached the meeting place she could be killed before she began asking questions.

His half-hour was gone and several minutes more. He hesitated briefly, then turned the next

corner and started up another hill toward Jones
Street.

"I'll walk several blocks back on Jones," he decided. "Then down to Mason—or go home." He
smiled wryly. "And I've always said: 'Let your
head save your heels.' Oh, that I had wings like
a dove. Even if I cover Jones and Mason besides
Taylor, there are at least five or six streets crossing
them that must be considered. Amalia might have
turned off any one of them. . . ."

He reached the top of the hill and whistled softly. He had driven by this corner house more than
once and not without noticing it when he did.
It wasn't the sort of building your eye slid over
quickly and carelessly—a big, squarish brownstone mansion, complacently ugly.

Hedges and an iron gate kept Jones Street in its
place, and a large side lawn held its neighbor on
the left at arm's length. Nor was it forced to look
any other house in the eye since the corner lot
across from it was vacant.

Michael folded his arms over the iron gate,
and his whistling became softer and very doleful.
"'Bury me beneath a willow, 'neath a weeping willow tree—'"

A brick walk led directly to the front door with
a wider walk branching off it to skirt the side of
the house. By twisting his neck to an uncomfort-
able angle he caught a glimpse of a sort of circular

court to the right of the house in back, finished off with a stone balustrade. He could see, too, the tops of trees in a garden below.

There must be steps leading down to that garden. The grounds evidently stretched more than halfway down the hill he had just climbed, and the slope was so steep the house must have either a very large and lofty basement or perhaps an extra half story for servants in back.

He stood erect, walked a few steps away and then came back to the gate, unwilling to leave this promising bone. The blinds were down in all the front windows, but one had not been lowered quite to the sash. He could make out a curtain at that window: Nottingham lace, he thought; distinctly passé and rather dingy.

The lawns and hedges were well kept but the place did have the look of being unlived-in. It always had, so far as he could recall. Valerie had commented on that once when they drove by. He couldn't remember ever seeing any "To Lease" sign on display, and he felt he should know who owned the house; that he had been told and forgotten. Of course if he had ever lived in this neighborhood—

He walked to the corner, looking up and down the streets. A block away, on Leavenworth, a corner grocery still showed its lights. He started toward it, whistling again. "'Rye whisky, rye whisky, rye whisky, I cry—'"

He bought bourbon; the most expensive brand the fat Italian proprietor could produce. And while his change was being counted out, began:

"Do you know if that big brownstone house on the corner of Jones could be rented? It doesn't look like anyone lived there—"

"You wanta rent it?" the Italian said doubtfully.

"Well, I've got five kids and we need a big house. We're out in St Francis Wood now, but it's too damn foggy. I don't like to live so far out either, and I'd like a marine view. Looks like that place would have a good one in back and be about the right size for us."

"Five kids, that's a nice family," the proprietor said approvingly. "I got six. But I don't think you could rent the house even if Mr. Steele never stays there more than a day or two— Something?"

Michael had snapped his fingers disgustedly. "No," he said quickly. "Only I'd hoped it might be rented, but if you mean Martin Steele—"

"That's him. He's gott-a, money enough he don't have to rent no house he don't live in. All-a time he travels and shoots-a wild animals in South America and places like that. Since his wife died it's like that. That was ten years ago: I've-a been here twenty, and the house she's only build about five years then."

"In 1914, that would be? It isn't so old then. It doesn't seem sensible just to let a house sit vacant."

"Oh, there's a caretaker. Been there a long time. He takes-a good care the place."

"Do you think if I talked to him he'd tell me how to get in touch with Mr. Steele? I certainly do like the location, and he might rent to someone reliable. What's the caretaker's name?"

The proprietor plucked a straw from the broom leaning against the counter and thoughtfully explored his teeth.

"I sell him groceries ten years and I don't know his name," he said finally. "That's-a how it is in a city. He's a quiet little man. But pleasant. My boy Pete once in a while he helps him trim the shrubbery where it grows up high. Pete, he says this man never talk much. But sure you could see him. He lives down in back the house."

"Thanks. Maybe I will try to see him," Michael said. "Well, good night—"

He put the bottle of whisky, not without sighing, into a trash can across the street. And continued back toward the brownstone house; down the hill again to Taylor Street and past the apartment house on the corner there.

Next to it he found what he thought he remembered: a wide, ornamental iron gate. It opened on

a stretch of pavement wide enough to accommo-
date a car. Apartment-house walls looked down on
it, but all their windows were dark.

The gate was not locked, though it creaked dis-
tressingly when he opened it. He pulled it to again
and went on past the apartment houses toward a
shallow flight of wide steps. They ended at a door
in a high board fence. It was unlocked too, and on
its other side was the sloping garden behind the
brownstone house.

Its back windows looked down from the hilltop
as he followed the path that led up and around the
garden's terraced slopes. The walls that enclosed
it were so high no one on the street could see into
it. These walls continued to the corner. When
Michael had climbed a long flight of steps from
the garden itself and found himself in the circular
court at the back of the house he still could not
be seen from the street.

From there he had to go down half-a-dozen
steps to reach the door to the caretaker's quarters,
built into the slope under the house proper. He
found at once that there was a key in the lock on
the other side of that door. It took him longer to
push it out than to unlock the door after he heard
its proper key strike the floor in the room beyond.

He stepped into that room, closed the door
and stood listening. When he heard no sound he

turned on his flashlight. He was in a small kitchen, specklessly neat though the linoleum was worn, none of the cooking utensils new and the stove an old-fashioned wood range.

Nevertheless it was well polished, while the cheap curtains and the slip cover of a cushion in an old rocker were clean if faded. There were potted begonias on the window sills; a few books—Shakespeare, the Bible, Emerson, Thoreau, Stevenson, Thackeray—on a shelf beneath an elderly wall clock. And a cage hanging on a hook near a window that would get the morning sun.

It was covered with a black cloth; when Michael lifted it a plump canary cheeped drowsily. There were seed and water in the cups, enough for some time, while on the kitchen table a quart bottle of milk bearing the name of a dairy delivery company stood unopened.

Afterward he felt that milk bottle had been warning enough and, as he ignored it, more than he deserved. Instead of stopping to consider what its presence inside the kitchen might mean, he turned the knob of a door near the stove.

He found himself in a square hall with three doors opening onto it. He guessed there must be bedrooms here but though he listened intently he heard none of the sounds sleepers make.

At last he chose a door at random and cautiously eased it open. When the silence persisted he turned on his flashlight again. There was a bed in the room and something on it, very still under a pink cotton spread.

Michael drew a deep breath, walked over to the bed and flung the cover aside. He looked down at a small man in blue trousers and worn white shirt; a man who had a gaping hole in the back of his head and very little face.

His arms were crossed over his breast; only his arms. His hands had been cut off above the wrist.

II

Michael was more than willing to leave the bedroom undisturbed for the police to examine later. He carried away from it an impression of the same sort of neatness that prevailed in the kitchen. If anyone had gone through the dead man's belongings they had been put in order again.

He made certain of that before he took the key from the inside of the bedroom door and locked it on the outside. The key was in his pocket, and now he should get to a telephone. There was none here in the kitchen but the grocery store must have one and it might be open until midnight. It was only eleven thirty-five now.

But what had he to report to Sullivan? That he had illegally gained entrance to the quarters of Martin Steele's caretaker and found him dead. That he was entirely convinced Amalia Landreth had been killed in this house; that the caretaker had died because he knew she had.

Sullivan would say: "Prove it." If nothing worse he would be heavily sarcastic. Michael smiled sourly.

"I might write him an anonymous letter," he muttered. "'It would be to your advantage to find out what has become of Martin Steele's caretaker. A Friend.' He's going to ask how I got into this place.

He's always suspected I've a set of old Hymie Rose's best picklocks and he'd like nothing better than to confiscate them.

"I'll be damned if he does! If I present him with not only that very unwholesome corpse but with proof it's part of the Landreth case he might be so elated he'd not ask embarrassing questions until I've invented good answers to them. Well, she certainly was not killed down here. . . ."

That was his excuse for not going immediately in search of a telephone. With or without excuse he could not have brought himself to leave the kitchen without discovering where its third door led. He was agreeably surprised to find it unlocked and not at all surprised that it opened onto a steep flight of stairs that ended at another door.

There was a key in this door, one of half a dozen on a steel ring. Staring at that, Michael felt cold crawl slowly down his spine. Now he asked himself who had seen to it the canary shouldn't lack food or water, and who had taken in a bottle of milk that wouldn't have been delivered before noon today. For if he was any judge the man in the bedroom had died long before noon. . . .

At that point he deliberately jerked his thoughts up and left them dangling. He opened the door slowly, sheltering himself behind it as long as he could. When finally he stood with his back against it, he risked flashing his torch on for a split second.

He was at the end of a long hall: he saw little more than that in the brief instant of light he allowed himself. Though, standing in the darkness again, he realized he was quite certain there was a mounted suit of armor halfway down the hall, if not just where were the doors that opened into it.

He shifted his flashlight to his right hand and felt for the wall with his left. He groped along the wall until he thought he had come more than ten feet down the hall without finding a door. Then he muttered impatiently: "Oh, the hell with it!" and put the flashlight on again.

That was the last use he ever had of that particular flashlight. It seemed to explode in his hand almost before he heard the cough of a gun across the hall and smelled burned powder. He dropped to the floor and tried to make himself part of it. Then, as another bullet whined into the wood above and behind him, rolled twice over and brought up with an elbow in sharp contact with cold metal.

His fingers promptly went numb but the sensation was as welcome as any he'd ever had. He squirmed around the feet of the hollow knight and safely into the space between him and the wall. For almost the first time in his life he was glad he was only five feet nine and weighed a scant hundred and fifty pounds. His protector was comfortingly broad and tall. Michael patted his helmet affectionately.

"We'll see this through together, Lancelot, my Lancelot, in whom I have most joy and affiance— or words to that effect. You won't hold it against me that I'm a trifle rusty on *Idylls of the King*—"

He broke off in this silent address to his barricade as he realized his hand on the helmet was damp and slippery. What he'd been told was true then: that when you'd been hit by a bullet you often felt nothing but shock. And apparently not always that if you had enough to keep your mind fully occupied at the moment.

He found a handkerchief and managed to knot it tightly about his right forearm with his left hand and his teeth. This complicated things. It might be only a pinprick but he didn't dare wait here until he was dizzy from loss of blood. Besides, the thing was beginning to feel not at all like a pinprick. . . .

If nothing else he knew now where one door was, and that someone behind it had a gun. He wished its owner would empty it into the "varray parfit gentil knight." He had fired three shots— well, perhaps only two. The bullet that demolished the flashlight might have taken a queer hop and be in Michael's arm.

And what the devil was the unseen enemy doing? He must guess by now that Michael was unarmed. If he thought he'd killed him, why didn't he come out to look at the remains? He evidently wasn't going to move hastily or waste bullets on a suit of armor if he knew his target was behind it.

Michael moved his arm gingerly. The damned thing was still bleeding, and it hurt abominably. He suspected he wasn't thinking too clearly. Otherwise why couldn't he remember the third line of "In days of old when knights were bold, and iron pants they wore—"?

"I'll have to run for it," he decided abruptly. "I'd like to play Indian with you, *amigo*—but not just now. This is the end of this game of hide-and-seek. 'Come out, come out, wherever you are!'"

He slipped cautiously out from behind his shelter, put his shoulder against its arm and shoved. Sir Lancelot toppled slowly sideways, struck the floor and disintegrated there. Before the clatter and clangor that followed his fall had subsided Michael had reached the door at the end of the hall.

He had a hazy notion the doughty knight had drawn two more shots. He wrenched at the door, felt something round and hard under his feet and kicked it down the stairs before him.

When he had locked that door, reached the kitchen and put on the lights there, he went back to find it: a coin bearing the head of Liberty, surrounded by thirteen stars with the date 1850 below and "Dubosq & Co." on Liberty's coronet. The reverse showed an eagle with outstretched wings and a shield on its breast. Its right talon grasped a laurel branch, its left three arrows. Around the border were the letters "S M V CALIFORNIA GOLD" and under that "TEN D."

Michael laughed weakly, went over to the cracked sink and put his head under the cold water faucet. "There's proof for Sullivan," he murmured.

"Come home: all is forgiven. Shall I crawl into the bathroom and lock myself in until daylight? He might wait for me outside—but not unless he is more stupid than I think. He should be several blocks away from here by now."

He shook the water out of his hair and looked at his watch. It still lacked ten minutes of being midnight. That grocery store might not be closed yet. . . .

The grocery store's proprietor woke his wife from a sound sleep at twelve-thirty. He had a story to tell of a man who had asked questions about Mr. Steele's house, gone away and then stumbled into the store again just before midnight.

With a bloody handkerchief tied around his arm, Luigi Ferrari said; his black hair wet and his face greenish-gray. He had telephoned some policeman and said he'd better come to the store right away. Then he had told him, Luigi Ferrari, to go dig a bottle of whisky out of the trash can across the street.

The same bottle he'd bought at their store not an hour ago, and what was it doing in the trash can? And then he'd sat there drinking it and looking at some kind of gold coin he had. Until the police came, and they went outside to talk and then away in a car down toward Mr. Steele's house. Yes, and stopped there too, because he watched to see if they did. . . .

III

When the telephone rang a second time and kept on ringing, Michael stopped trying to convince himself he was asleep. He rolled over, hitched himself painfully up against the pillows and snapped: "Well?" at the telephone.

"It's me," Sullivan said. "I gave you half an hour more when I rang once, and you didn't answer. It's eleven-thirty—"

"And if it were five-thirty—what of it?"

"Not feeling so good?"

"There is lack of woman's nursing: there is dearth of woman's tears. I'm all right. It might have been my left arm—"

"Come to think of it, you are about as left-handed as they come. Well, that accounts for it. All southpaws are screwballs. You forget to say it might 've been your neck. Oh, I'm not going to talk about that damfool stunt of yours—as such."

"What are you going to talk about? Are you going to tell me or ask me? Because if it's the latter—"

"Oh, I'm going to tell you. It may not be easy to find anyone who knows anything about that caretaker," Sullivan said pessimistically. "No one in the neighborhood knows any more about him than the owner of that grocery store told you. People have seen him around or working in the grounds, but they never saw anyone go in there but the milkman and mailman.

"His milk account was in the name of Fletcher. He paid cash for everything else. Yesterday's milk was delivered about one in the afternoon. So someone did take it in last night so the milkman wouldn't wonder why Fletcher hadn't. I've an idea if you hadn't busted in we'd never have found Fletcher's body in that house. It might or might not have turned up somewhere, someday."

"I thought of that—afterward," Michael said. "You weren't having anyone watched?"

"Yes, but you know how that is. If you can't put a man right in their homes, they can give you the slip if they want to get out badly enough. I can't absolutely surround the places they live; didn't feel the situation yesterday evening justified that.

"There wasn't one thing in the place to tell us anything about Fletcher," Sullivan went on. "I think his things had been gone through. But the doctor says he'd been dead close to twenty-four hours when you found him, so the guy that killed him had plenty of time to find anything he wanted, clean up the place and so on. And he did clean it up. There isn't one damn fingerprint in the whole place.

"That must 've taken plenty of time, and that's probably one reason he didn't take Fletcher's body away right after he killed him—if he ever intended to. It must have seemed safe to leave things for a while. He couldn't know we were going to find out about those coins yesterday. Or what ideas knowing Mrs. Landreth thought she was going out to meet a wealthy collector would put into your head."

"And after the doctor banished me, almost before the preliminaries were over—did you find any more coins?"

"The whole kit'n boodle," Sullivan said triumphantly. "Two more near that suit of armor. Evidently the one you picked up rolled down the hall with you. We were well enough pleased to have three. Then we go into a kind of breakfast room the fellow shot at you from. And there's a paper sack sitting on the floor there with the other coins in it, ingots and all. A paper sack!"

"They're easy to come by and can't be traced. Do you think he'd hidden the coins in various places about the house and was gathering them up while I was down in the caretaker's quarters?"

"That's my idea. And that he was just going to get the last three out of the suit of armor when you busted in up there. After your little fracas he didn't dare hang around and didn't dare risk taking the coins with him and maybe be caught with them in his possession. So he left 'em there. I suppose he'd already gotten rid of Mrs. Landreth's purse as soon as he could.

"I guess he knew, yesterday evening, that he'd never dare try to sell the coins since we knew about them, and that they belonged to Mrs. Landreth. But he probably wanted to get them out of the house so we wouldn't find them and connect Fletcher's death with hers that way. Evidently he never took them away at all after he killed her."

"Why should he?" Michael said. "We agreed that renting a safe-deposit box even under a fictitious name would have been dangerous. It would be even more dangerous to hide the coins in your own home. So that house was an excellent hiding place for them."

"For a while, anyway. It's a pretty swell joint. Besides that armor that came in so handy for you there's a lot of things in the house I'd call antiques. I've just been wondering—"

"If any of them came from Sturtevant's? Martha Ferris could tell you that—if she will."

"I don't have to ask her. Steele's lawyer tells me Steele is in Santa Barbara right now. Or he was. Because when I got in touch with him he said he didn't want to talk over the phone—"

Sullivan chuckled. "He shouts into phones," he explained. "Like he had a grudge at them, you know? He seems to be kind of impatient too. He's got his own plane, and he's flying up here. I'm to meet him at the Palace at four if he doesn't call me sooner. He said he didn't want to go to that house. It would have taken so long to tell him everything over the phone that I didn't try. You've got a right to hear what he can tell us, so if you're up to it, I'll come by for you this afternoon."

"Certainly I'm up to it," Michael said irritably. "You heard the doctor say I'd be as good as ever after a night's sleep. All I lack is the night's sleep. Did you turn up anything else in the house besides the coins?"

"Not in the main part of the house. But you know its location and grounds made an ideal set-up. Mrs. Landreth wouldn't have hesitated to enter a place like that. It was built after she left here in 1908 so she wouldn't know who it belonged to. She'd think it was just the right kind of house for a wealthy collector to live in. You got results, going about it the way you did, quicker than we would have," Sullivan admitted generously. "Though I still don't officially approve of what you did.

"But after she was killed it was pretty safe to leave her body there even for a day or two—if Fletcher was the murderer's accomplice. I haven't made up my mind about that yet. Offhand, it seems Fletcher must have been, for the murderer to get the use of the house—"

"If Fletcher was a willing accomplice why did her body have to be moved Monday night?" Michael said.

"Yes, that was riskier than leaving the body in the house for a while—if Fletcher was willing. There's even several not very pleasant ways it could have been destroyed right there. But since the body was taken away the risk was about as little as you'd ever expect in that kind of job. It could be carried down to Fletcher's kitchen, out that door and then down through the garden without any danger of anyone seeing over those walls—"

"And through the gate on Taylor Street to a car parked there. Of course there are apartment houses on either side of the stretch of pavement up to the Taylor Street gate," Michael said. "But you obviously haven't learned anything from inquiries in them."

"No. No one saw anything. And the windows are all kitchen or clouded-glass bathroom windows in those walls. Of course if Fletcher was in on the job, the murderer didn't have to worry about being caught carrying the body out through the kitchen. If Fletcher wasn't his accomplice, he'd be sleeping in that bedroom, shut off from the kitchen. The only danger would be him waking up.

"That would call for the murderer to provide himself with keys. But he must have done that

by Monday if Fletcher didn't just give them to
him. Keys that would get him in the upper part
of the house so he could let Mrs. Landreth in at
the front door. You'd think Fletcher would have
a duplicate set of keys but we haven't found any
but those on that key ring. If Fletcher kept those
on him, of course the murderer got 'em after he
liquidated Fletcher."

Sullivan stopped to clear his throat. "But we
did find something in the kitchen the murderer
missed," he continued. "Under the linoleum in the
bird cage—a handkerchief with Mrs. Landreth's
initials and two feathers that must be from that
bird that was missing from her hat when we found
her. They're draggled like they'd laid out in the
fog and dirt."

"Patton told me the threads that held the bird
on the hat were loose," Michael said. "And on Monday morning Mrs. Landreth was wearing a white
handkerchief in the breast pocket of her suit."

"And it must have dropped out of her pocket
some time or other. And her hat looked like it had
been stepped on. Well, some place in the house
or garden Fletcher must have found those things.
And that's about all—"

"All? Why are Fletcher's hands missing?"

"I'm hoping Steele can give us some clue to
that," Sullivan said. "Of course the fact all his

fingerprints were wiped off everything in the place shows the murderer don't want us to have Fletcher's prints. That looks like he had a record and could be identified by them. But I can't imagine Steele leaving his house in charge of an ex-con—if he knew Fletcher was. The doctor says his hands were cut off quite a while after he died."

"That is a comforting thought. Were your interviews with Lona and Roger Keith satisfactory?"

Sullivan snorted disgustedly. "Keith claims he never read that article of old Sturtevant's after Martha Ferris gave it to him. He made a great show of having a hard time finding it. I'll admit it was dusty enough, and he's got books and magazines and stacks of papers all over his room. That Miss Blessing in the reference room at the library last night couldn't remember that Keith took out any other book that wasn't recorded on the slip he signed."

"And Lona Keith?"

Sullivan snorted again. "She says one thing, and ten minutes later it dawns on you maybe she meant something entirely different by it. She says her husband made that coin collection before she ever knew him. Since he was about thirty-five before she met him, maybe she's telling the truth about that. But it seems he might still have had some catalogues around that she might have read. She says not. And that she didn't know old Sturtevant, any more than Roger Keith will admit he did. I tell you, I was dead beat when I finally got home last night."

"And did you talk to Nora too?" Michael asked.

"Yes. And went to the old Keith place and looked over that bedroom with her. We couldn't see that anything is missing. There's those bundles of old letters and pictures. We wouldn't know if some of them were gone, but we went through 'em once, and none of them was important.

"But Roger Keith was right about there not being a sign of a print on that letterweight, and you do have to turn it upside down for the snow to start falling down on the figures in it. But it's the thing not having a print on it when two or three people handled it yesterday morning that convinces me, more than Miss Keith's story does.

"I saw that fellow Leroy that Conklin mentioned as having a good collection of private gold coins," Sullivan added. "Jaloff has been out of town for a week. Leroy agreed with everything Conklin said. He says if anyone brought him that unique Dubosq, for example, he'd have wanted to know where they got it. But if they'd told a story like Mrs. Landreth's he'd have bought it—quick. Before Jaloff could, he said. Nice fellow, Leroy is.

"He also said that once it got around that Mrs. Landreth owned that coin or any other rare specimens, he wouldn't have bought any of them from anyone but her or her accredited agent. And that while there might be a few who would if they thought the coin was only stolen, no reputable dealer would. And once it was known those coins were the motive for a murder, no collector or dealer would risk touching them. Or damn few anyway, and the seller wouldn't be able to ask what they were worth.

"Well, I'll get back to work now. Thanksgiving's a bad day for interviewing people. I'll have to let the other coin dealers go today. This new angle is more important. You'll be ready about three-thirty?"

"I'll be ready," Michael promised. "What I need now is coffee—and a great deal of it."

IV

He was finishing his fourth cup when the doorbell rang. Through a living-room window he saw Nora on the doorstep, frowning sulkily, with an equally sulky back turned ostentatiously on Lona Keith.

"I wanted to see you," she began, stepping into the living room. "And Lona said— Why, you look perfectly ghastly, Michael. Why is your arm in a sling?"

"You appear slightly pea green yourself. And not at all elated, as an heiress should be."

"Oh—that. I hate the very thought of those coins. And wouldn't you be pea green yourself if you'd had to look at what we've just been made to look at? But perhaps you have seen him. Something certainly happened to you—"

"Did Sullivan ask you to view the body?" Michael said. "But of course he'd have to. And you might as well save your questions because I'm not going to answer them."

"You see, dear?" Lona said. "I told you Mr. Dundas must naturally put his duty as a citizen first, though of course he wants to help you too."

"My duty as a citizen be hanged!" Mr. Dundas muttered. Nora smiled maliciously.

"When I said I was coming here to talk to you, Lona wouldn't let me come alone. She said it wouldn't look well; that your wife and Neil wouldn't like it."

"It would be rather indiscreet. You see," Michael said blandly, "I've only been waiting until Valerie was away to go on the loose. If other events hadn't interfered I'd meant to stage an orgy here last night. I had five blondes and four brunettes lined up. But no saucy little redhead. I'd have been glad to include you—but you would have had to wait your turn."

"Well, really!" Lona said. "Of course you're joking—"

"Exaggerating—perhaps," Michael said pensively.

"Joking," Lona said firmly. "But perhaps it's as well your wife doesn't hear you say that."

"His wife has a sense of humor," Nora said. "But Lona may have been right about Neil not wanting me to come here, Michael."

"I suppose he was also at the morgue, and you knew he wouldn't care to come here with you so you made your excuses and slipped away from him?"

"Y-yes. We none of us had ever seen that man before—or could imagine we might have." Nora shivered. "And I was sick afterward, and it was very humiliating."

"Then would you like replacements? Food, that is?"

"No. I don't ever want to eat again."

"A drink, then? I shall have several whether or not you join me."

"Let me fix one for you." Lona was suddenly all sweet womanliness again. "Having your right arm in a sling must make things very difficult for you."

"It's very inconvenient," Michael agreed. Nora was staring unhappily out the window, not listening to him. "You'll find everything in the dining room over there. I'll take whisky and soda. You may measure the soda with an eye dropper but not, *por Dios!* the whisky. . . . Did you have something to say regarding Cornelius, Nora?"

"N-no. He came by and took me for a ride last night and—"

Nora hesitated, trying to decide how much she should tell Michael. She didn't want him to think Neil had come to her crying for sympathy. He'd only told her what had happened between Martha and himself and given her an account of their joint interview with Sullivan. He'd been unusually thoughtful and solicitous, and when she told him so, he said uneasily:

"I guess I'm not—not demonstrative enough. I mean, it's hard for me to make a fuss over people, even you. But I am very fond—I mean, I do love you a lot, Nora. If you didn't marry me I'd take it pretty hard though no one would think I was."

"But I am going to marry you," Nora said quickly. "Has Lona, maybe, hinted to you I mightn't?"

"She just said it was too bad that after Mrs. Landreth came home you and Roger Keith began to see each other quite a lot again. That it was only a boy-and-girl affair—"

VIRGINIA RATH

"Affair! Roger used to be around our house before Mother died. And then he—he put her in a book, and I hated him for it. And I'd thank Lona to mind her own business! You didn't believe her?"

"Well, women know about things like that sometimes. And some people might think Keith is attractive. It's bothered me the last couple of weeks."

"It needn't. I'll marry you any time you set."

"You know I'd like to say right away. But we always said we'd wait till business picked up—"

"You mean you've always said we'd wait until you have an income that will support me in a style to which I am not accustomed. You know I wouldn't care."

"A fellow likes to have something to offer a girl. I don't want you ever to have to worry about money again. And to be able to give you everything you want—"

"I know you do, dear," Nora said.

And she had always known that Cornelius wanted to be the indulgent husband—with complete control of the purse strings. As she was feckless about money she thought it would be very restful simply to hand him her bills at the first of the month and ask for cash when she needed it.

That would bolster up his ego. It had occurred to her lately that perhaps he was more conscious than she'd supposed of his inability to talk entertainingly about nothing. And that while he claimed it was best to be slow but sure in thinking, he might really rather be hare than tortoise. Also, she was surprised he could speak of anyone as vindictively as he did of Martha Ferris.

"She won't get another job if I can help it. I wouldn't put it past her to have killed your aunt. But we aren't going to talk any more about that tonight. . . ."

"Probably nothing we said is worth repeating to you," Nora told Michael hastily, realizing he was watching her speculatively. "Only Neil thought you were his friend—and so did I."

"Why? I'm entirely surrounded by females at Gisele's, so it's a welcome change to have Mr. Sturtevant clump into the office now and then, bringing a reassuring whiff of masculinity with him. But frankly, several hours in his company would send me into a near coma."

"I know you don't talk the same language. So I wouldn't have thought you'd consider he was clever enough to—to engineer these murders."

"I don't consider Cornelius stupid," Michael said. "Though it isn't very intelligent to try to convince yourself you already know everything that's worth knowing. Oh, he does, my child. He is every inch a materialist. He looks at almost everything with only two questions in mind: 'How much did it cost?' or 'What's it useful for?'

"That has handicapped him at Sturtevant's. He'll never understand why people collect things unless they are items so valuable they can always be sold for as much or more than they cost. But if he wasn't inclined to agree with Mark Twain that for a male person hunting bric-a-brac is about as robust a business as making doll clothes—or women's clothes—he'd know all Martha could teach him by now."

"I suppose he's stepped on your toes," Nora said. "Made some condescending remark about your designing women's clothes—"

"Yes, he has," Michael said honestly. "And I know it is childish to resent that sort of condescension—but I do, and I am afraid I always will. Making women's clothes may not be a robust, male occupation but, my dear, no one gave me an old established business like Sturtevant's. I started Gisele's on a very frayed shoestring. And no one has ever pulled a trick on me like Martha Ferris has on Cornelius. No one ever will. So don't expect me to sympathize with Cornelius. But if he'd really set his mind to it, he'd know antiques by now, and he wouldn't forget what he learned. He's intensely practical; he has no nerves; once he'd made a plan he'd follow it through—"

"Oh, you needn't go on," Nora said. "I still say it's only—only an unfortunate coincidence that's involved him in this. And I'm going to marry him!"

"Why, whoever said you weren't, Leonora?"

"Don't *you* call me Leonora! And I don't like the way you are smiling, either. Tell me one thing: do you know who killed Aunt Amalia?"

"No. And I'm not lying, as your face too plainly suggests—"

"I'm sure this drink is strong enough," Lona said, coming back into the room. She offered her tray to Michael and then to Nora. "This is brandy, dear. Try it: it may settle your stomach."

"Ugh! You would bring that up just when I was forgetting it. Are you sure," Nora asked unpleasantly, "that there's only brandy in this glass?"

"Treat that remark with the contempt it deserves, Mrs. Keith," Michael said.

Nora scowled at him. There's simply no depending on him, she thought resentfully. Now he's making Lona think he's on her side—and maybe he is, on that subject.

"But you'll make allowances for all the nerve-racking experiences she's had lately and not scold her," he went on. Lona smiled contentedly and put the tray on a table, her wide silver bracelet clanging against it. "And regarding the last one, Nora—I understand it wasn't you but Roger

who went back into Mrs. Landreth's bedroom yesterday afternoon to see if anything had been taken
from it."

"Yes, I sat on the stairs while he did. But he
was only gone a minute. If it wasn't he who'd already been there, he couldn't have carried anything much away from the bedroom without my
noticing. He could have wiped the fingerprints
off that letter-weight then. But I don't see why he
would because he had handled it that morning, so
it wouldn't mean anything if his were on it."

"And you hadn't taken anything from that bedroom?"

"Not one thing. I still don't think I left the
front door open," Nora said. "But I can't remember hearing the lock click either so maybe I did,
and it swung open later. I do wonder if Roger often carries razor blades in his pockets—"

"Razor blades?" Michael said sharply.

"Well, one blade. This one fell out of his pocket
when he pulled out his handkerchief. If he hadn't
looked so—so disgusted with himself, I wouldn't
have given it a second thought. He wasn't as glib
as usual either. He just said one might find almost
anything in his pockets: Do you think it's important?"

"No, except that it does make you think of—
You didn't look to see if the family . . . No, of

course you didn't," Michael said exasperatingly. "And it doesn't matter—yet. I dislike being inhospitable, but Sullivan is coming by for me presently, and I must shave."

"We're going. And this is the Thanksgiving Aunt Amalia could hardly wait to celebrate! What right has it to be warm as summer and— Well, I'm thankful for just one thing: that the person who killed her won't profit by her death."

"But you do, dear," Lona said. "And we're all so glad for you. You'll have the money to enjoy while you're young. If poor Amalia had died a natural death she might have lived for twenty years more; longer, if she took after her mother. Besides, she was going to make a will and remember others in it. Though you know, whatever her good intentions, she'd never have lived on her income. Cornelius isn't going to like you having your own money and so much of it, but I'm sure you're clever enough to solve that problem. But I do wonder at the murderer's simply leaving those coins in the house where the inspector says Amalia was killed—"

"He may not have told us all we wanted to know, but he certainly made it clear no one 'd dare try to sell those coins now—but me."

"Yes, Nora—but perhaps he doesn't realize that some collectors wouldn't stop at murder to add to their collections."

"Oh, I don't believe that," Nora said flatly.

"But it's so. Why, half the famous paintings in the Louvre and places like that are really only copies. The originals have been stolen and bought by millionaire collectors," Lona said. "But of course the museums don't let the public hear about the thefts. You really should read more, Nora. Goodby, Mr. Dundas. I'll come up again tomorrow night and get the measurements of some of these windows. . . ."

V

Martin Steele was a wiry, dark brown man who never sat still when he could move about. He spoke so rapidly that after a few minutes you felt yourself to be tête-à-tête with a benevolent machine gun. When the role of narrator fell to you, Mr. Steele did his best to keep you going full gallop with his constant "Yes! Yes!" that was like the pricking of spurs. Even Sullivan found this trying; he was in a fine lather before he had given Steele the story up to date.

"Amazing," Mr. Steele said then. He eyed Michael approvingly. "How did you get into Fletcher's quarters?"

"The kitchen door wasn't locked," Michael said baldly.

"That's what he says, and maybe you'd better take his word for it even if it doesn't seem reasonable to you."

"I don't believe he would care if I picked the lock, Inspector," Michael said. "I don't think he would want to discourage private enterprise."

A whinny was crossed with a bray to produce Martin Steele's laugh. In time one could hear it without wincing even imperceptibly. This first time it jerked Sullivan erect in his chair while Michael closed his eyes in silent protest.

"Quite right," Steele said then. "Like to see a fellow make up his mind and go ahead. Not very sensible though; you going on upstairs when you thought someone was there."

"I know." Michael looked disgustedly at his bandaged arm. "But it was the chance of a lifetime to get a glimpse of the murderer. He might not have had a gun, and I'd have risked a rough-and-tumble fight in the dark—"

"No reason why you shouldn't," Sullivan said. "You're one of the two dirtiest fighters I ever saw, and you haven't any scruples against hitting a woman. Well—"

"Yes. I'll tell you what I know about Fletcher," Steele said. "My wife engaged him in 1924. Suppose you know she died five years later? Never stayed long in one place since then. She liked Fletcher's looks, and he turned out to be a good gardener. When she died, had to have a caretaker. The other servants were English; wanted to go home. Preferred Fletcher anyway. Thunderstruck when he told me he was an ex-convict—"

Sullivan looked at Michael and nodded complacently. "Know what you're thinking, and it's not so," Steele snapped. "Told me of his own accord. Left him in charge ten years and not one thing missing. Did more work than he had to; never hired help till lately, though I told him to."

"The son of the owner of that grocery store?" Michael said. "The one that helped Fletcher trim the hedges and shrubbery now and then?"

Sullivan nodded. "Pete Ferrari. They live across the street from the store. I talked to the kid this morning. He said Fletcher never had much to say, though he was always very pleasant."

"Always," Steele said belligerently. "Let me finish. His name wasn't Fletcher. And whatever name he'd been convicted under wasn't his real name either. He'd gone under two false names in the last twenty or so years; 'Fletcher' for the last fifteen. Is that clear?"

"Yeah," Sullivan said unhappily. "It means he won't be on record anywhere as Fletcher, and we haven't his fingerprints or enough of his face for a picture. Did he tell you what he was sent up for? Or where?"

"Not in California, but just where he didn't say. Why? Suspect he got hungry. Tried to stage a holdup and didn't succeed. He said that much. Pleaded guilty, got off lightly, no publicity to speak of. When it was all over, came back to San Francisco. How soon afterward he didn't say. And very wisely changed his name again."

"You said he 'came back to San Francisco'?" Michael said.

"Yes. Certain he'd been born here. Never said so; just gathered that from things he let drop. You can tell. Melancholy sort of fellow, pleasant as he was. No joy in living. Never could get him to say anything about his family. Asked him once who I'd notify if he died. Said there was no one he'd want notified."

"That doesn't make it any easier," Sullivan grunted.

"No. 'Fraid you'll have a dev'lish hard time finding out who he was. One of these small wiry men whose age is hard to judge. Thought he was in his forties when he came to us, but couldn't say he looked much older the last time I saw him, six months ago.

"About this family angle— Told him he oughtn't to take it to heart he'd made one mistake; ought to get in touch with any old friends or relatives he had. Shook his head and smiled the melancholy way he had. Think that's all. Except I thought he'd been around boats a lot when he was younger, or in the navy. Everything always neat and ship-shape in his quarters. He could tie all kinds of knots too."

"And he's just gone on for the last ten years, never mixing with anyone; just living there, looking after the house and grounds?"

"Far as I know, Inspector. Haven't been here much myself in the last ten years. Often don't even sleep at the house. Only relaxation he ever took was to have dinner once a week at a French restaurant called Madelon's—"

"And was it on Mondays that he always went to Madelon's?" Michael asked. "And for an early dinner?"

"Yes! Yes, now that you speak of it. Always on Mondays. Left the house at five and walked. Remember being there once on a Monday. He offered not to go. I said: 'Nonsense! just dropped by to ask how things are. Go ahead,' I told him. He smiled and said he was afraid he was a creature of habit. Went to a movie sometimes, afterward. Other times too. Also took long walks. Why?"

"There you are, Inspector," Michael said. "Now we know why Mrs. Landreth wasn't killed until Monday. It was because her murderer had planned the setup to include that house he hoped no one would ever link him with. But he couldn't have the use of the house and be sure he'd not be disturbed there until after five o'clock on Monday. And that explains why he chose five-fifteen as the time for Mrs. Landreth to come there. He couldn't wait until later in the evening. Fletcher might come straight home from his dinner at Madelon's. And it means Fletcher wasn't an accomplice."

"Always knew that," Steele said. "Knew Fletcher couldn't be. You'll find out he was at Madelon's the usual hour. Quiet family place; no crowd—"

Sullivan picked up the telephone, got through to his office and ordered a man sent to make inquiries at Madelon's.

"But I've been doubtful all along that Fletcher was in on the business," he said. "And this afternoon one of our men who was trying to keep the crowd back at the park after her body was found there came in with a funny story. He'd just looked at Fletcher and said he could be the man that 'd come walking along toward the park and into the crowd. And nearly fainted when we started bringing her body out of the brush.

"Healy remembers it was just after some fellow in the crowd had been repeating a description of Mrs. Landreth; mentioned her name and what she wore, including that red-and-green bird on her hat. Healy started him off down Taylor; told him it was no place for him. He remembers this man said: 'You're quite right, officer: I shouldn't be—here.'"

"Yes, yes, yes! Shock to Fletcher to learn she was dead," Steele said. "Never took a morning paper; hadn't known she was missing. But uneasy already because of the handkerchief and feathers you think he'd found somewhere about the place. All fits in; knew he should go to the police at once. What he meant when he said 'I shouldn't be—here.'"

"Yes, probably that was what he meant. But he kept still till Tuesday night to give someone a chance to explain. Someone who must have known him and your place pretty well even if no one has ever noticed anyone going there to see Fletcher. Someone that came to see him before Monday and managed to grab his extra keys— Did he have extras?"

"Yes, yes! Of course. A full set to his own quarters and the house itself. Kept them hanging on a nail in the kitchen; other set in his pocket. If he found they were missing, that would make him suspicious, eh? Murderer had to keep them to get back in the house later to carry the lady's body away. Took a chance Fletcher wouldn't go up into the main house after he was home from Madelon's. Probably tucked the body away somewhere. Plenty of good hiding places; that house is an ark."

"If we knew who Fletcher really was!" Sullivan said. "Then we could trace back and find out what friends or relatives he might have gotten in touch with. Because he must have changed his mind about that or made friends with somebody—"

"Man does change his mind when he gets older. Spite of what he said to me may have wanted to talk to someone he knew when he was young before he died. Wouldn't expect to know them socially again; be grateful for what they were willing to give. He was like that. Think he'd been born a gentleman. Felt he'd come down in the world; didn't think highly of himself."

"Well, since his hands were cut off to keep us from identifying him by his fingerprints—"

"If you had his fingerprints, what would you learn by them?" Michael said. "Only what name he was using when he was tried and convicted. What good would that do you? It was also an assumed name. Of course, working backward from that, you might in time find out what his baptismal name was. And you might not, since he apparently protected his anonymity very successfully from the time of his arrest on."

"But then why were his hands cut off?" Sullivan said.

"Oh, the fingerprint angle did enter into it. But why were his hands cut off so far above the wrist?"

"Well—yes, the right one was hacked off a good three inches above the wrist. You think he had some identifying mark on his hands or wrists?"

"And if he had it was certainly noted down on his identification card at whatever prison he was sent to. If you had his fingerprints, and they got you the name he served time under, they'd also get you any other identifying marks that were on his body. And that last point, I think, would tell you what his real name was."

"You've got no proof of that, and it sounds pretty farfetched," Sullivan said.

"I know. Did you ever see Fletcher with his shirt sleeves rolled up, Mr. Steele?"

"No, can't remember at all that I ever did. Remember him working in the grounds, usually with a sweater on. Not often warm enough here to go about in your shirt sleeves, you know. Not unless you're doing strenuous work."

Michael glanced quickly at Sullivan, but he seemed not to be paying very close attention to what Steele was saying. Michael started to speak, remembered Sullivan's: "you're too intriguing to dames like Mrs. Gerard," and decided this was as good a time as any to pay off that score. He said nothing at all, and Sullivan abruptly changed the subject.

"Did anything in your house come from Sturtevant's, Mr. Steele?" he asked.

"Yes! Yes, any number of things. 'Fraid I can't tell you what. My wife chose the furnishings. Some tapestries though— Got to thinking, one day: might be rotting away, hanging on the walls in a damp house. Wrote to Fletcher; suggested he ask Miss Ferris to look at them. Didn't know what you do with the things; clean them, pack them away in moth balls—"

It was Sullivan's turn to say "Yes!" impatiently. Steele grinned at him.

"Want to know if she did look at them? Yes, and bought them back for Sturtevant. Wrote me about them: said it was too bad for them just to hang there, inviting dust and moth. Let her take them and lost money on the deal. That was about three years ago."

"And that," Sullivan said, "is going to give me material for a very interesting little talk with Miss Ferris. Why, the truth isn't in the woman!"

VI

He sat brooding over Martha's complete lack of veracity during the time it took Steele to shout an order to Room Service and mix fresh drinks when the bellboy had appeared with more ice and soda. The telephone rang as Steele said: "Here's health!" and Michael: "*Salud!*"

Sullivan answered it; remarked: "Quick work. He was there this Monday? . . . Usual time? . . . I see . . . O.K. I'll see 'em myself if it's necessary."

"Told you so," Steele said. "Fletcher was at Madelon's Monday night, eh?"

"Yeah, usual time, about five-twenty to -thirty. They'd got to know him and always gave him the same table. But they never got to know anything about him, and he never mixed with any of their other regular guests. He ate slowly and appreciated his food, the dame that runs the place says. So he took all of an hour for dinner."

"Knew it was that way, knowing Fletcher. About this Ferris woman," Steele said. "She wanted to buy back more than those tapestries. At bargain prices of course. I refused. Had a letter or two from her, but sorry to say I never keep letters. But don't think Fletcher would have let her in the house without my express permission.

"Of course if they got friendly he had a perfect right to have her visit him in his own quarters. Can't see him doing that unless they found they were old friends or relatives. Just thinking: isn't a man who changes his name apt to choose one that begins with the same letter as his real name?"

"Yes," Sullivan said. "Sometimes they do it almost unconsciously. And it's more convenient if you have anything you have to use that's marked with your right initials."

"And sometimes we cast the initial aside along with the name," Michael said. "I was born Maclean—"

"The hell you were!"

"I supposed you knew. I quarreled rather violently with my grandfather and changed my name—legally. Dundas was my grandmother's maiden name. I preferred it to my mother's—Marquina—which would be constantly misspelled and mispronounced. So I had my reasons, and so must Mr. Fletcher. Unfortunately we don't know what they were, or if he merely opened a telephone directory and took the first name his eye or finger happened to light on."

"That's the trouble. All I think of in connection with Fletcher is Castoria—"

"You— Will you say that again?"

"You know: Fletcher's Castoria? 'Children cry for it,' or something like that. What's the matter with you, anyway? You look like something had just bit you."

"Something has," Michael said. "You thought Fletcher had been born a gentleman, Mr. Steele— whatever that may mean. But I suppose you also

meant he appeared to you a man of some educa-
tion— But of course he was if he read the books
he kept in the kitchen. He was probably fairly
well informed—"

"Oh, he read his books. Used to quote Shakespeare—"

"And other early dramatists?"

"Couldn't say. Not a reading man myself."

"Look!" Sullivan said. "Whatever's biting you,
I want to know—"

The telephone rang again, and again he dealt
with it in a series of "I sees," "yeses," and "O.K.s."
"Well," he said, putting it down, "that's interesting. One of the D. A.'s bright young fellows who's
been checking up on background—what these
people have been up to the last five years or so—
turned up an item about Lacey. Seems he has a
client named St John: an old fellow past seventy
who's lived in a couple of rooms in one of these
family hotels for the last twenty years.

"His money goes to some cousin in the East, but
Lacey's been good to him, so he's left him all his
personal belongings. And his rooms are crammed
full of old things, same as in the old Keith house.
And he can't live much longer. His doctor told the
hotel people he'd give him three months—"

"Well," Sullivan said aggrievedly as Michael
made no comment, "don't you see how handy that

would have been for Lacey if he was thinking ahead to disposing of those coins? He could say they came to him from old St John, who's also a member of a pioneer family here. A perfect set-up—"

"As Mr. Lacey will no doubt admit when you point that out to him," Michael said.

"And I certainly will talk to him about it before tonight. Oh, by the way—I told the whole gang to choose a meeting place for eight tonight. I said I'd bring them up to date then—"

"A gathering of the suspects according to the best tradition of detective novels? There they sit until you level a threatening forefinger at someone and bark: 'You are the murderer!'"

"Hell, no! But don't I wish I could. I'm just going to tell the story to all of them at the same time."

"Thought you fellows always acted mysterious," Steele said. "Refuse to give out information; that kind of thing."

"Oh, I've found when you're dealing with people like these you don't lose anything by letting 'em think you're telling them everything even if you're really keeping some things to yourself. I made all of them look at Fletcher. And the Ferris woman never batted an eye," Sullivan said sourly. "But I didn't tell them much this morning. Now

I'm hoping that learning we know or can guess just how he pulled off these murders may make the guilty person pretty uneasy. Might make him lose his nerve and decide to run for it. Besides, I'd rather have them out of the way while we search their apartments again."

"For what?" Michael said.

"Anything that might look interesting, including a gun. We do know what kind we want from the bullet the doctor took out of your arm. We've searched their places once, but that was before we knew what we do now. I like to do these things without any fuss when I can.

"Lona Keith said they could meet at her place. We looked it over before she got home. No one to say anything there; that Miss Montmorency that lives under her is deaf and spends a lot of time in the back of the house. Well, will you be with us at eight? You can go there with me if you want to stick around with me till then."

"I will be there, thank you. And you might take that chance to examine the suspects' hands and wrists." Michael finished his drink and got up. "I must be going along now."

"Going along where?" Sullivan said suspiciously. "I can take you home if you want to go there."

"Inspector, you force me to tell you that I wa-ant to be alo-one."

"That's what I'm afraid of. I've let you off easy as far as your escapade last night is concerned. But whatever you're thinking of doing, don't do it!" Sullivan said. And then spoiled his effect by adding: "What are you thinking of doing?"

"Have you no idea?"

"No. Should I?" Sullivan eyed Michael uneasily. There was a dull flush over his cheekbones and his blue eyes were too bright. "You've got a little fever, and you're screwy enough when you're in good health."

Michael disregarded that. "You know everything I do. Except that I've taken part in several interesting conversations that I've only repeated to you. And however faithfully you try to repeat what people say, it isn't as good as hearing them say it. And I may have skipped too lightly over remarks that seemed unimportant at the time."

He had reached the door of Steele's suite and paused for an instant with his hand on the doorknob.

"But I will be generous and give you two hints. What do sailors sometimes do on shore leave? And who wrote the 'Mikado'? You certainly should know that, Inspector. Good afternoon, Mr. Steele. . . ."

"Mikado! Mikado?" said Steele. "He means the Gilbert and Sullivan thing?"

"I guess so. Maybe that's his idea of a joke. I met a guy once who said: 'Where's Gilbert?' when he heard my name. As to what sailors do on shore leave—"

"Look for women."

"Yeah, but Michael said 'sometimes,' and there's no sometimes about that. Well, maybe he didn't mean anything at all and was talking so I wouldn't guess what he really has in mind. That's the hell of it: you never know. And I have to be going too, Mr. Steele. . . ."

While Sullivan was interviewing Edwin Lacey and getting from him, in the final analysis, only a weary smile and: "I suppose you're right, Inspector, though Mr. St John and his legacy haven't been much on my mind lately—" Michael was dragging young Pete Ferrari away from his Thanksgiving dinner. He left Pete at the end of five minutes, bewildered but grinning over a five-dollar bill.

He went to his own office after that, took the two old photographs from his desk drawer and sat studying them for some time. Meanwhile Sullivan was hammering away at Martha Ferris, finally reducing her to something approaching meekness, though she still insisted she had only been in the Steele house twice, "once to look at the tapestries and then to take them away. I didn't even know the caretaker's name and hardly noticed him. Of course I shouldn't have lied this morning at the morgue. But who wouldn't? And I certainly couldn't truthfully say I recognized him, as he looks now. . . ."

Sullivan left her and went back to his office as Michael finally closed the door on his, after making a telephone call that interrupted another person's Thanksgiving dinner. He took a taxi to Post Street and half an hour later hailed another to take him home.

It was six o'clock when, having eaten a sketchy meal, he went into the bedroom, picked up the telephone and dialed Nora's number.

"Who," he said without preamble, "is the missing Keith?"

"W-what? I don't understand—"

"Do you remember saying to me on Monday morning that Mrs. Landreth had gotten in touch with everyone that could be called a Keith or related to a Keith? But that most of the ones she'd known are dead and 'one is reported missing?'"

"Oh. Oh, did I say that?"

"You know you did, Leonora. Who is reported missing? Who is the black sheep that strayed away and didn't return?"

"I—I won't tell you!" Nora said desperately.

"Then tell me why your grandmother didn't think highly of—"

He shrugged and put the telephone back on the table. Nora had broken the connection.

VII

Nora thought Sullivan had almost done talking and would have finished before if Michael had been there. Sullivan had waited some time before beginning, and he still kept glancing hopefully toward the door though it was after nine now. After nine, and she hadn't been able to speak to Roger yet—

She'd kept trying to get him on the telephone between six and a quarter of eight when Cornelius stopped to pick her up. Roger wasn't at Lona's when they reached the house; he'd arrived only a few minutes before Sullivan did. It seemed he and Edwin had had dinner together and then, as he told Sullivan:

"I went home and wrote a note warning your cops I'll have the law on them if they mess up my manuscript when they search my rooms."

When Sullivan called them to order Roger sat down across the room from Nora. She couldn't go over to sit beside him. Everyone would wonder why she did; why she left Cornelius who had taken up his favorite position, leaning on the back of her chair. There was nothing to do but wait and hope she could speak to Roger without anyone's hearing what she had to say when the gathering broke up. . . .

And now Sullivan paused, cleared his throat and said slowly: "Well, that's all, unless there's some questions—"

On the steps outside someone began whistling "La Golondrina." Michael came in, stopped and regarded the group with a benign smile. He appeared not only affable but very nearly jaunty. Moreover, his entrance into the room had the same effect on it as a strong breeze blowing off a distillery.

"Ah," he said, "the old familiar faces. 'Earth seemed a desert I was bound to traverse, seeking to find the old familiar faces—' And here they are, not looking very happy. Ah well, 'he that would be rich in a year, will be hanged in half a year.' S'too bad."

Nora giggled hysterically. "Holy mother!" said James Sullivan. "Are you tight?"

Michael looked at him reproachfully. "You know me better 'n that, Inspector. Do I stammer, do I st-stutter, do I avoid the letter ess? Do I see more than one of you? No. Would I let you down by becoming vulgarly inebriated at this point? Again: no! Not tight; merely contented."

"That is just swell." Sullivan was ponderously ironic. "Admitting you didn't feel any too good when you left me, you had time for a good nap instead of sitting over a bottle. And do you know what time it is? Why bother to show up at all?"

"*Más vale tarde que nunca.* I'm late, perhaps, but I'm here. And what is time? An invention of the methodical. 'Time is an arrow, sharp and strong— No, that's wrong. That's two other poems. 'Again I hear the Lindis flow, swift as an arrow, sharp and strong—' All mixed up," Mr. Dundas said sadly.

"You've confused your Jean Ingelow and your Longfellow," Roger chuckled. "You mean you shot an arrow into the air and it's a long way from falling to earth yet."

"*Muchas gracias, amigo.* You are a scholar and a gentleman. The looks these other persons are casting my way hurt me to the core. However, as the sage s-sayeth"—he burst into song—"'They say I drink whisky, my money's my own, and them that don't like me, can leave me alone.'"

Even Martha, who had sat all evening glowering at her small feet, laughed at that. "Will you sit down?" Sullivan said. "Or go home? I don't care which."

"I will sit down," Michael decided, and did so without mishap. Sullivan was plainly out of temper now. He turned to Nora who was nearest him.

"I want to look at your hands and wrists. If you wouldn't mind turning up your sleeves, all of you—"

"Turning up our sleeves?" Nora echoed stupidly.

Sullivan had told them Fletcher's hands were missing but not what he thought might be the possible significance of that mutilation. They had been left to guess it must have some connection with Fletcher's fingerprints since he was an ex-convict. But why look at their wrists too, Nora wondered as she turned up her rumpled cuffs.

She presented thin, blue-veined wrists for Sullivan's inspection. He looked at them perfunctorily and passed on. Martha's hands were plump and white with unusually short little fingers, and her wrists were surprisingly slim. Cornelius' were thick, red and hairy; his hands broad and square.

"What's happened to the knuckle to your little finger on the right hand?" Sullivan asked abruptly.

"Hunh? Oh, it's been like that since I was a baby. Got stepped on and broken down somehow."

"Oh," Sullivan said ungraciously and went on to Roger. His hands and Edwin's were much alike; well-shaped with long fingers, though only Roger's bent back a little at the tips.

"Typewriter," he said. "And I played at the banjo once. Try that some time; spraddling your hand out and clamping your finger tips down on the strings. Take a good look at our wrists too. No birthmarks, no scars, no peculiar vein formations—”

“‘Look well, oh wolves, look well,’” Michael said sleepily. “And no tattoo marks. What, a sailor and not tattooed? The day of romance is over.”

“Romance?” Sullivan said.

“‘And on my breast just carve a turtle dove, to signify I died of love.’ Names and hearts pierced with arrows,” Michael said vaguely. “‘What’s in a name—’ ‘Deny thy father and refuse thy name—’ ‘The rank is but the guinea’s stamp’; ‘The man’s the gowd for a’ that.’”

Roger grinned. “Next time I think I’ll consult you instead of Bartlett. . . . O.K., Inspector?”

“Yes,” Sullivan said grumpily. “You, too, Lacey—”

“‘O master! we are seven,’” Michael said suddenly from where he sat humming happily to himself. “That is, we are eight. But where is the seventh?”

“Perhaps he is referring to Patton,” Edwin suggested.

“Well, since you mention her name, I’ve been wondering why she isn’t here too,” Lona said. “I’m convinced she knows far more than she’s told.”

“Lying in wait for anyone who does think so— with an ice pick,” Mr. Dundas said succinctly.

“An ice pick!”

"Won'erful weapon. Doesn't make any noise; no danger you might shoot yourself with it. Much prefer knives to guns. Never have liked guns—"

"Sure, I know!" Sullivan snapped. "You take that nap you should 've had this afternoon. I haven't looked at your hands, Mrs. Keith."

Lona smiled indulgently and spread out her large strong hands. Her nails were well kept, though broad and coarse in texture.

"Dishpan hands, I'm afraid. And I've never learned to like nail polish even if most women would feel almost undressed without it. But I'd rather not be fashionable than—"

"Don't blame you. Would you mind taking off that bracelet?"

Lona's smile faded. She drew her right hand back quickly. "I—I always wear this, Inspector. I—"

"Better take it off, Lona," Roger said gently. "He can't force you to but he'll wonder why you won't."

Lona slowly unclasped the bracelet and held out a wrist disfigured by a jagged white scar. "You see why I always wear it? I tried to kill myself once," she said flatly. "Years ago, before I ever came to San Francisco. You don't need to know why, do you, Inspector?"

"Uh—no, I guess not," Sullivan said uncomfortably.

Nora thought they were all glad the telephone rang just then and Lona went into her bedroom to answer it. When she returned she was again the perfect hostess who is still obviously aware she has a difficult set of guests.

"It's for you, Inspector."

"Hunh? Oh, I did leave your number at head-quarters but I don't know what—"

Sullivan grumbled his way out of the room. Lona glanced toward Michael.

"Wouldn't we all like some coffee?" she said tactfully.

Michael opened his eyes, apparently greatly re-freshed by a short nap. "Told Valerie I'd take to strong drink if she stayed away too long," he ob-served. "And my pal Sullivan has washed his hands of me. I don't know that I blame him, but he isn't carrying this blasted arm around with him."

He got up, wincing as he adjusted his bandaged arm in its sling. "About as pleasant as an aching tooth, and I can't very well have it yanked out. Not to speak of the hazard of shaving with your left hand—"

He indicated a small cut on his chin and turned toward Nora so swiftly she had barely opened her lips before she met his eyes and closed them again.

"Have you the keys to the old homestead?" he asked.

"Y-yes. I have, but—"

"May I have them?" Michael said.

"No. No, you can't. Why do you—"

"Say no more about it. Merely asked; don't really need them. You should put the family records in safe deposit though; not leave them lying in that house. I'm going home before Sullivan can take me there and lecture me in transit on the error of my ways. Good night, my little chickadees—"

"Hey!" said Sullivan, coming back into the living room. The slamming of the front door was the only answer he received.

"Oh, well," he said resignedly, "he's a better driver soused than most people are sober, I suppose. And I don't hear any car so I guess he walked. I'll catch him at home."

"Was the telephone call important?" Roger asked brazenly.

"Hunh? No, just some fellow in the D. A.'s office wanting to know if I'd be home at all this evening. Well, that's all, I guess—"

This was her chance. Roger was standing up, and her coat was lying across the couch where he'd been sitting. Nora started toward it, opening her purse as she went. She reached for the coat and dropped the purse.

"Don't bother," she said frigidly as its contents scattered over the floor, and Roger, grinning, stooped to gather them up. That was for Cornelius' benefit, but luckily Lona was talking to him. Nora stooped down until her head was close to Roger's.

"Don't act like I'm talking to you. . . . Michael asked me this evening what Keith is reported missing. I didn't tell him your father walked out on your mother years ago, and you don't know if he's dead or alive. Or didn't know. But I did tell him about that razor blade in your pocket yesterday afternoon. And he was interested in that. That's— that's all. You needn't say anything, but I wanted you to—to know."

She stood erect and walked away without looking at him. "Let's go home," she said, slipping her arm through Cornelius'. "I'm tired, and my head aches."

The only remark Cornelius made during the few minutes it took to drive to Nora's housekeeping room on Pine was: "Funny, how little Martha had to say for herself tonight. You'd almost say she acted scared— Is your head bad, dear?"

"Splitting," Nora said briefly.

When Cornelius parked the car in front of the respectably shabby tan house, she put her head against his shoulder, not thinking, only passively existing. He bent and kissed her cheek.

"You better go to bed. Take some aspirin. Sullivan hadn't any right to make you look at that fellow Fletcher. I'm surprised at Michael taking on a load like that even if he was feeling rotten, but I always had a hunch he's kind of flighty. He had something to do with discovering Fletcher's body even if Sullivan didn't say so— Why, what's the matter, Nora?"

"Oh, I'm a selfish, thoughtless beast!" Nora said confusedly. "I'm fond of Valerie, but I was so wrapped up in my own problems I wasn't even thinking about her and Michael. And it isn't fair to her— Neil, he wasn't drunk—"

"What! Well, he certainly acted like—"

"Of course he did. But when he spoke of the hazard of shaving left-handed . . . You know he is left-handed!"

"Now you speak of it, I guess he is—"

"And his eyes warned me not to tell everyone he is. Then he asked me for the keys to the house and said he didn't really need them. He's going there for some reason and everyone will know he is—except Inspector Sullivan who thinks he's gone home. You must get in touch with the inspector, Neil! Or go to the house yourself— No, that might be dangerous for you—"

"Never mind about that," Cornelius said stolidly. "Two against one—"

"Yes, even if the one is . . . But you've no gun. I mean, someone must have a gun. Michael wouldn't have one even if he was as handicapped by that arm in a sling as he wanted people to think—"

"You're wasting time," Cornelius said. "Get out— dear. I'll see if I can find Sullivan, but I won't take too much time for that. . . ."

VIII

The lock on the front door of the old Keith house presented no difficulties that Hymie Rose's picklocks could not quickly solve. Michael pushed the door open, stepped into the hall and stood there for an instant considering the dozens of excellent hiding places the old dark house afforded.

He was tempted to go to ground in the best of them. But two people might play hide-and-seek here for some time, perhaps without one ever getting a good look at the other. He had gambled last night at the Steele house: the chance the intruder there had a gun against his own chances of catching a glimpse of a murderer's face.

He'd lost because the odds are always with the dealer. But the deal had passed to him tonight. Still, no trap would ever spring shut until the mouse had nibbled at the cheese. And he was supposed to be drunk enough to be foolhardy, so it would be best to be caught in an appropriate attitude.

He started up the stairway, recalling the Duke of Wellington's comment when confronted with certain of his own troops for the first time. "I don't know if they'll frighten the enemy but by God! they frighten me."

"I don't know," Michael muttered, turning toward Amalia's bedroom, "if I've frightened the enemy, but if my knees were well informed on this situation they'd be making a noise like a pair of castanets—"

He stepped into the bedroom, felt for and found the light switch. There was a shaded lamp on the bedside table; when he had turned it on he put out the glaring central lights. That left the room half in shadow and himself not so clearly defined a target.

Thinking over a probable time schedule, he decided it could not be improved on. He had walked very slowly and quick action by the murderer would be necessary. Because while Sullivan was probably at Russian Hill Place now, he wouldn't wait long in front of an empty house. He'd soon go looking for Mr. Dundas. It might even occur to him that the telephone call that had taken him out of Lona Keith's living room had been a phony.

So he hadn't long to wait. Something would happen very soon—or nothing would happen. Michael went over to Amalia's desk, untied the ribbons that held one stack of old letters together and strewed them over the floor. He added hall-a-dozen photographs to this stage setting, picked up the old family Bible and the small red leather volume marked "Diary."

He laid the Bible on the desk and opened it. Or rather, it opened of itself to what should have been the pages in its center meant for births, deaths and marriages. But that section had been neatly cut out of the book.

Michael's smile verged on complacency. He'd been right when he guessed that razor blade had been used to cut pages from a book; carefully, in the hope they wouldn't be missed. And it had been enough for Nora and Sullivan that the Bible was still in this room. . . .

A voice at the door said: "You asked for it!" and a gun spat venomously. The shot spun Michael completely around. Spinning, he caught at the desk and, for all its solid weight, took it crashing to the floor with him.

It was shelter, but one foot was pinned under it. He doubted if he could get to his feet in any case. A huge hand was gripping his right shoulder,

and the numbness was spreading over the rest of
his body. It was only a matter of seconds until the
desk was no shelter but simply one of the fetters
of a condemned man.

In the time it would take to walk from the door
and around the desk . . . Those eight or ten steps
against the movements of his own fingers, groping
in his left-hand pocket. Fingers gauntleted with
marble—

He had his hand about the gun now: the one
Rocky Allan had given him this summer. If he
could get it out of his pocket; keep it close to his
side— Somehow he managed that. When he saw
the murderer's face, he pulled the trigger. . . .

After a long time, voices slit the darkness. He
didn't need to open his eyes to identify Sullivan's,
muttering: "Why the goddamned hell don't that
doctor get here!" Or to know Sullivan was kneel-
ing beside him, tightening a bandage about his
shoulder. He didn't want to talk, but there was a
joke he must share with someone.

"Left-handed," he said. "You know that—"

He was annoyed because Sullivan received this
lucid remark with a soothing: "Sure, I know. Don't
talk."

"But you didn't know Rocky Allan taught me
how to handle a gun this summer," Michael said
fretfully. "Per-perfectly true I don't like guns.

J-just as true Mr. Allan well pleased with his pupil. Never boast though— Well, not often. And you do see it's—very funny?"

"I'm laughing my head off," Sullivan said grimly. "You didn't miss if that's any comfort to you."

"And not fatal? Didn't want that—" He broke off, biting his under lip. "D-do you have to do that?"

"This bandage has got to be tight. And no; your shot wasn't fatal."

"Then I think I'll—take that nap you—kept harping on this evening. Letter for you—in my— desk—at home. . . ."

When it became necessary to open his eyes again he was prepared for the immaculate white of a hospital room. He expected to see a nurse spring to attention with a cheery: "And how are we feeling now?" but he was not too surprised to discover his wife in a chair close to the bed, her head down on one arm.

After several minutes he cleared his throat humbly. Valerie sprang up, came over to the bed and knelt down beside it. After one brief look into her hazel eyes, Michael hastily shut his own again.

"Don't look at me like that, my dear. You convince me I'm the world's worst heel."

"Just a damned fool who won't mind his own business," Valerie said sweetly. "And you're not to talk back—or at all."

"Is it Friday night? No, it isn't night—"

"But it's Friday. And when you are in good health again we're going to talk about how I walked the floor after I got the letter you wrote Wednesday night. Honestly, Michael! Don't you suppose I know you well enough by now so that when I'd finished reading that letter I knew you meant to go out not only to mail it, but to prowl around looking for a house Mrs. Landreth could have been killed in?

"The only thing that comforted me was that you hadn't wired me yesterday to come home and bail you out for housebreaking. I thought you must have escaped any trouble Wednesday night. That was no sign you would another night. I didn't get your letter until yesterday evening, and then I had a perfectly fiendish time chartering a plane—"

"Chartering?"

"I couldn't get a seat on any regular plane. So I arrived here at ten-thirty last night, and what I found when I did is something else we'll talk about when you are able to put up a good argument."

"I wrote you another letter last night," Michael said diplomatically.

"Did you? A sort of 'morituri te salutant,' I suppose? I'll find it when I go home again—"

"I wish you would go home and catch up on your sleep. I'm—I'm sorry, Valerie. I know this sort of thing isn't fair to you but I—well, I get so blasted fed-up with designing clothes for women!"

"I know," Valerie said. "And with big strong he-men who think it's amusing that you do."

Michael flushed darkly. "You're entitled to that little dig—and I can't deny it. Moreover, if I hadn't taken time to admire myself wholeheartedly for one minute, I probably wouldn't be here. Though I couldn't very well shoot first. But little Narcissus did let himself be caught daydreaming—"

"You mustn't talk. I had strict orders about that. But no one said anything about kissing you. . . ."

Several minutes later someone behind them coughed disapprovingly. Valerie got to her feet and looked the nurse undauntedly in the eye.

"I'm going home now," she said. "And you may take his temperature as a matter of scientific interest—"

"And if she wants to risk her thermometer's exploding," Michael said appreciatively. "And when you come back, my love, for God's sake bring me some pajamas. The lower half at least. No man can preserve his self-respect—or feel himself prepared for all emergencies—in a hospital nightshirt."

IX

Inspector Sullivan threw the morning paper on the floor, then scooped it up hastily and folded it

neatly. This because Patton had let him in and informed him primly that she had gone to the hospital this morning to offer her services to Mrs.
Dundas, and that the offer had been promptly ac-
cepted. With Patton in mind, Sullivan drew his foot
over the ashes he had dropped on the floor and put
his cigarette out very carefully—in an ash tray—
instead of dropping it into a more convenient vase.

He yawned, glancing toward the door that led
from the living room to Valerie's bedroom. He
didn't blame her if she felt like making him wait,
and if she wanted to, Nora Keith's being here gave
her a good excuse.

Still she didn't need to spend half an hour
talking to Nora even if the girl was taking it hard.
It had been a shock to her, but you had to learn
sometime that people weren't always at all like
you'd always thought they were. Valerie could tell
her that—

He sprang to his feet as Valerie came into the
room, eying her apprehensively. "Oh, I don't
blame you," she said, smiling. "Michael deliberately planned the whole thing so you couldn't
protect him and everyone would know he hadn't
confided in you."

"That's right. And here's a letter we found in
the desk, not addressed yet. I knew it must be for
you because it's in Spanish. We didn't even try to
translate."

Valerie took the sheet of paper he handed her, closely covered with Michael's precise backhand.

"I'm glad you didn't," she said, reddening. "Michael does sometimes let himself go—in Spanish."

"Well, there's one he left for me I want to read you. He wrote it by hand between six and nine-thirty. And I'll tell you that the things he said we'd have to check on today are all just as he guessed they'd be. I'll skip this first paragraph where he says we've got to concentrate on Fletcher now, not the coins as coins. Well, he goes on:

"'I still say that if only Fletcher's fingerprints had to be taken into account, there was no need to cut off his hands. If his fingerprints brought you only the other assumed name under which he served a sentence at some prison, you still wouldn't know what his name had been originally. But if his prints also brought you information regarding some distinctive mark on his hands—or wrists, since they were removed too . . .

"'There must have been some such mark. Not on his hands: Steele would have noticed that. But on one of his wrists—something that would link Fletcher with his killer if the police ever saw it or learned what it was.

"'It was Steele's saying Fletcher might have been in the navy that made me think one of his wrists might have been tattooed. A favorite device is a heart with a woman's name across it. Of course Steele said he thought Fletcher had been "born a gentleman," but there's no telling what even a sensible man will do when he's young and in love.

"'And his right wrist was tattooed, Inspector. You should have listened when Steele remarked that Fletcher probably worked with his sleeves rolled up only when he was doing some strenuous job. You should have gone to see young Pete Ferrari who helped Fletcher trim hedges and shrubbery. Pete noticed that Fletcher was tattooed, and he was curious enough to contrive a good look at the heart and the name across it. . . .

"'What name? I'd rather you'd wait, because that alone wouldn't have been quite enough for you. Though you did say Fletcher's killer must have been "someone he was pretty fond of." And Steele that he'd have been grateful for whatever any old friend or relative was willing to give him. You were both right. I doubt, once Fletcher was fairly certain Amalia Landreth had been murdered in that house, that he cared a great deal whether he lived or died.

"'But let us consider why he chose the name of "Fletcher." You put me on the right track when you said it made you think of Castoria. Because as Gilbert brings Sullivan to mind and the name of Weber makes you think of Fields, so might Fletcher be linked with Beaumont in the minds of some men. Beaumont and Fletcher who wrote plays together in the sixteenth and seventeenth centuries.

"'Farfetched? But there was once a young man named Lucian Beaumont living in San Francisco. I refer you now to those two photographs I so nearly tossed away.

"'In the picture taken in May of 1908 you can pick out Martha Ferris, the elder Cornelius Sturtevant, Roger Keith's mother and father, the three Keiths of the main branch—Amalia, Nora's father and Stephen—Edwin Lacey, his mother and father, two young men named Falconer and Bernard who were beaux of Amalia's according to Martha. Amalia's mother was not present, therefore Roger's mother did not have to face her disapproval because she disported herself at picnics when Roger was already on his way.

"'The other picture was taken in 1899 and it is also, with some exceptions, a family group. Martha is missing, but Cornelius' uncle Sturtevant is there along with a coquettish damsel named Beatrice Palmer, who may, Martha says, have been his lost love who died young.

"'You have the three Keiths again; the four Keiths, counting Roger's father who was not married in '99. Then there are Amalia's mother and father and Mr. and Mrs. Falconer, plus their son and young Bernard again. Which, since those two boys were still attending Keith picnics in 1908, only proves you still have decidedly a family group in 1899.

"'With, that is, the exception of Sturtevant, Miss Palmer and a young man in a yachting cap named Lucian Beaumont. Who is he? And where is Mrs. Lacey? The rest of the family is present—but this is 1899. Edwin was born in San Francisco in 1899 and remember, old Mrs. Keith didn't think picnics the place for pregnant women.

"'So Edwin's mother didn't go on that picnic and Lacey, you might guess, stayed at home with her. Lacey, who Roger says always lived in the South. But, again according to Roger, Edwin Lacey and his mother didn't move South until 1901—

"'So where was Beaumont when the Keith family picnicked in 1908—uninvited or unavailable? Had Lacey, since 1899, taken Beaumont's place with Edwina Lacey, whose given name was tattooed on Fletcher's wrist? Not a common name, and one that would immediately bring her son to mind. And that son's middle name, indicated only by an initial on his office door, is Beaumont. I found that out easily enough by calling one of the lawyers who shares offices with him.

"'Then I talked to Martha Ferris, and she remembered that at the 1908 picnic Amalia whispered to her that "Edwina had actually been divorced." That still wasn't quite the thing in 1908, especially to a woman like Amalia's mother. Another item I had from Roger was that old Mrs. Keith didn't approve of Edwin's mother, and also: "I don't suppose she approved of his divorce either. Her viewpoint hadn't changed any since 1900—" Suggestive, if nothing more, that particular date coming into his mind.

"'Martha, being only seven when Edwin was born, honestly couldn't remember if Edwina Lacey had ever been married to a man named Beaumont. I think Roger must know; perhaps Lona Keith does too. I wouldn't trust Roger not to warn Edwin: I think he realizes perfectly that Lacey can't forget his ex-wife. And I wouldn't trust Lona Keith not to talk, but I'm quite certain Martha won't.

"'I think you'll find Edwin's mother divorced a man named Beaumont when Edwin was very young; married Lacey, and that Lacey adopted her son. Naturally he and everyone else would come to think of Lacey as his father. And that Beaumont, returning finally to San Francisco, wouldn't make himself known to his son while Edwin was riding the crest of the wave.

"'But watched for news of him, knew when he lost his high-salaried position and his wife. And finally got in touch with him despite his previous resolution not to. Without ever asking Edwin to make the relationship public and being grateful for whatever he cared to give.

"'I believe you'll also find the records have been cut from the Keith family Bible with a razor blade which Lacey dropped when he heard Nora coming upstairs yesterday afternoon. And that Roger Keith picked it up later in that bedroom—and may or may not know what it was used for.

"'When Lacey went back to that bedroom Monday night, he couldn't know that Fletcher-Beaumont would ever learn he'd killed Amalia. He was still dealing with the problem of profiting by his killing by eventually selling those coins. But by yesterday we knew they were the motive for Amalia's death, and Edwin's problem had changed.

"'He'd had to kill Fletcher meanwhile, and now his problem was to keep his connection with Fletcher hidden. So he had to return to the house yesterday afternoon for those family records in the birth section of the old Bible that would show who his real father was.

"'Well, that's all—and not enough. At least, a confession would simplify matters. I'm going to

join you at Lona Keith's now and—God forgive
me!—put on an act I hope will convince Lacey I
am thoroughly soused and a plain damned fool.

"'I hope Nora will forgive me too—for fright-
ening her with my inquiries. Not that it's important, but I suspect Roger Keith's father simply
walked out on him and his mother one fine day. It
did occur to me, before I knew what name was on
Fletcher's wrist or connected him with Beaumont,
that he might be Roger's father. But it won't harm
Nora to be frightened: it may help her make up
her mind. I'm not above matchmaking.

"To resume: on my way to Lona Keith's I shall
stop at—well, never mind where—and ask a young
man I know to call Mrs. Keith's at nine-thirty and
ask to speak to you. He has a pleasant cultured
voice; you should accept him as an ornament of
the D. A.'s office if he doesn't say too much.

"'It's a dirty trick, but I must have you out of
the room long enough to let Lacey know I'm going
to the Keith house instead of to my own. And that
you don't know I am. That, with a few hints I have
in mind—remarks regarding tattooing; "Deny thy
father and refuse thy name"—should draw him.'"

Sullivan folded the letter and put it back in his
pocket. "So that's it," he said. "We got a complete
confession from Lacey before he died—"

"Did—did Michael kill him?"

"What if he had, in self-defense? But he didn't. He didn't try to because he wanted a confession. He got him through the shoulder but in spite of that Lacey tried to get away from us. He grabbed his gun again, and I had to shoot—twice. He died about midnight—

"He'd been hit bad enough to stop him for a while, but Michael was out cold when we got there. But I don't think Lacey would have finished him off. At least, he asked after Michael and said he was glad he hadn't killed him. I guess he regretted it all at the last. Seemed like then he was the person everyone had always thought him again. He said wanting more money and his wife back seemed to get to be kind of an obsession with him.

"So when he saw his chance to get money he took it. Mrs. Landreth did consult him after all. He told her he wasn't certain those coins couldn't be confiscated. That kept her from talking all day Friday.

"Saturday he had to tell her it was all right, but by then he'd made his plans. Told her he thought he had a buyer for her and all the rest of it like we figured it out—that the buyer was eccentric and had to be handled carefully and have things done his way.

"She promised so faithfully not to talk and was so anxious to get a lump sum for the coins that

Lacey thought she'd keep still. She did try and succeeded fairly well till the last. But she was so impatient she had to be doing something. So she asked Roger Keith if he knew where she could find out anything about stamps—"

"Stamps?" Valerie said. "Oh, she argued that wherever you could get information about stamps you might also get it about coins."

"Evidently. And Roger recommended the library. Her going there and making those notes was the first thing that went wrong with Lacey's scheme. He missed the original notes in the bedroom Monday night. Besides, he found a fair copy in her purse and supposed that was the only notes she'd ever made.

"If we had those notes it was almost a certainty we'd eventually find out about the coins. There's a kind of—of poetic justice about the fact it was Mrs. Landreth herself who made his murder profitless. Because she got impatient again and went to see Conklin Monday. And he gave us definite proof she had had the coins. When Lacey learned that, he knew he'd never be able to sell the coins."

"There's also a sort of poetic justice in the fact that it was his own clever scheme to get her out of the house carrying the coins with her that led to his being caught," Valerie said. "Michael always says a murderer makes a bad mistake when he tries to be too clever. If Mr. Lacey had killed Amalia in her own home Friday night he probably would have gotten away with it. But no; he had to plan an elaborate setup that included Mr. Steele's house. And because he used that house he had to kill Fletcher—and then try to hide his connection with Fletcher. And that was what he couldn't do."

"You're right. Well, Lacey's ex-wife was at the hospital before he died. Pretty subdued, probably for the first time in her life. He looked at her once and said with a funny smile: 'The woman tempted me and I did eat.' But Michael can thank Roger Keith that we got there when we did. He's smart; he guessed Michael wasn't really drunk. He started off in his car, got uneasy about the whole thing and turned around and caught me up here."

"And Nora had sent Cornelius off on the same errand," Valerie said. "She guessed too that Michael was going to the old Keith house."

Sullivan grinned. "He just missed me. Turned up at the house after it was all over. Young Sturtevant is a little slow in his movements."

"Well, if even the things Michael guessed at are right—"

"They are. Edwin's mother did divorce Beaumont and married Lacey who had more money. Beaumont was crazy about Edwin's mother but let her have her divorce, and then he just disappeared.

He got in touch with Edwin about three years ago. He used to go to see his father now and then, but Edwin said he always had in mind he was an ex-con and wouldn't let him make the relationship public. And I guess Edwin wasn't anxious to."

"But how did Beaumont—or Fletcher—find out Mrs. Landreth had been killed in that house?" Valerie asked. "I know you said you could guess at that, but—"

"Oh, Beaumont missed his extra keys, and no one but Edwin could have taken them. He went up into the main house Tuesday and found that initialed handkerchief of hers. It had dropped out of her pocket, Edwin thinks, when he was carrying her body out of the house. And her hat fell off in the garden. He stepped on it and that bird came off. He thought he got all of it but he was in a hurry—naturally—and missed two feathers that came loose. Beaumont found them next morning too.

"Well, Edwin had talked to him about Mrs. Landreth, but he didn't know anything about the coins of course. He didn't come across any of them where Edwin had hidden them about the house. He didn't even know Mrs. Landreth was missing when he started out for a walk Tuesday morning. But he found out she was not only missing but murdered when he got to that park just after her body had been found there.

"He knew something was wrong then and telephoned Edwin to come to see him Tuesday night. Edwin couldn't give a satisfactory explanation; his father said he'd have to go to the police and Edwin shot him. I guess Beaumont just didn't care enough to take any precautions against something like that.

"Well, the only loose thread I can think of is that Lona Keith did doctor up Nora Keith's malted milk Monday night—for her own good, she says. I guess we'll never know why Lona Keith tried to kill herself when she was a girl. It's none of our business now.

"Everything," Sullivan added complacently, "was just the way we figured it out as we went along. I mean, the case seemed to kind of divide itself into sections. You'd get one phase all doped out—and still find yourself not knowing who did it. Well, I'd better get along and let you get some sleep."

"I need it and I think I deserve it," Valerie said. "Before I came in here I was persuading Nora she's a damned fool if she doesn't marry Roger—"

"But she's engaged to young Sturtevant."

"I don't like Cornelius. He's narrow-minded and materialistic. But that has nothing to do with it. Nora didn't think she could bear it last night after Michael had made her think Roger was the

murderer. She'd much rather it had been Cornelius. She knows that now. I told her if I can sur-
vive being married to Michael she certainly should
be able to take on Roger. She's never loved anyone
else. So of course when she got herself engaged she
picked a man as different from Roger as possible."

"Oh. I mean—sure, of course," Sullivan said
uncomprehendingly. "And so now she's going to
marry Roger—"

"Of course!" said Valerie.